THE EXES

JANE LYTHELL

Print ISBN: 978-1-5040-8526-7

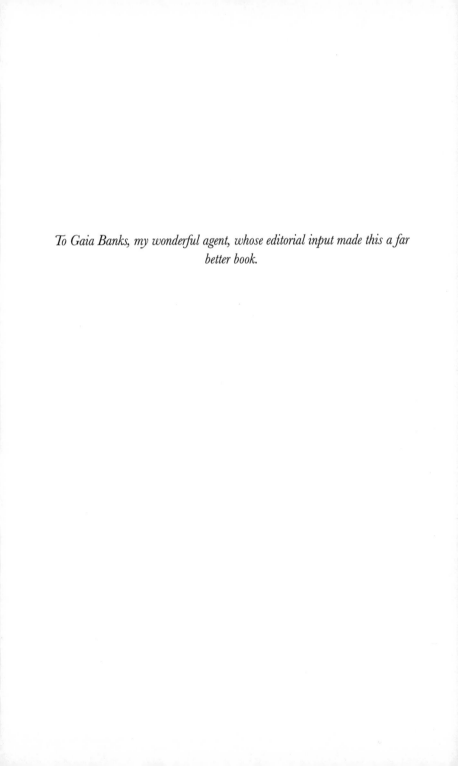

To Gaia Banks, my wonderful agent, whose editorial input made this a far better book.

NOVEMBER 1999

PENUMBRA HOUSE, BRIGHTON

The soil around the trunk of the fig tree is spongy after days of rain and makes the digging easier, but the low, almost-horizontal, branches of the tree are an obstacle. He must duck down as he wields the shovel or else crack his head. Digging bent over is hard and dirty work, and it will take him hours to dig a channel deep enough to prevent a scavenging fox from unearthing anything buried here.

The wind buffets the thorn bushes by the wall, and they whistle against the bricks which constrain them and his shovel squelches as he excavates the saturated soil. The earth beneath the fig tree has lain undisturbed for years and is thick with small living roots and stones. He has propped her body against the trunk of the fig tree, wrapped in layers of black bin bags and sealed with duct tape. Her body sits stiff and erect, like a masked observer.

It is nearly two in the morning and there is no one on the street at the front of the house. The glow from the street lamp does not penetrate this dark corner of the garden at the back. But he noticed the tower block which overlooks the end of the garden. A single light still shines out from the block, a square of sodium yellow. Can he be seen from that high vantage point? He thinks he is shielded by the fig tree, but its branches are bare of leaves and a worm of anxiety gnaws his gut.

The trench is knee-deep when a twig snaps, sending out a small sharp noise and something moves close by. He freezes and stills the shovel for several minutes and listens intently. He hears only the sound of rain on fallen leaves and the whistle of the thorn bushes scratching the wall. It must have been a cat or a fox prowling the garden. No homeless person would seek shelter in this inhospitable place.

He is sweating hard, and he wipes his eyes and looks up and notices for the first time a figure standing by the lit window in the block of flats. He thinks it is a man, that silhouette with those wide shoulders must surely be male, and the man is standing there looking out into the night. How long has he been there? Watching. How much can he see in the dark garden below?

He inches towards the trunk of the fig tree and stands very still in its shadow looking up at the silhouetted figure. He must not move until the watching man retreats. A sudden gust of wind surges through the garden and the body by the trunk tips to one side and comes to a stop at a lopsided angle. Does the watching man see this? He curses the onlooker as sweat trickles under his armpits and down his torso but he dare not make a move to right the body against the tree trunk.

The figure moves away from the window. Has he gone to report suspicious activity in the garden of Penumbra House? Should he run for it? But he cannot risk dragging her body back to the car. Police may be on their way. His body tells him to run but his mind tells him to stay. Wait. Just wait. Panic and hasty action gets you caught.

Time passes. His sweat cools and he shivers. The light at the window goes out. After five more minutes, he moves away from the fig tree and resumes his digging.

At last, the trench is deep enough. There are several inches of water in the bottom and as he rolls the body into its last resting place, it makes a thump and a splash. Covering the corpse with soil and levelling the earth takes him far less time.

He knows the house is only visited once a year in April. Grass and weeds will have grown over by then and will disguise any sign of his digging. It is the ideal burial place, the forgotten garden of a near-abandoned house.

He walks down the side alley, onto the street and away. At last, he feels safe.

Chapter One

JANUARY
PENUMBRA HOUSE, BRIGHTON

'A commune of your exes. Good luck with that!' Laura says.

'It's not a commune,' Holly protests.

'They're all moving in with you, sharing your house. Ray in your basement, for heaven's sake.'

'I thought you liked him. You said he made you laugh.'

'In small doses. He was fine as your rebound relationship to get you out of your separation slump. But I think he'd be impossible to live with.'

'He was more than a rebound relationship, Laura. And he's very good at what he does. I trust him.' Holly says this slightly too loudly.

'Isn't Spencer obsessive about his painting? He'll be here day in, day out.'

'Fine by me. What this house needs most is people living

and working here, bringing it back to life. And Spencer's only using the first floor during the day.'

'What mystifies me the most is you agreeing to James moving in after the way he behaved.'

'We went through a lot together. I prefer to get on with my exes.'

'You've got a big heart.'

'He asked if I'd do him a favour, just until he got established. It was hard to say no.'

'I hope you'll charge *him* rent.'

'Don't worry. I *insisted* on rent.'

Laura rolls her eyes. 'I'm glad you're being more assertive with him at last. Watch out he doesn't try to take over. You know what he's like. Or maybe he wants to get back with you.'

'No way! The chances of James and me getting back together are zero. He used to take me to these fancy restaurants but then he'd be critical of the wine list, or the dish he'd chosen. I just wanted him to take pleasure in the meal and be nice to the waiter. But it was glass half empty with James; never glass half full. If I could give advice to my younger self, I'd say marry a man who is glass half full.'

Laura won't let it go. 'I can't see James getting along with Ray.'

Holly's worried too but wants her best friend's support.

'They're your *exes* for a reason. I don't get why you're doing this, Holly. I really don't. Most people can't wait to get away from their exes and if it was possible to live with them, you'd still be with one of them.'

'I won't be living with them; not in that way.'

'They'll be a permanent fixture in your life.'

'It'll be great to have Ray close by when things go wrong in the house. He understands buildings.'

'I think you're paying far too high a price for that benefit.'

'But look at the house! I need his help.'

'Penumbra House, *Penury House* more like. You do know most building projects turn into bottomless pits.' Laura has a habit of giving unflattering nicknames to people and places.

'Which is why I need Ray.'

Holly regrets inviting Laura to walk through Penumbra House with her, the house she inherited three months ago from her reclusive aunt Lillian. Laura always says what she thinks in an unvarnished way and today this grates on Holly.

They are standing in the sitting room, which smells musty, like a cupboard unopened in decades. The house is dirty, creaky, and unloved, but underneath the neglect is a fine and substantial Victorian villa. The interior has magnificent proportions, high ceilings, massive rooms, generous windows, and the ground floor alone is twice the size of Holly's one-bedroom London flat.

It's *her house* now: the words give her a tingle. But from the moment Holly walked in, she'd experienced something uneasy in the air. Houses emanate their own unique atmosphere and Penumbra House is mournful and desolate. Her aunt Lillian only lived here one month a year, every April. Her main residence was in Brittany.

Holly knows she can't renovate the house on her own. She's a single woman with few practical skills. Sure, she can paint a wall and hang a picture. But, unlike her aunt Lillian, she's not a brave person. It's why she invited her ex-lover Ray, a builder, to live in the basement rent-free for the long term if he would manage the renovation. They're no longer a couple, but he has all the project management skills and the contacts to make it happen.

'Come on, let's have a cuppa,' Holly says, walking into the kitchen and hoping to change the subject.

She has brought a kettle and provisions with her. The kitchen is dirty. The fridge door has been wedged open and turned off, but it still smells of mould. Holly fills the kettle and recalls helping wash the dishes for her aunt in the large butler sink with its upright brass taps. The wooden draining board is mottled black with water damage and looks unsanitary. Holly fills the kettle as Laura plonks herself down at the kitchen table, looking at the cracked ceiling thoughtfully.

'I've got a better plan to get your house done up. We'll make a video of you going round and pitch it to that Channel Four programme. You know the one. They send in teams to transform problem homes.'

'You're not serious?' Holly dunks tea bags into the boiling water in two mugs.

'Why not? I make videos all the time and it's a good story. Cash-strapped teacher is left a wreck of a large house by her aunt and seeks help to restore it to its former grandeur.'

'It's not exactly a wreck, is it?'

'It's near enough and they'll *love* the fact it's called Penumbra House.'

'I looked up Penumbra. It means partial illumination during an eclipse, and also means something that shrouds or obscures. Odd choice of name for a house. Lillian told me the original owner was an astronomer, one of those Victorians who collected knowledge.'

'And she never changed it.'

Holly passes Laura a mug of tea. 'Lillian was a purist and if that was the name they gave the house in 1881, it would stay its name.'

It's a cold and sunny afternoon and they start the shoot outside. Laura has jotted down some keywords for Holly to use.

'Talk into the camera as if you're telling a friend about the house,' she says.

She starts the video camera on her phone and makes Holly

walk up the front path. This is made of small black-and-white tiles which look elegant when they are all in place, but there are lots of tiles missing. Holly turns and stops in front of the red-brick façade which boasts ornamental flourishes and a wide front door.

'Three months ago, to my astonishment, I inherited Penumbra House from my aunt Lillian, who lived in Brittany. She left me a short letter saying: *I believe you have it in you to rise to the challenge of Penumbra House.* Come inside and see for yourselves why it is a challenge and why I need your renovation team to help me restore what could be such a lovely house.'

'Cut. Good words, but we'll do it again and speak more slowly this time, Holly, especially when you say Penumbra House.'

They do the second take and Laura moves the camera up to shoot the name of the house which is painted in thick black letters on the fanlight. They head down to the basement. The entrance has a separate front door which sticks, and Holly has to push hard to get it open. Large flagstones cover the floors, and the rooms smell strongly of damp. There are three rooms and to one side is a scullery and a kitchen of sorts. The whole floor is empty and untouched for years. She wonders if her aunt ever came down here.

'Not very interesting.' Laura is decisive. 'Let's focus on the upper floors.'

'Ray said he'll put a shower in the old scullery and refit the kitchen.' Holly's glad he's already thinking about the basement as his new home, but she won't share her gladness with Laura.

'Who wouldn't. He's getting it rent-free, isn't he?' Laura positions Holly in front of the enormous window of the sitting room and lifts her hand. 'Action.'

'See what a magnificent room this could be, but the skirting boards are warped, the walls are cracked, and the door frame is out of square,' Holly says to camera.

Laura pans away from Holly to show the grand dimensions of the room and the cracks which disfigure it.

The women go up to the first floor. There are no carpets anywhere in the house and the bare floorboards make their passage echoey and forlorn. They enter Lillian's bedroom and Holly stops in front of an ancient gas fire with a tap you turn on at the side.

'My aunt only visited the house every April, and this is the room she slept in. The rest of the time she was in France while Penumbra House stood empty. I'm told this is a Kenmore gas heater, a period piece.'

The two rooms on the other side of the staircase have connecting doors which open to create a lovely long light-filled room, although cracks also zigzag down these walls. This is the space Holly has offered Spencer as a studio. Laura gets Holly to walk through these rooms to the window overlooking the garden.

'Talk about the garden,' she instructs Holly.

'My aunt told me the garden is a hundred and twenty feet long, but sadly it has been neglected for years and is now an overgrown wilderness.'

Laura moves over to shoot from the window and signals with her hand for Holly to keep on talking.

'A giant fig tree has taken over the top half of the garden. And look how the side wall is deep in brambles grown high and impenetrable, like Sleeping Beauty's castle during her long sleep.'

'Cut. Nice touch, poetic,' Laura says.

On the top floor, the ceilings aren't as high, and the rooms smell of dust and decay. There are two decent-sized rooms, a second kitchen and the small bathroom, which Holly remembers from her visits to see her aunt at the house every April. In the back room Holly points out the trail of amoeba-shaped brown blobs staining the ceiling.

'Maybe we should film those stains, Laura. Ray said there are broken roof tiles and water is getting in.'

Laura moves her phone up and films the stains on the ceiling. She moves the camera back to Holly's face. 'Sum it up and ask for help,' Laura says.

Holly takes a breath and looks into the phone's camera lens.

'I need your help. The house has stood empty for so long. It's in a state and I'm totally out of my depth. Please help me restore Penumbra House.'

'Good.' Laura ends the recording. 'I've got enough footage. I'll edit it, and it should run under five minutes.'

'Thank you so much for doing it. You're awfully clever with the camera.'

'Part of my skill set. I'll do the first draft of the letter to the man who presents the show. You know I'd like to meet him. He's attractive.'

Laura works as a top event organiser in London and is used to bashing out pitches and can be very persuasive when necessary.

'Fingers crossed it leads to something,' Holly says. 'Did you see that small box on Lillian's bed? It may contain something important, and I'll take it back with me.'

The small cardboard box is covered in thick dust, and Holly sweeps it clean before double locking the front door. They reach the street, wide, leafy, and prosperous, and are greeted by a friendly looking woman, probably in her sixties.

'Hello. I'm Hazel. I live next door. Are you moving in?'

'I'm Holly Hilborne and this is my friend, Laura. Yes, I'm moving in soon and I plan to renovate the house.'

'It's excellent news you'll be living there. Welcome.'

'There'll be a lot of building work, a scaffold, some noise and dust for a while, I'm afraid, but...' Holly peters out.

'But it will be worth it,' Hazel finishes her sentence for her.

'A house that's been empty for so long, it's just so dismal, isn't it? Not to mention the threat of squatters moving in.'

Hazel glances beyond them, up at the façade of Penumbra House, with a look of aversion on her face. There's an awkward moment as Holly tries to think what to say. Should she apologise for the obvious neglect of the house?

'I'm sure you will make it lovely. I was told it was owned by a famous French writer who was a recluse,' Hazel adds.

'A translator actually, my aunt Lillian. She was based in France most of the time.'

'It's odd, but I don't think I ever spoke to her.'

'She wasn't here very much,' Holly says.

'I'd invite you both in for tea but I'm about to go to my *Purl and Plonk* group.'

They smile at the name of the group.

'Are you a knitter, Holly?'

'Not since my schooldays.'

'To be honest, it's often more plonk than purl.'

'Sounds fun. It's nice to meet you, Hazel.'

'Likewise.'

Holly and Laura walk away.

'I'm glad I warned her there will be months of building works,' Holly says to Laura. 'People have a passion for their properties and they must have hated the signs of decay next door to them.'

'She'll share this intelligence with the other people on the road. There's bound to be a neighbourhood bush telegraph in a street like this.'

They reach Brighton station and buy two small bottles of rosé in the M&S on the station concourse. Finding a four-seater, they sit opposite each other on the train back to St Pancras. By the time they reach Gatwick, they've both finished their little bottles and harmony is fully restored between them.

'You know I'd love it if you'd join my "commune",' Holly

says, 'but you're such a London person, and anyway you have the most beautiful home.'

'Oh God, yes, you'll never get me out of Camden Square or London.'

'I want to live a bigger, braver life and the inheritance is the moment to make changes. Restoring Penumbra House will be my major project.'

'I get it, Holly. And it could be a beautiful house, a palace after your flat. It's just recruiting your three exes as your helpers strikes me as high risk. Once they're in the house you'll be lumbered with them.'

Laura's phone rings and she switches seamlessly into work mode.

Holly looks out of the window. She's still married to James, even though they separated four and a half years ago. It was a difficult separation, but as the resentments faded, they've managed a kind of friendship.

Following the 2008 financial crash James had to reinvent himself from city high-flyer to trainee osteopath. He's in his last year at the University College of Osteopathy. She recalls their awkward conversation when James phoned to ask if he could use the top floor in Penumbra House as a treatment room for patients. Foolishly, she'd told him Ray and Spencer would be involved in her restoration project.

'Hang on. You mean you want to *work* out of the top floor?' Holly had said.

'Exactly, for the first year, while I build my practice.'

'So, clients will come to the house?'

'Patients, not clients. There won't be many to begin with, I can promise you that.' He gave a bark of laughter, which sounded false, and she guessed he was embarrassed to ask her for this favour. 'The first year of building a practice is critical, you see. As soon as I get established, I'd move out.'

'But I thought you planned to practice in London?'

'Brighton's actually an ideal location. I've done some research.'

He'd done some research! Probably after their December lunch when she'd told him about her inheritance and her plans for Penumbra House.

'But what about your mum?'

'Easy to travel up from Brighton and my sister is nearby.'

'I'm not sure about this at all.'

'Why's that?'

'It's the idea of people coming to the house. The disruption. They'll ring the bell and–'

'I'll install a separate bell. Of course I will. My patients will be middle-aged and older folk and all very well behaved. Nothing to alarm you.'

She found that comment patronising, as if he implied she was easily alarmed. 'I mean, it's a *family* house.'

There was a pause, and she knew James was marshalling his arguments.

'Actually, lots of osteopaths work out of private houses and you'll hardly know I'm there.'

'But you don't get on with Ray *or* Spencer. You never have.'

'Oh, we'll rub along just fine. Water under the bridge, you know. You'd be doing me an enormous favour. For old times' sake, Holly.'

For old times' sake. She can't forget how he treated her in their last years together. James was ruthless when he wanted something.

'It will be a building site for months, noisy and dusty, hardly ideal for a treatment room.'

'But I won't be practising fully till the summer.'

She had run out of arguments to dissuade him. When James got an idea, he was like a terrier with a bone.

'If I said yes, you'd have to pay rent for the rooms and a

contribution to the council tax, water and utility bills,' she said crisply.

There was a pause at the end of the line, and she hoped her demand for money had put him off the idea. To have her *three* exes involved in her house was getting absurd.

'Ray and Spencer are paying rent, are they?'

She recalls her hot flash of irritation and she'd snapped at him.

'How long have we been separated?'

'Um, a while…'

'Coming up for *five years*, James, and I don't intend to share my financial arrangements with you.'

'I was only asking. How much would the rent for the top floor be?'

'Less than the market price.'

'Fair enough. It's a deal then?'

'I suppose so; but only till you're established. Not for the long term.'

'Thank you, Holly. I appreciate it and I'll move in sometime during April.'

As the outskirts of London flash by, she reflects the major difference is that *she invited* Ray and Spencer into the house because she wants them there. James has invited himself. Sure, they have a shared history, and it's the longest relationship she's had. But why did she agree? Is it because she knows James is short of money, and he was generous to her when he was earning big in the city?

She won't accept rent from Ray; his contribution is managing the renovation, a huge task. Spencer is strapped for cash and probably won't even heat the first-floor rooms. He once told her he is more creative when he's cold. He'll probably give her a painting and she likes his paintings; and now she'll have plenty of wall space on which to hang them.

Oh well, the die is cast, and James will join the house in April. Best not to brood on it.

But Laura's vehemence on the subject of her exes has had a dampening effect on Holly's mood. It's not a commune! It's four people, all in their mid to late forties, coming together under her roof because she's been gifted this big old house. Holly can afford to be generous. And she tells herself it will be wonderful to have more space to live in after her tiny flat. Once it's done, she'll feel proud to say I did this – I restored Penumbra House to its former elegance.

Laura was harsh to dismiss Ray as Holly's rebound relationship. It's true they got together eighteen months after Holly had given up on her marriage to James and moved out. Ray *isn't* impossible. He is an excellent and reliable builder who understands how houses work. Then she recalls how Ray will smoke a joint from time to time.

'You can only tile a bathroom so many times before you go loco,' he told her when she caught him sitting on the toilet seat in her flat with a large spliff.

She has seen him stoned a few times, and he gets noisy and plays his music at full volume. *Can* she rely on Ray? *Will* the cost of the renovation be a bottomless pit? Will it become Penury House? She chews on her thumbnail, doubting herself. Her brave aunt Lillian would despise such defeatism and had faith in Holly to rise to the challenge of Penumbra House. This time she will *not* be a coward and will not let herself be ruled by fear.

Laura has been talking business all the way from Gatwick to Farringdon. Finally, she snaps her phone shut. 'That client is *so* demanding. This is supposed to be my day off.'

They get out at St Pancras and share a taxi back to

Camden Town. They hug before they part outside Laura's flat. Holly's flat is a short walk around the corner.

'Ray, Spencer and James all under your roof. Look, sweetheart, it's your bed and you'll have to lie on it.' Laura says then waves goodbye.

Chapter Two

HOLLY'S LONDON FLAT
THAT EVENING

Holly is glad to be back in her cosy flat, which she'll be leaving next week. She had put her flat on the market to give herself a building fund for the renovation of Penumbra House. The flat sold quickly to an American woman, a cash buyer who met the asking price.

Things are happening almost too fast, and Holly is still stunned at the bequest. She thought her aunt didn't totally approve of her. Lillian would look at her with an odd expression, puzzled and sometimes even pained. Holly thinks it's because Lillian thought she hadn't done enough with her qualifications and rather despised her for not showing more ambition in her career. But few people could live up to Lillian's exacting intellectual standards. To be left Penumbra House is both thrilling *and* bewildering. It's mortgage-free and now belongs to Holly, all four storeys of it. She's a lottery winner who never bought a ticket.

She puts the small box she found in Lillian's bedroom on her kitchen table and slides her nail under the rotten tape. At the top, something is wrapped in wads of tissue paper. Holly unrolls this carefully to reveal two small liqueur glasses, each about five inches high. They are crystal and engraved with flowers and a bird in flight. They look antique, probably Victorian, and are exquisite. She doubts she'll ever use them, as they would hold only a mouthful of liqueur, but these little glasses appeal to her. And they must have meant something special to Lillian.

Below are two photographs held together with a rusty paper clip, and a piece of yellowing paper at the back. The first photograph is black and white and shows Lillian sitting with a man at a table in what looks like a French square. It's a younger Lillian, maybe early forties, and she has her trademark Gauloises in her right hand. She's wearing a dress with bold stripes and chic sandals and looks almost glamorous. The man is a few years older than her, handsome with striking thick eyebrows. There is something about their body language, the way their torsos and arms mirror each other, which makes Holly feel sure they were intimate. Written on the back in ink is one word: *Jacques*.

The second photograph is in colour. It's the same man, those eyebrows are unmistakable, but many years on. He's sitting at a desk with his hand resting on a volume, a gentle smile on his face. He is probably eighty, yet still a handsome man. Holly turns the photo round and deciphers the name on the spine of the book: *Jacques Pichois*. There must be a love story here.

She examines the sheet of yellowing paper. It looks like a letter, or a draft of a letter, because a line is scored diagonally across the text. It's in English on one side and in French on the

other and she recognises Lillian's handwriting from the
birthday cards she got from her aunt as a child, always with a
book token enclosed. She reads the letter.

> *September 1996*
> *My darling,*
> *I met her mother in the village. She is broken, has aged ten years
> and says their future has been taken from them. I have hardly slept
> since so deep is my dread. I am consumed with the thought I have not
> done the right thing and should have reported my suspicions.*
> *He was in the area, and I know he is capable of killing.
> Remember Rabbit.*
> *I am frightened of him. I have decided I cannot and will not see
> him anymore. I urge you to seek professional help for him.*
> *My love as always,*
> *L.*

The letter disturbs Holly. Her brave aunt was frightened of
someone, someone connected with this Jacques, who surely
must be the *My darling* at the top. The draft is dated September
1996, twenty-three years ago. Why did Lillian keep this draft
letter with the photographs and the liqueur glasses? These
things were important to her. And what does *Remember Rabbit*
mean?

At the bottom of the box are three hardback books. She
takes these out and examines them; they are in French and the
author is Jacques Pichois. It seems Lillian had a lover, probably
for many years. It would explain why she spent most of her
time in Brittany. Holly finds she is glad her aunt had a lover,
that her life was a happier one, less lonely than she previously
thought. Yet her father never mentioned a man in Lillian's life.
Did he know anything about this Jacques Pichois? Or could he
have been a married man and Lillian had to keep him a secret
all her life? It's a mystery.

Chapter Three

ONE WEEK LATER

I t's Holly's moving day. She thinks, *I'm leaving London and all I know.*

Cooper, Laura's cockapoo, is at her side because Laura is away at a conference and said Holly must have a dog to keep her company and guard her *'for the first few days in that big old empty house'*. Cooper is adorable, apricot in colour with bright affectionate eyes and Holly loves him dearly, but she has never thought of him as a guard dog.

She says goodbye to her pretty little flat with a pang. When she reaches St Pancras station she wonders if she'll ever live in London again. When people leave the capital, they rarely come back.

She finds a four-seater on the train to Brighton and Cooper settles at her feet with a little sigh.

Spencer is waiting for her when she arrives at Penumbra House.

'A big day. Tell me what you need doing,' he says.

Shortly afterwards the two removal men pull up and park their van. They manoeuvre her double bed into the dining room which is going to be her bedroom. It will make a grand bedroom with its ornate cornicing and long windows which overlook the garden. They put her sofa in the centre of the sitting room which faces the street. Her furniture, which fitted like a glove in her small flat, is dwarfed in so much space and Cooper is unsettled by the size of the house. He skitters in the hall and hovers at doorways as if tensed and ready to spring into action. Spencer unpacks the box of kitchen utensils so they can all have tea.

Holly only unpacks the most essential things because the house is dirty. The rest will have to wait until the house has been thoroughly cleaned and she'll live out of her suitcase for the next few days. The removal men head off. Holly is covered in dust and exhausted. Spencer sweeps the hall.

'That's enough for today,' she says and they go into the kitchen. It's cold and Holly retrieves the small fan heater which belonged to Lillian, still in its original box, and plugs it into the wall socket. It throws out a meagre heat and a smell of singed dust.

Holly holds out a bag. 'I brought us some sandwiches and apples. No cooked supper tonight I'm afraid.'

She washes a couple of plates and puts the sandwiches on them.

'Sorry it's dirty in here. I'll clean the kitchen tomorrow. Thanks for the help, Spencer. You've made it easier all round,' she smiles at him.

'My pleasure. What the hell?' he exclaims, his fond smile falling away.

Sparks are shooting out of the plug in the wall. They both leap up and Holly moves towards the fan heater.

'Don't touch it!' Spencer shouts.

She steps back. The sparks crackle and spit dangerously and there is the strongest smell of burning rubber.

'I need to turn the power off. And *no water* anywhere near it.'

'The fuse box is in the cupboard under the stairs.'

They go into the hall and Spencer throws the big switch. The lights in the kitchen go out and the flying sparks stop, but the smell of burning rubber persists. He pushes the kitchen window open. 'Do you have any rubber gloves?'

She gives him a pair.

'I'll pull the plug out once it's cooled down.'

They finish their sandwiches, and Spencer tugs the heater plug out of the wall and half of it has melted. He puts the power back on. The kitchen bulb flickers but remains on.

'Dodgy electrics,' Holly says.

He packs the ruined fan heater back into its box. 'I'll take this with me and dispose of it,' he says.

The day has tired her out, so Cooper only gets a short walk round the block. When they return Cooper will not settle on the old towel she's put by her bed. He keeps circling the room, sniffing at the skirting boards, making exploratory scratches. The creaks of the house have started up, and he is skittish at the slightest sound. This is unlike him because Cooper is not usually a highly strung dog.

'You're missing Laura,' Holly says fondly.

She stands by the window looking into the back garden. How monstrous the giant fig tree appears in the cold-blooded moonlight; like something from a nightmare. Those long branches would catch at your hair and drag you back. She wishes everything about the house would stop unsettling her as she pulls the curtains together and wriggles under her duvet. The wind is up, the windows rattle and the thin curtains balloon and flutter. She watches the eerie dance of the curtains.

The room is chilly as well as damp, and she shivers and rolls over onto her other side with her back to the curtains. She can't get to sleep because she's cold. She'd spotted a hot water bottle in a kitchen cupboard and goes to find it.

It's made of faded orange rubber and looks ancient. She boils a kettle and fills the hot water bottle and can't remember the last time she used one. Her small London flat was easily heated. She puts a jumper on over her pyjamas as it occurs to her for the first time that the heating bills for Penumbra House will be huge.

Lying down, she hugs the bottle to her chest. The warmth is comforting, and she is drifting into sleep when the dining-room door swings open slowly and with a slight groan. She feels the change of air in the room. Cooper growls, and she uses her elbows to get up into a sitting position as she stares at the opening door in terror.

'Hello?' she calls out, alarmed at how fast her heart is beating. Cooper's growl gets deeper.

Sure she closed the door properly when she came back from the kitchen, she notices how fear makes her limbs go weak and useless. She gets up gingerly and tiptoes across the room, switching on the overhead light. The bare bulb swings and the curtains are still stirring in the draught from the window.

She approaches the door with caution and does not look out into the hall. When she closes the door, she hears it click shut. But to make sure she drags a small wooden chest across the room and pushes it in front of the door. She leaves the light on and climbs back into bed thoroughly awake. Cooper has finally stopped growling and she is glad of his presence.

Ray had told her that most of the houses on the road are sliding down the hill. Old houses move and shift, he'd said. Is that why the door swung open? She looks up at the ceiling and the bare bulb. There is a long crack running from the ceiling rose all the way to the left-hand corner. What *has* she taken on?

She wakes very early because she's wet and freezing. The hot water bottle is perished and has leaked, soaking her jumper and sheet.

'Hell!'

She flings the useless thing across the room in disgust and Cooper barks as it splats on the bare floorboards. It feels as if everything in Penumbra House is rejecting her, wanting her gone. It's still dark outside, but there's no choice except to get up and dressed and be active.

A cup of tea warms her, and she lets Cooper out. He skips down the kitchen steps into the back garden, relieves himself against the fig tree and gets very interested in the soil at the base of the trunk, sniffing the earth as he digs enthusiastically. Holly watches him as the sun rises slowly over the garden wall.

She yawns hugely. A long day stretches ahead of her with much to do and she's only had a few hours' sleep. She knew it would be a challenge to spend her first night alone in such a large empty house.

In London she is used to hearing her neighbours, a couple, moving around above her. They sometimes had rows which travelled through to her floor. Now she has learned silence can be more disturbing than noise. It isn't exactly silence either; there are creaks and exhalations coming from the walls and the floors as if Penumbra House is not used to a living being inhabiting these rooms.

She'd found a Brighton cleaning company online called *Pam and Paige* and has hired the two women for the morning and a window cleaner for the afternoon. She needs them to give the basement a deep clean as Ray is moving in tomorrow.

Holly ties a scarf around her hair and uses a broom to sweep away the grey and sticky cobwebs high up in the corners of the kitchen. They are thick with the sucked-out carcasses of flies.

She pulls the mess off the head of the broom, grimacing as she does it. She wields her broom on the dresser next, releasing clouds of dust. She scours the large table with hot soapy water before taking down the two dinner sets from the dresser. Some plates are mottled with brown spots and will have to go.

There's a rap on the front door and she opens it to two women in pink overalls carrying a bucket of cleaning materials.

'Morning. I'm Pam and this is Paige,' the older woman says.

'Good to see you. I'm Holly. I'd like you to blitz the basement, only the basement today.'

She leads them down to the side entrance.

'This place has been empty for years, hasn't it? My granddaughter went to the nursery on the corner and asked if a witch lived here,' Pam says cheerily. 'She's at secondary school now.'

Holly laughs nervously. 'It does look a bit like a witch's house at the moment. It belonged to my aunt, and she was based in France.'

'No offence meant,' Pam says.

'None taken. Will you give the rooms a real going over please? They haven't been cleaned for ages.'

Paige, the younger woman, is looking around watchfully.

Holly returns to the kitchen thinking about Pam's

comment, the house of a witch. It was said light-heartedly but Lillian was stand-offish and it was telling that she had never spoken to Hazel, her next door neighbour.

Holly carries on washing the dinner sets, adding to the discard pile and stacking the good pieces she'll keep. She recalls the meals she's eaten off these gilt-edged plates. Lillian cooked French dishes that took a long time and were rich and meaty: coq au vin; beef bourguignon; duck confit. She rarely served puddings, but there was invariably a good cheeseboard. Holly can't eat cheese, or any dairy, and Lillian would forget this.

Two hours later Pam comes upstairs to say the basement is done. Paige is standing at the bottom of the path by the gate, waiting for her.

'Do you want to take a look?' Pam asks.

The basement rooms are dust-free, and the floors are scrubbed. They've pushed the windows open to let in air, but she still smells the damp underneath the citric tang of the floor cleaner.

'You've done a great job. Thank you.'

'We found three dead frogs, squashed flat they were,' Pam says.

Holly pays Pam with cash.

'Would you be able to come back next week? The rest of the house needs a deep clean from top to bottom.'

'We're all booked up. Sorry.'

'If not next week, sometime soon?' Holly persists.

'We work as a couple, you see. I can't take on solo jobs.'

'I'd book you both, of course.'

'Sorry, but Paige's really spooked by the basement. Says it's got bad vibes. There's no way I could persuade her to come back here. Was all I could do to get her to complete today's work.'

'That's fine, not a problem,' Holly says, though it does not feel fine at all; it makes her thoroughly despondent. A witch's house with bad vibes! She's glad Ray will be joining her tomorrow.

Chapter Four

PENUMBRA HOUSE

F renzied screams in the garden wake her. An animal in distress. There it is again, high-pitched, pain-drenched, awful. Cats fighting over their territory. Or a fox tearing some prey apart?

Hearing it in the dark makes it worse and Holly wonders if Ray hears it in the basement. The scream comes again, and she tenses. What should she do? She gets out of bed and peers out at the garden. The giant fig tree looks sinister, absorbing the light, and nothing will make her venture out into the waist-high nettles. It's been raining and hordes of snails will be out. How she hates to stand on snails, the sickening crunch followed by a squelch, knowing she's killed them.

She can't see any wildlife moving out there. At last, the cries stop; silence returns and she un-tenses her body. Back in bed she turns on her side, pulls the duvet right up to her chin and tucks it round her tightly thinking how the garden at night is transformed into a fearsome place.

That afternoon she gets to work with her retractable tape measure, jotting down measurements in a notebook. The sheer size of the sitting room is daunting. How do you furnish a room like this? The sealed cupboards on either side of the fireplace intrigue her and she'll ask Ray to get them open.

He is settling into the basement and seems glad to be here. She knows the nearness of the house to the sea is the major draw for Ray agreeing to move to Brighton, rather than any lingering feelings he might have for her. Sea fishing is his passion.

He's told her he'll come up with his plan and outline budget for the renovation. When he arrives, he's carrying a four-pack of London Pride beer. They sit down opposite each other in the sitting room, and he unloads his bottles on the table and makes a roll-up. His green eyes have always attracted her, and she watches him squint as the smoke rises. Suddenly a weird knocking sound starts up. Holly leaps to her feet as it reverberates around the room. 'What *is* that?'

'It's the radiators warming up. Might have an airlock.'

She walks over to one of the cast iron radiators. 'That's all it is?'

'Yeah. They put out a good heat but weigh a ton. They're gonna be a bugger to move.'

'I don't want to move them.'

'You want to keep them?'

'Yes. They're an original architectural feature and I think they look good.'

He raises his eyebrows and grins at her.

'I'm not being pretentious,' she says.

29

He offers her a London Pride.

'No thanks. I'll get you a glass.'

He pours one for himself carefully and takes a swig before handing her the plan he's produced.

'The roof needs work and we'll have to dig up the drains. Whole place needs rewiring and replastering. You're gonna need your building fund, Hol.'

'The drains? Is that why it smells so damp downstairs?'

'A cracked drainpipe. Wouldn't be surprised if that bloody great fig tree's roots did the damage. You might have to take it down.'

'But surely the fig tree didn't—'

'You wouldn't believe the damage tree roots do.'

'Cutting it down is drastic.'

He shrugs. 'There are other options. You could dig down and check the roots. Big job though. Now, it looks like your aunt upgraded some switches a while back, but the fuse box is ancient.'

'Is it dangerous?'

'It needs to be changed.'

She looks at the spreadsheet he handed her, a detailed month-by-month breakdown of work required and the likely cost. The work could go on until June or even into July.

'The roof repairs are the big item. This is *not* a good time to be doing the roof, but we have to get the house weatherproof as soon as we can.'

'This is really helpful, Ray. Thanks so much.'

'I'll find us the lads to do the work. You pay them cash, and it helps you too because they won't charge VAT.'

'Isn't that sort of, well, illegal?'

Ray laughs and opens a second bottle.

'What about those sealed cupboards, Ray? Do you think you'll be able to open them?'

'Yeah. I'll come up with my tools tomorrow and take a look.'

THE NEXT DAY

Lillian has a sizeable collection of vases and lamps scattered through the house, and Holly plans to sell most of these on eBay. She gathers them together on the first floor and photographs them in the washed-out light. Outside the window, she hears the harsh cry of a seagull and sees him standing on her garden wall, looking noble. He has pale yellow eyes and looks as if he belongs on the wall, whereas she still feels she does not belong in Penumbra House.

A sharp rap on the front door and Ray is carrying his toolbox, as promised. He surveys the sealed cupboards in the sitting room before laying a dust sheet on the floor and selecting a range of sharp-edged tools.

'This'll be messy.'

She watches as he chisels at the years of paint which hold the door of the left-hand cupboard fast. Flakes of old paint fall away as he presses and gouges. Finally, he gets back to the wood and uses a bendy knife to work an opening from the top to the bottom of the cupboard. Holly moves nearer, intrigued at what the cupboards might hold.

He works his fingers in and slowly inches the door open. There's an exhalation as the door swings free with a loud creak. The cupboard is empty and is lined with green wallpaper with a repeating pattern of pastoral scenes. It gives off a strange smell, reminiscent of garlic.

'Well, look at that,' she says in wonder.

The scenes show two men with shotguns and a dog at their

side and a courting couple sitting in a wagon. The figures are picked out in vibrant green on a cream background.

'Amazing.' She reaches out to touch the pretty wallpaper.

'Don't touch it! Step back.'

'What?'

'Looks like Victorian wallpaper. There'll be arsenic in the dye.'

Holly drops her hand and steps back. She stares at the picturesque and benign scenes lining the cupboard, they're very much the work of a lost time. 'Such a pretty design.'

'It's a find but it has to go. I need to check how to get rid of it safely. Meanwhile we leave the cupboard shut.' He closes the door firmly and sticks two pieces of duct tape across it to stop it from swinging open.

They head to the kitchen, and Ray washes his hands thoroughly as she makes them tea.

'You're sure we can't conserve it. You'll have to rip it out?'

'We don't have a choice, Hol.'

'It's a shame. It's probably from the time of the original owner. Maybe that's why Lillian left the cupboards sealed.'

'How long did your aunt have this house?'

'She bought it in 1971. I've got the deeds.'

'Nearly fifty years. Why did she leave the cupboards like that? Big oversight.'

'She may not have known the wallpaper was toxic.'

'Oh, come on! Fifty years? And she didn't investigate? Looks to me like a case of postponing a problem; waiting for someone else to sort it out.'

He seems irritated with her as well as with Lillian. Yet another job to add to his long list.

After Ray has gone, Holly googles Victorian wallpaper and finds a review of a book on the poisonous pigments in the nineteenth century home. It's fascinating stuff, and she reads that a growing wallpaper trade in Britain used arsenic in the mix to produce bright colours. The vibrant emerald colour this produced was especially popular but also the most dangerous.

Victorians knew arsenic was poisonous and most homes had some lying around to kill mice and rats. But the belief was you would only get poisoned if you licked the wallpaper. Yet even left untouched, it released flakes of arsenic into the air or produced arsenical gas if conditions were damp. And after years of standing empty Penumbra House is certainly damp.

The wallpaper *is* a health hazard. Ray's criticism of Lillian was right, and her aunt has been remiss. It *is* in character though for her to have left the wallpaper untouched. Lillian often said how she respected the past more than the present and how our Victorian predecessors were better educated than us. She had sealed the poisonous wallpaper away, letting it become part of the very fabric of the house.

Chapter Five

PENUMBRA HOUSE

A grey mist hangs over the garden and a grey dawn breaks.

It's still early when she hears a sharp rap on the front door and goes to open it.

'She was never any good for this house.' The man standing on her doorstep looks to be in his sixties and has a weathered look about him.

'I beg your pardon?' Holly struggles to recover from the abruptness of this stranger.

'Lillian Hilborne. She never meant to live here. This house has suffered because of her.'

'I'm sorry, who are you?'

'Pumphrey. Barry Pumphrey.'

'And you knew my aunt?'

'Your aunt? I thought you were the new owner.'

'I am.'

'She sold this place to her own flesh and blood?'

'She *left* it to me.'

Why is she telling this strange man her business?

'I thought she must have died. Been a while since she made her yearly visit.'

'What do you know about that?'

'My wife used to clean the house before Miss Hilborne arrived. Scrubbed it from top to bottom every March.'

This partly reassures Holly that the man is less dangerous than she'd initially feared. 'I'm Holly, Lillian's niece.'

He gives a small nod. 'I've been worried about her garden.'

'You mean the wilderness at the back of the house.'

'That's nothing to do with me,' he says defensively.

'Why would it be?'

'I'm a gardener.'

'You did some work on it when my aunt...'

He cuts her short with a snort of derision. 'Wouldn't let me near it. I offered, but Lillian Hilborne was of the opinion nature should have its way.'

'Well, that's not an opinion I share—'

'Course not,' he butts in again. 'I mean it's a disgrace. So? Do you want me or not?'

There is something about the forthrightness of Barry Pumphrey she finds oddly appealing.

'It does need sorting out, but there's so much to do in the house first.'

'Not now. I'll come back in March and take a look.'

'Well, thank you.'

Why is she agreeing to this? The man is brusque to the point of rudeness.

'You won't find anyone who'll give you a better rate,' and with these words he turns to leave.

'Your wife…'

He stops abruptly and looks back at her.

'Does your wife still offer cleaning services?'

'My wife died years ago.'

'I'm sorry.'

'I'll see you in March.'

She watches him trudge up the road and turn at the corner. He is wearing an old brown overcoat which reaches below his knees. They spoke for only a matter of minutes, and in that time this gruff and abrupt man has more or less told her he'll be her gardener. She asks herself why she agreed to that, even though she hadn't actually said yes to him.

Holly watches as Ray pulls on gloves and a face mask.

'Really?' she says.

'Yeah, and if you're gonna watch put this mask on,' he says.

She loops the mask over her ears. Ray has contacted a specialist waste company who supplied him with bags marked 'hazardous waste'. He pushes open the large window and chilly air blows into the room. As he opens the left-hand cupboard she steps back and watches from near the door. There's still that strange smell from the cupboard. He scrapes at the wallpaper with a tool and the paper comes away in strips, which he bags at once.

'This bag goes straight to a licensed landfill,' he mutters through his mask.

She watches for a while until the coldness of the room drives her out. As she puts the kettle on, she considers how lucky she is to have Ray in her life.

Chapter Six

FEBRUARY

PENUMBRA HOUSE

All week there have been warnings of a great storm heading towards the country and due to make landfall on Sunday. Holly watches the weather bulletins which show vivid maps of the trajectory of the storm. Brighton will be affected. The weather woman advises people to avoid unnecessary travel and to lock away garden furniture.

That night Penumbra House is battered by gale-force winds and rain lashes the windows. Wheelie bins left out on the pavement are overturned, tarpaulins are ripped, and recycling boxes are tossed into the air like toys.

The hollow roar of the wind, a sound like no other, wakes Holly at five in the morning. The roar is followed by a high-pitched whistling, and she lies in the dark with a sense of foreboding. Something crashes into the garden, and she sits up. She pulls on her kimono and goes to the window.

A roof tile sails past and shatters on the ground. Two more

follow in its wake, smashing as they land. Gusts are convulsing the fig tree, pushing it back and forth in a frenzy. The thorn bushes by the walls judder and shriek as they scrape the bricks.

Moving into the kitchen, Holly puts on the kettle and hears more roof tiles plucked from the roof disintegrate outside. Surely Ray can't sleep through this commotion? The tiles are crashing right outside his windows.

As she stands and watches the wreckage in the garden, she wonders what happens to the birds in such a tumult. Do they hide deep in the hedges as their world swoops and heaves around them?

There's a rapping on the front door and Ray stands there gasping, his hair wet and sticking to his head from the short run from the basement.

'There'll be leaks up top and nothing to be done till it's light, except get the buckets out,' he says.

They make several journeys carrying buckets and pans to the top floor. The back room has taken the worst hit and rain is coming in through the gaps in the roof. They cover the floor with buckets and pans of all sizes and watch as the rain fills them. The front rooms are largely unaffected.

They settle at her kitchen table, and she makes them mugs of tea. There is a pattern to the storm; a break in the wind and for a moment blessed silence follows and the tree and thorn bushes are stilled. Then the wind roars back with renewed force and the fig tree bends and groans and more tiles are prised from the roof and crash on the paving stones right outside the window.

'We've lost so many tiles,' she says gloomily.

'Rotten luck this happening before we'd secured the roof,' Ray says.

They don't go back to bed. They empty the pans upstairs and sit in the kitchen.

'Best we keep watch till sunrise, not long now,' Ray says.

'I couldn't sleep with this going on anyway. I'll make more tea.'

Holly brings a fresh teapot to the table. Takes a breath.

'I wanted to let you know that James will be joining us in the house. He'll be living and practising as an osteopath on the top floor, only for a year,' she says.

She resisted telling Ray this before, not wanting to put him off moving in and helping her and she is stupidly nervous about his reaction. The two men do *not* like each other.

'When is he moving in?' Ray asks.

'Sometime in April, he said.'

'I'm surprised you agreed to that, Hol.'

She looks at him recalling how much she told Ray about James when they got together. It was eighteen months after her separation from James and she was still an emotional mess. Ray helped her put herself back together, but she had told him too much, far too much.

'Because he was unkind to me?' she says quietly.

'Yeah. You're a far more forgiving person than I could ever be.'

'It's not permanent. Just till he establishes himself.'

Ray doesn't look convinced. 'One big happy family,' he says grimly.

He gets up and stretches and clicks his neck. 'I'm knackered. I need a shower and a shave. Then we can go out and assess the damage in a bit.'

After Ray's gone Holly sits on at the table. His reaction to James joining the house, while it's to be expected, unsettles her. It echoes what Laura said. Doubts crowd her mind and peck away at her resolve.

'I'm tired,' she says aloud. 'I always doubt myself when I'm tired.'

By nine the wind drops, and the rain peters out. Ray and Holly pull on wellington boots and go out to survey the damage. The garden is littered with broken roof tiles, severed branches, and roots, and there's a strong smell of wet earth. Spencer joins them in the garden soon after, and he helps them sweep the debris and stack the larger pieces of tiles at the top of the garden. They gather the broken branches and make a pile.

'Sodden wood. It will be months before we can have a bonfire with these,' Spencer says.

They stand at the top of the garden and see the many gaps in the back half of the roof.

'Oh well, we had to mend the roof anyway,' Ray says.

Ray has found a scaffolding company who offer good rates. They can start at once as few people are putting up scaffolds in February.

'Do you want to pay for the scaffold to be alarmed, Hol? There's an extra charge if you do.'

'I don't know. What do you think?'

'The house is occupied so there's little threat of burglars. And once it's up we'd hear anyone climbing on it. I probably wouldn't bother but it's your call.'

'I think we'll leave it,' she says.

Two days later a team of three men arrive early with a lorry loaded with tubes, couplers, and boards, and for once it isn't raining. There follows a day of non-stop clanking and grinding, shouted instructions and their radio playing pop music at top volume as they build the scaffold to reach the roof at the back of the house.

Holly spends the day ferrying mugs of tea and ginger nut biscuits to the men, asking if they'd like to come in out of the cold to have their breaks. All three say they'll take their breaks outside ta, and Ray tells her that in the building trade scaffolders are known to be the toughest crew of the lot.

By sunset the scaffold is in place and it's a significant moment for Holly. She watches Ray hand the boss an envelope bulging with twenty-pound notes. She and Ray have agreed Ray will do all the paying of the workmen.

'We're on our way,' she says, cheerful because there is nothing worse than a house that leaks.

'Do you fancy a drink at The Wounded Hart to celebrate?' Ray suggests.

It has become Ray's local, and she agrees, wanting to mark the moment the renovation of Penumbra House has truly begun. There's no going back now. The house has a hold on her.

Chapter Seven

PENUMBRA HOUSE

I t turns into the wettest February on record. Gardens are saturated with nowhere for rainwater to run off. Roadside puddles grow to the size of ponds. Holly is up and down the stairs emptying the buckets on the top floor. The work on the roof gets going for one day and then has to stop. She frets about the delay, but Ray is philosophical.

'It'll get done,' he says.

There are signs of a good atmosphere developing in the house. Ray settles into his basement and is working through his plan. Spencer arrives early most mornings and spends hours upstairs painting. The two men like each other. Holly is less settled. They both have work to do, but she does not. For the first few weeks she is mildly panicked about how to spend her days. If she isn't a teacher, who is she?

She spends a lot of time cleaning the house, dusting and sweeping. Ray says the old plaster dust will just keep falling and why not learn to live with it until there's new plaster on the walls. But she keeps on cleaning anyway.

James calls her and says he wants to move in early, indeed next week, two months earlier than she expected.

'I really wouldn't. The back room took a hit in the storm and it's full of buckets catching the leaks.'

'How about the front rooms?'

'They're dry.'

'I'll base myself there to start with,' he says.

With his arrival imminent, Holly sets herself the task of blitzing the top floor. As she carries the hoover and broom upstairs, she meets Spencer on the landing.

'I'm done for today. Let me take that.' He carries the hoover to the second floor.

'James is moving in *next week*,' she says.

They look at the rooms and at each other.

'I know, but he would *not* be put off. He told me, finally, that the lease on his flat is expiring and he doesn't want to sign up for another six months. That's the reason for his early arrival.'

'You OK with that?'

'I think it's crazy to move in with the room in such a state. But when James gets an idea in his head there's no shifting him.'

'We'll be full house then.'

'Yes, we will.' She sounds doubtful, hears it in her voice.

'A big house like this, plenty of room to get away from each other,' Spencer says. 'Can I do anything to help now?'

'Thanks for the offer but no need. I'm going to give the rooms a clean and it shouldn't take me long.'

'At least let me help you take the buckets out of the back room.'

They shift the buckets into the hall, and he leaves.

She tackles the dry front rooms first, hoovering the bare boards and wiping the skirting boards with a damp cloth. The kitchen is old fashioned but perfectly functional. The main back room that overlooks the garden is a different matter altogether. The floor planks are wet and slippery. One of the floorboards in the corner is black and as she steps on it the rotten wood gives way, splinters, and her right foot goes straight through. She thumps onto her bottom, jars her spine and feels something sharp pierce her ankle and lower leg.

'Damn!'

She tries to pull her foot out but it is caught tight in a lattice of sharp wood splinters, and she feels something moist on her leg. Is she bleeding? Looking down she can't see her foot. She flexes it hoping to lever it out. The network of broken wood holds her fast, and it hurts even to move her foot. If she wrenches her foot out, she'll cut herself more deeply.

She manoeuvres gingerly and gets into a kneeling position on her left leg. She rolls up her sleeve and puts her right hand down into the hole which is deep and gritty. She tries to work her foot free from the shards of wood which are gripping her. A long splinter has embedded itself in her leg. She inches this splinter out, gasping with the pain. When she withdraws her hand, her fingers are covered in blood.

'Shit!'

Her left leg is cramping, from the awkward angle of her kneeling, and she has to straighten it out and jig it up and down till the muscle pain passes. The base of her spine is throbbing where she landed hard. She wipes her bloody fingers on her jeans thinking she is trapped because Ray is in the basement and won't hear her cries for help. Spencer won't be back till tomorrow morning. She can't sit in this room all night, she just can't. The room is getting dark, and she is already shivering. If only she had brought her mobile with her.

She'll have to grit her teeth and tug her leg out in spite of the pain. Be brave. Do it. But she keeps delaying the moment, fearful of the damage she might do to herself. Isn't there a big artery in the leg? She tells herself to get a grip, count to three, and pull her leg out.

'One, two, three…'

She tugs with all her might and there is a ripping sound and the sharpest pain in her leg as something gives below. But her foot is still caught.

'Again!' she says loudly. 'Come on! One, two, three…'

She screams as her foot finally breaks free and is out of the hole. There is a lot of blood around her ankle. She crawls to the other side of the room, away from the evil hole, and looks at her bleeding leg.

'OK. It's OK. Get downstairs and ring Ray.'

He drives her to A&E in his white van. They have to wait, and Ray consumes a cup of machine coffee every hour, which stokes his impatience.

He goes outside for a roll-up and when he comes back, he looks disgusted to see Holly is still sitting there waiting to be treated. She sits slumped on the white plastic chair. She knows he's thinking she should have been more careful. Her leg is throbbing, her back hurts. And she is thoroughly miserable. It's as if the house doesn't want her there and is working against her. I'm not an uninvited guest; I'm *the owner* she keeps saying to herself.

'Please go, Ray. I'll get a taxi back,' she says, after two hours.

'I'm not leaving till they patch you up.'

He's impatient but also chivalrous.

Finally, they call her name. A deep flesh wound, and she needs stitches and a tetanus shot because the wood was rotten and dirty.

Ray drives her home, and they say good night quickly. It is clear he can't wait to get back to his basement and to bed.

She hobbles into her bedroom and sits on the edge of her bed feeling rattled. Those words in Lillian's draft letter pop into her mind as they have done many times since she found it.

I have hardly slept since so deep is my dread. I am consumed with the thought I have not done the right thing and should have reported my suspicions.

What information had Lillian kept to herself which tormented her conscience so badly? Holly curses Penumbra House with its dark corners, its rotten floorboards, poisonous materials, and its secrets.

Chapter Eight

BRIGHTON

By noon it stops raining, and she gets the bus to the clock tower. James is arriving at two and they are meeting at the station. Brighton is looking shabby. Holly does not remember it looking so run-down on her annual visits to Lillian. London Road is a procession of nail bars, pound shops and charity shops. The centre of town shows signs of decay too with faded fascia boards, stained pavements, and the public buildings need a coat of paint. Ten years of austerity has left their mark.

She walks the last brief stretch to the station slowly. Her right foot and leg are healing but are still tender. She passes a pub called The Hope and Ruin, a memorable name and one she hopes does *not* apply to Penumbra House.

Will the arrival of James, earlier than expected, disrupt the harmony of the house? When she started dating Ray, James referred to him as Holly's 'bit of rough' and 'a horny-handed son of toil'. She was so angry James has never dared to be snobbish about Ray again. But James has a need to be in control of things, though the shock of the financial crash has knocked the edges off him. Ray is also an alpha male, and the two men might well compete to be top dog. It's a good thing James will be on the top floor and Ray has his own entrance to the basement, avoiding any awkward encounters on the staircase.

James also has issues with Spencer. During the early years of their marriage, James would complain that Spencer was hovering around too much, 'sniffing around her' was the unpleasant phrase he used. But Spencer is not the reason they split up, even if James invoked his name bitterly to cover the truth which was too painful to acknowledge. From tonight her three exes will be under one roof, her roof. She hopes Laura's warnings turn out to be wrong. What did Ray say? One big happy family!

Standing at the barrier she watches James wheel his large suitcase along the platform with a rolled-up yoga mat slung on his shoulder. Since becoming a student, he has grown a beard and shaved his head. He is three years younger than her so will be a qualified osteopath at forty-six which gives him at least twenty years to practice. James kisses her on both cheeks.

'My furniture's arriving tomorrow. Do you have a spare bed?'

'There's a single bed on the top floor. Not the most comfortable and I was thinking of throwing it out.'

'It'll do me fine.'

'The taxi rank is close,' she says.

'We can walk, can't we? My case is on wheels.'

'It's a twenty-minute walk and my foot is still healing.'

He glances at her bandaged leg. 'OK.'

They wait in line then get into a taxi.

'I've cleaned the top floor as best I can, but the back room got the brunt of the damage during the storm and it's a mess. There's a working kitchen and an antiquated shower,' Holly says.

'Great. Thanks.'

When they pull up outside the house, James does not reach for his wallet until Holly suggests they split the fare between them. How he's changed, she thinks, this new frugal James. He once made a pile of money in financial services and enjoyed spending big, buying her designer dresses, and taking her to fancy restaurants.

But that was before the crash of 2008. Now he has found his vocation but is financially challenged. It's why they haven't got round to divorcing yet as Holly agreed they could wait until he's back on his feet financially.

James looks at the façade of Penumbra House and raises one eyebrow. 'It's so *big*, Holly.'

'Yes, and the rooms are huge.'

'What a change from your flat.'

'I'm very lucky.'

She pushes open the front gate and the wheels of his case get caught in the path where the tiles are missing. He tugs to free his suitcase.

'I plan to fix the path,' she says. Why is she apologising to him?

She leads him up the stairs to the top floor. He walks into the room overlooking the garden where the floorboards are beginning to dry out slowly.

'Be careful about the hole in the corner,' she says.

Ray has cut away the rotten wood and left a neat square aperture ready to replace with new wood.

'OK.'

'That's where my foot went through. I needed stitches and a tetanus shot.'

'This will be a good space to meditate,' he says.

Typical James, ignoring my troubles, she thinks.

They move to the front room, which is clean and dry, but it strikes her how spartan it is, and the bed, with its old-fashioned iron bedstead, looks forlorn stripped of bedding.

'That's the bed I always slept in when I came to stay,' she says.

'Why did she put you all the way up here?'

'I used to wonder about that.'

She laughs. 'Maybe she wanted to make sure I only stayed the one night. I've got a spare duvet and pillows, I'll get them.'

Later, James joins her in the kitchen, and she makes them a cafetière of coffee.

'I bumped into Spencer,' he says.

'He works here most days.'

'Where does he live now?'

'Saltdean, in a house-share.'

'A house-share? Does he make a living from his paintings?'

'He gets by. His work has got better over the years and if anyone deserves to succeed it's Spencer.'

James has always rather despised the fact Spencer doesn't care about money. She notices he still has the tidy gene and is lining up the two cartons of milk – dairy and soya and placing a teaspoon next to each carton. James likes order and symmetry and hates clutter of any kind.

When they lived together, there was a constant battle between them over the state of the surfaces. He liked them clear but Holly would often leave papers on the table. And he hated it if she brought in the milk bottles from the doorstep and forgot to wipe them before putting them in the fridge. He was committed to getting their milk delivered in glass bottles, even though they didn't deliver soya then, so she'd had to buy hers from the supermarket. Their marriage was made up of these small daily battles and resentments, she remembers, as she pours him a mug of coffee.

'Welcome to the house. There's plenty of space and we each have our own floor which is a good thing.'

'Thanks. I'm glad to be here, a good place to prepare for my exams. It's quite some house and your aunt Lillian did you proud.'

It is Saturday and Spencer has not come to the house. It's raining again, and she is in the sitting room with Ray when she sees a large van pull up outside and steer around a puddle before parking. She calls up to James.

'The removal men are here.'

One of the men brings in a box marked 'Fragile' and parks it in the hall. James hurries down the stairs and opens the box at once.

'I just want to check something's travelled OK,' he says.

He pulls away the bubble wrap and lifts out a heavy stone figure of the Buddha, about a foot high, to show them.

'I bought this to put in my treatment room. It's a fine piece, isn't it?'

She nods. 'It is.'

'Looks like he ate too many Indian takeaways,' Ray says.

'Thanks for the casual racism, Ray,' James says.

'Bollocks! I love a curry,' Ray retorts.

The rain makes the move more difficult and there are tracks of muddy footprints in the hall and up the stairs. The buckets are in the back room again and James tells the men to

JANE LYTHELL

put everything in the front. He has a double bed and a professional treatment bed which moves up and down at the touch of a button.

'I'd like to keep the single bed too if that's OK with you?' he asks Holly.

'Sure, if you've got a use for it.'

She carries up his two large framed prints. One is of a skeleton and the other is a coloured illustration showing all the muscles and tendons of the body in nasty shades of pink and orange. He has boxes of textbooks, and she knows he'll take an age ordering these alphabetically.

'I'll leave you to it,' she says.

'Would you mind making the guys a drink?'

'OK.'

In the evening James comes down to her bedroom carrying his flattened cardboard boxes.

'For recycling,' he says.

Holly is sitting on her bed looking at Ray's latest budget.

'You settling in OK?'

'It'll be fine once the back room dries out. My treatment room will be at the front and my personal space at the back. Will Ray mend the hole in the floor?'

'It's on the list,' she says.

'And how long will the scaffold be up?'

'The roofers are working whenever they can. There's two of them, one does the tiling and the other the lead work.'

James glances at her. 'Never thought you'd be interested in building processes, must be Mr DIY's influence.'

She gives him a look. 'I'm paying for it, so I like to know what they're doing.'

'Fair enough. I'll meditate first thing before they come or after they've gone.'

James started meditating when he became a student, and a day doesn't go by when he doesn't practise.

'The hall and stairs are muddy, James, from your removal men.'

He nods.

'Would you give them a quick mop.'

He looks bemused.

'Mop the mud off the stairs. I don't have a cleaner.'

'I don't have the equipment,' he says.

'You can use my mop and bucket. And tomorrow will be fine,' she says.

She gets off her bed and takes them from the cupboard underneath the stairs, leaving them in the hall.

'OK,' he relents.

She hears him climb the stairs to his floor and sees he has left the mop and bucket in the hall. *I won't be cleaning up after you anymore, James*, she thinks.

———

The next morning Holly is in her sitting room when she hears James ask Spencer if he'll give him a hand with washing the mud off the stairs. She feels like stepping in when she hears Spencer agree but holds back.

At the end of the day, when he's finished painting, she follows Spencer out onto the street.

'You helped James clean the stairs, Spencer. You didn't have to do that. It was *his* removal men who tracked in all that mud.'

'It's not a problem.'

'James can be a user. I had years of it and it's something to look out for.'

'It didn't take me long.'

'Maybe. Anyway, it was nice of you, thanks.'

He smiles, such a winning smile, and gets onto his bike.

'See you tomorrow.' He waves and cycles off.

She watches him leave, sighs, and turns back to the house, thinking, *Am I being petty?*

Chapter Nine

PENUMBRA HOUSE

Holly has been out shopping and when she opens her front door, she sees a sheet of paper lying on the doormat. She kneels and picks it up. No envelope and it's Aunt Lillian's distinctive handwriting which startles her. Where did this come from? Standing in the hall, she reads it at once.

BRITTANY 1973

I was not cut out to be a mother. I knew it early on and made a vow as a teenager never to have children. Small children irritate and bore me, and teenagers are absurdly self-obsessed.

I arranged to see a doctor in Rennes privately and not the doctor in the village whose discretion I do not trust. Too many stories emanate from his surgery. The doctor sat at his table and his expression was mildly benevolent. He told me the pregnancy test was positive, and I was well into the third month which meant I was out of the danger zone. At forty-one, he said, they would monitor my pregnancy, but the signs were good. I was deeply shaken. Pregnant at forty-one was worse than an inconvenience; it was not who I was or wanted to be.

It was a week before I could bring myself to tell Jacques and his reaction was completely different from mine. I prepared him by saying I had some difficult news to share. When I said I was three months pregnant his face softened and there was a light in his eyes. There are no children in his marriage, and I knew at that moment he wanted a child, had probably hoped for one for years. This surprised me, and it upset me too. I thought we shared the same attitude towards children.

He kissed my hands and said he welcomed the pregnancy with all his heart. He would do all he could to support me, and it would not change anything fundamentally. What he meant was he would not tell his wife and we would go on living separately, meeting at my house whenever we could.

I love him and I cannot break with him so the pregnancy will have to proceed.

When Jacques left, I stood in my garden and watched a tractor moving slowly up and down the field which borders my house. Birds were wheeling above the tractor, following its path. I chose this house because of its location. I am in walking distance of the village but have no close neighbours. There is a field and a copse beyond, and a day will pass and the only person I see will be a farm labourer and, occasionally, the postman on his bicycle. The house gives Jacques and me the privacy we desire. It is not a large house, but it has always been big enough for me. It is old, made of stone, the windows are narrow, and the walls are thick. The house is quiet, and it is a good place to work on my translations. I am productive here.

And now this wretched pregnancy. My body has betrayed me.

Holly feels almost dizzy as she walks into her bedroom, clutching the piece of paper to her chest. She sits at her desk and reads it again, then examines the sheet. It looks like a page that has been cut out of a book. The cut is very precise, as if a Stanley knife was used. She is focusing on these small details because the content is so startling and she can't quite take it in.

She reads it a third time. Lillian was *pregnant*. By the man in the photograph. And he wanted the baby, and she didn't. It goes against everything she thought she knew about her aunt – the solitary intellectual who didn't need people. Yet this sounds like Lillian's voice speaking to her, as if from a private journal. And it *is* Lillian's handwriting. She recognises those loops and the dark blue ink.

I love him and I cannot break with him so the pregnancy will have to proceed.

Lillian continued with the pregnancy, but no child has *ever* been mentioned, has ever existed as far as she and her father knew. Had Lillian miscarried? As Holly had, twice. Lillian would have been forty-one in 1973, only eight years younger than Holly now. Lillian *may* have miscarried.

Holly walks over to her bedroom window and looks out at the overgrown garden. She was right about Lillian having a lover. But he was married and was not willing to leave his wife when his mistress became pregnant. Strangely, Holly does not feel like sharing this information with Laura. Usually, she is the first person she tells things to, but it feels disloyal to her aunt to reveal her secret torment.

How had that page arrived on her doormat? *Who* posted it through the letter box?

She shivers. Someone knows personal stuff about her aunt, stuff which she does not know. And it must be someone in Brighton who knows Holly is living at Penumbra House.

She's been thinking a lot about her aunt, piecing together the stories her father told her about his older sister. Lillian was a sought-after translator of French into English. Two of her early fiction translations were international bestsellers and Lillian bought Penumbra House with the proceeds. Houses were cheaper fifty years ago, Holly reflects, thinking of her own struggle to buy her tiny flat in London.

Later, Lillian bought a house in Brittany as well. Holly's dad told her Lillian had big plans for the Brighton house but something changed that. Did meeting Jacques Pichois change that? The house in Brittany became Lillian's primary residence, and there was speculation about her life there. What was the draw which kept her living in an isolated village? Holly thinks she knows the answer now.

She retrieves the plastic folder from her desk where she put the draft letter found in the box and also the short letter from Lillian which her English solicitor in Brittany gave her when he informed her of her inheritance. She had been disappointed in that letter, the last words of her aunt to her. It was a single sheet of paper, and she reads it again.

> *My dear Holly,*
> *I believe you have it in you to rise to the challenge of Penumbra House.*
> *Courage!*
> *Lillian*

She had expected more from her aunt. After all, Lillian was a translator who had a way with words. The letter was so short and cryptic. And there was her use of the word *Courage*; probably to be understood in the French way: Cou-rage, like a call to arms or something. What did Lillian mean by that?

Chapter Ten

PENUMBRA HOUSE

Holly is on her knees giving the oven a clean when she hears raised voices in the hall. It is Ray and James, and she hurries to join them.

'One day I'll meet a builder who'll give me a straight answer.' James directs his exasperation at Holly.

'I'll get to it when I can. Is that straight enough?' Ray barks back.

'Get to what?' Holly feels the need to intervene.

'The hole in the floor in my back room,' says James.

'He's not stopped banging on about it,' Ray says.

Both men are using her as an intermediary.

'Because it needs fixing,' James says.

'I'll do it, but it doesn't stop you using the room. Getting the house weatherproofed is the priority,' Ray snaps.

'It's still dangerous. I could put my foot through it.'

'So look where you're going!' Ray stomps into Holly's kitchen.

James looks at her and slowly shakes his head.

'Please drop it, James. He's working flat out,' she says.

'How do you deal with someone like that?'

She's never known James not to have the last word. As he goes upstairs, she joins Ray in the kitchen.

'Well, you two have obviously hit it off,' she says.

'He's been here five minutes and straight away it's all about what he wants.'

'That's James. Tea?'

'Ta. I'm not surprised you kicked him out, Hol.'

'Let's not get too personal. Biscuits?'

'But I'm amazed he was ever your old man.'

Holly momentarily freezes, a packet of digestives in her hand. Has Ray gone too far? They look at one another for a few seconds before they burst out laughing.

Early Saturday morning and the house is quiet. Spencer has not turned up and the roofers won't be back till Monday. Two days without rain has let them get on with the work at last.

Holly enjoys the silence as she makes a pot of tea and looks out at the garden, her garden, in the morning light. There are a few green shoots at the base of the fig tree, and she watches a blackbird pecking at a tuft. She found a biscuit barrel in one of the cupboards and washes it. It has a design of pink roses and blue birds, and this surprises her because it is sweetly pretty, and she doesn't think of Lillian as a blue bird and roses type of person.

Footsteps sound down the stairs and James walks in dressed in jogging pants, a sweatshirt and grey felt slippers.

'Morning. Can you loan me a few tea bags? I'm right out.'

'Sure. I've just made a pot. Do you want a cup?'

James takes a sip. 'Thanks. I see you've abandoned Earl Grey.'

'Yes, back on English Breakfast. And the workmen prefer it.'

'Those first-floor rooms could be really nice.'

'I think they're really nice as a working studio.'

'You don't object to the smell of solvent?'

'Not at all.'

'It's a strong smell and it lingers. I'd be willing to pay more rent if you let me have the first floor. And Spencer could do his painting at the top of the house.'

'No can-do, James. I offered Spencer that floor months ago and I'm not going back on it.'

'Why not? I'm sure he wouldn't mind. He's very laid-back and don't artists usually work in garrets?'

'I think he would mind. He loves the light in those rooms. And anyway, *I would mind.*'

He shrugs and picks up his mug. James is never slow to make demands and she tries to quell her irritation as she goes through the mail she's found on the front mat – a leaflet from the Labour Party on homelessness in the city, a pizza flier and a card offering chimney sweeping services.

'Do you think I should get the chimneys swept?'

'Might be an idea. I'm about to do a mindfulness meditation, would you like to join me? Best way to begin the day.'

'OK, why not.'

She follows him to the top floor. The back room is empty except for his yoga mat. He places two cushions on the floor and sits with his back to the window as she sits cross-legged opposite him. He scrolls through his phone.

'I like this one. It's a guided meditation and lasts about twenty-five minutes.'

JANE LYTHELL

He presses 'start' and the room fills with the low sound of waves and a woman's soft voice telling them to breathe in deeply through the nose and release the breath through the mouth with an audible sigh to empty out the old stale air.

Holly closes her eyes and does as instructed.

Now breathe in and out through your nostrils and focus on the physical sensation of breathing; notice how the air coming in is colder than the air going out.

Holly tries to focus. She has not meditated before and finds her mind running over the tasks planned for the week ahead. She wants to buy a new duvet cover for the sofa bed in the sitting room before Laura comes.

When thoughts arise let them go and gently bring your attention back to your breath, the woman's voice intones.

Holly tries to empty her mind, but she hears something outside the window. It's the scrape of scaffold tubes. There it is again. Could it be a seagull landing?

Holly opens one eye. James is sitting entirely still; his palms open on his knees, his eyes closed and his breathing regular. He looks the image of a practised meditator.

The scraping noise continues, and she sees, with mild alarm, the shaking of the scaffold. James remains unmoved, breathing slowly and rhythmically. Ray looms into view on the scaffold plank right outside and seeing the scene in front of him pulls a silly face, waggling his eyebrows up and down.

She gives him a warning look, but he flattens his face against the glass and his splayed cheeks and lips look so ridiculous a giggle bursts out of her.

James opens his eyes, turns around and sees Ray. 'For heaven's sake! The man's a child!' He turns off the meditation with an angry stab of his finger.

'Shall we go on with it?' Holly says.

'No point, my focus has gone.'

She gets to her feet, walks over to the window, and pushes it open. A blast of cold air comes into the room.

'What are you doing up here?' James snaps.

'I climbed up to check the guttering and downpipes,' Ray says.

James is still looking cross and ignores Ray who is inching along the plank out of view. James puts the cushions away and Ray comes back soon after.

'As I thought, some of the downpipes need replacing,' he calls cheerily through the open window.

'Thanks for checking that,' she says.

'Ohmmm…' Ray intones.

He disappears from view, climbing down the scaffolding.

'He just loves to be Mr Indispensable, doesn't he?' James says.

With time on her hands, Holly turns her attention to cooking. After the break-up of her marriage, she hadn't cooked much and would often settle for hummus on toast or a salad pot after a day of teaching. Now she experiences the simple pleasures of cooking from scratch, browsing through recipe books and selecting the ingredients. It's a way of relaxing into her new life in the house.

First of all, she has to learn the quirks of Aunt Lillian's oven, which puts out a tremendous heat only distantly related to what the dials say. There have been a couple of disasters which ended in the bin. She perseveres with the oven and gradually makes a friend of it. She likes making soups. Her pea and pesto is an old favourite, but now she experiments with a mushroom soup and roasted red pepper and tomato. Some evenings Spencer joins her for a bowl before he cycles back to Saltdean.

Now James is installed upstairs an idea starts to form. Maybe she'll cook a roast dinner, once a month, and invite the men to come together on her floor. She'll do it on a Sunday, and she likes the notion of a monthly get-together. It will give them an opportunity to discuss any issues about the house and maybe build a sense of shared endeavour.

Chapter Eleven

LATE FEBRUARY

PENUMBRA HOUSE

H olly comes out of her bedroom and gives an involuntary shiver when she sees a piece of paper lying on the doormat. She runs to the front door, flings it open and scans the street in both directions. There is no one about. It is early and she has no idea how long the paper has been lying there.

Reluctantly she picks it up feeling a desire to hiccup build in her diaphragm. She goes back into her bedroom, closes the door, and reads the two sheets of Lillian's handwriting.

> *BRITTANY 1974*
> *My labour lasted thirty-six painful hours. I gave birth to a boy.*
> *Jacques had booked me into a private hospital in Rennes and I had my own room. I asked him to stay away until the baby was delivered, and he did as I asked.*
> *He came to the hospital and the nurse handed him the baby. He*

was joyful and thanked me for giving him a son. He said he would like to call him Emmanuel and I agreed.

I caught an infection from the bathroom there and had to stay in hospital for a week. On the third day after the birth, I could not stop weeping. The maternity nurse said that was normal, it was the hormones. She showed me how to bath a newborn baby and it is not an easy thing to do.

I longed to be back in my home with my books around me, but when I got home, I was the bleakest I have ever been.

I can find no comfort, not even from reading. I am losing a lot of weight.

Emmanuel cries all the time. He has not taken to breastfeeding and is not gaining weight. I was advised to move him onto formula which I did. He is gaining weight at last but remains the most fretful infant.

Jacques visits us regularly and brings toys for Emmanuel. The latest is a box of coloured wooden bricks. How many times can you build a tower and watch a child knock it over and build it up again?

I will not be able to get to Brighton for a while. It is too much of an effort to think about travelling there with all the equipment an infant needs. I will have to set something up; find a cleaner for the house. Yet days pass and I have little energy to do anything. I am sometimes still in my dressing gown in the afternoon.

Bleak and pointless.

Why is it so difficult? Where has my old life gone? I am used to spending hours on my own, with my books and my work. I crave the luxury of empty time to produce beautiful translations. Never being able to get away from a small crotchety child with his endless demands is hell. Yet I cook and puree vegetables for him now that he is on solids. I hope a full stomach will make him more content and better able to sleep through the night.

We discussed employing someone from the village to help look after Emmanuel but decided against it. We wish to keep our life as private as possible. And people in the village love to talk.

The health visitor has been here and tells me to sleep when Emmanuel sleeps. She said if I'm sleep deprived it makes everything more difficult. I don't tell her that the only time I do any work is when he sleeps. I manage a few pages at most and my translations are suffering. Is it wrong to care so much about my reputation as a translator?

Holly reads Lillian's words through twice. Her aunt had gone through with it and given birth to a son; a son she and her father knew nothing about. It is truly extraordinary. Why did Lillian keep this huge thing a secret from her family, from her brother whom she was close to? *Hell* is her description of being with the baby.

I have a cousin Emmanuel, Holly thinks. Or I *had* a cousin. Is he still alive? Maybe he died as an infant. Maybe that is why the house came to me. It might also explain why Lillian buried his existence. How sad that would be. The short life and death of an unknown boy.

Holly inspects the edges of the pages. As with the first entry, it has been carefully cut out from a book. Lillian must have kept a journal, and Holly senses there is more to come. What is sinister is the thought someone, an unknown person, has this bombshell information about her aunt and is posting it through her door bit by bit.

Is someone watching the house, waiting for their moment to post the pages through Holly's letter box; unseen and unknown? The thought thoroughly unnerves her. If whoever is doing this intends to unbalance her, they are succeeding.

Laura is coming to stay for two nights, and Holly expects her on Saturday morning. They hadn't heard back from the Channel Four TV programme, which doesn't really surprise Holly. They must get countless requests for their team to renovate old houses. But Laura was disappointed.

Holly wipes down all the surfaces, scrubs the bathroom and makes up the sofa bed in the sitting room with the pretty new duvet cover she's bought. There are no curtains at the huge windows, so she pushes the sofa bed as far away from the window as possible. Will Laura mind the possibility of being overlooked.

It is well after 1pm when her phone pings:

On my way in a taxi. See you soon. Xx

Laura and her dog Cooper step out of the taxi, and she is wearing big sunglasses.

'Sorry I'm later than intended, sweetie. I've got a hell of a head. My team bought me a gin journey voucher for my birthday, and I did it last night.'

Holly kneels down to caress Cooper.

'What's a gin journey?'

'You have this guide, and he takes you to five different venues to sample five different gin cocktails. Seemed like a good idea last night!'

'Was it fun?'

'It sort of was, you know. There were ten of us and we were raucous by the end. You get chauffeured from place to place, which was just as well.'

'Black coffee?'

'Please, extra strong.'

Laura follows her into the kitchen. Holly runs her a large glass of water, puts down a bowl for Cooper and makes the coffee strong. Cooper scampers to the back kitchen door.

'Shall I let him out?'

'Thanks.'

Cooper is down the steps and heads straight for the fig tree. He relieves himself and starts to dig enthusiastically at the base of the trunk.

'He's doing it again,' Holly says.

'Doing what?'

'Digging a hole by the fig tree.'

'We need to take him for a proper walk,' Laura says.

'I've made up a bed in the sitting room. Do you want to leave your bag in there?'

They enter the sitting room.

'This will be spectacular when it's decorated,' Laura says.

'Yes, best room in the house.'

'You're Holly the Heiress now and you better make sure you change your will!' Laura quips. 'Now, poor Cooper is overdue a walk.'

They take Cooper to Preston Park and let him off his lead. Laura is wearing her heeled boots with her jeans, and she'll happily walk miles in them, which always strikes Holly as an achievement. Her injured foot has healed but she is sticking to sneakers.

After the park they head for the North Laine where the independent shops cluster: vintage dresses; vegetarian shoes; a shop which sells nothing but spices and a fudge emporium from which the sweet smell of butter, sugar, and vanilla wafts. They peer in and see a woman rolling out warm fudge on a marble slab.

'I'd like her job,' Holly says.

'Step away from the fudge.'

'You're right. Let's go down to the sea.'

Laura is revived by their bracing walk along the seafront and finally takes off her sunglasses. When they reach the derelict West Pier, she lets Cooper off the lead, and he scampers joyfully in front of them. The metal skeleton of the pier is black against the sky and yellowish waves foam at its foundation.

'I can't believe they're letting great chunks of metal fall into the sea like that. Surely it's a danger?' Laura says.

'You'd think, but it's been like this for years. I guess swimmers know to give it a wide berth.'

'Well, I think it's bizarre.'

Two young women hurry past them chatting happily.

'Have you noticed how young girls wear false eyelashes all the time these days?' Laura says. 'I mean I used to put them on for a party. They wear them for a stroll on the beach.'

'Thick and black and they remind me of spiders' legs. Yuk.'

They head back into town.

'Maybe a bus home? It's an uphill walk,' Holly says.

'A taxi and it's on me.'

Laura opens the door at the front of the rank, a massive eight-seater with heavy doors, and white with the outline of the Pavilion printed in turquoise on its side.

'What's it like having the Three Stooges as your housemates?'

Holly smiles wryly at Laura's latest unflattering nickname for her exes. 'So far so good, though James thinks I'm wasting the first-floor rooms on Spencer.'

'He'll be angling to get them for himself.'

'Of course he is. But that isn't going to happen. I don't want him to get too comfortable. The big difference, Laura, is that I invited Ray and Spencer into the house and James invited himself.'

'Is he paying you rent?'

'Oh yes. I asked to have it in advance.'

'Good gal. How is Ray working out?'

'He's been brilliant. Gets me good deals and takes the stress out of the renovation.'

'No late night spliff and loud music sessions then?'

'If he does, I haven't heard him,' Holly says.

———

That night, Laura is stylish in silk pyjamas and sits cross-legged on the sofa bed scanning her phone.

'I've been whatsapping Charlie,' she says.

'Is everything OK with him?'

Holly's fond of Laura's grown-up son.

'He's got this new girlfriend, Iona. They met a few months ago and it's getting serious.'

Laura pulls a mock-tragic face.

'What's wrong with that?'

'I know it's massively shallow of me but I'm not ready to be a grandmother.'

'That's jumping the gun, isn't it?'

Though it's likely Laura *will* become a grandmother in her fifties, Holly thinks, and how wonderful it would be to have a grandchild to love and help care for. They never dwell on the fact that Laura managed to get pregnant so easily and deliver a healthy son, a son she adores.

'You would be an exceedingly *glam gran*,' Holly says.

Laura throws down her mobile and picks up a bottle of overnight reset serum, peering into a small round magnifying mirror with its own light. Holly is always struck at how well-equipped Laura is with her products and her accessories. Laura does not look entirely happy as she dabs serum delicately onto the skin under her eyes.

'Well, there's nothing I can do about it. I'll be better company tomorrow, sweetie. I needed to get the gin out of my system.'

Laura wriggles under the duvet and Cooper is lying at her feet. She puts on her eye mask and Holly turns off the light and leaves the room.

Chapter Twelve

L aura helps Holly prepare for the inaugural roast dinner.
'A traditional roast: chicken, roast potatoes, carrots, peas, broccoli, stuffing balls and lots of gravy,' Holly says.

'Men love their meat and two veg,' Laura says.

They put the finishing touches to the table, laying out Lillian's gilt-edged plates, the matching serving bowls and a gravy jug. Holly had found some linen napkins in a drawer and has washed and ironed these, marvelling at how she is morphing into a domestic goddess.

She wants the meal to be a success. This will be the first social event in the house for Ray, Spencer, and James. She is serving the food at six and hopes it will become a house tradition.

The kitchen fills with the delightful smell of roasting chicken, an extra-large one she got from a traditional butcher shop. She grips the roasting tin with ovenproof gloves and sticks a fork in the side. The juice runs clear, and the breast is crispy and golden brown. She gazes at it with pride and satisfaction.

'I'm happy with that. I got the oven right this time.'

Laura places a bunch of early daffodils in a vase in the centre of the table.

'Oh dear,' Holly says.

'What's wrong?'

'It just occurred to me it might be an issue if I ask Ray to do the carving.'

'Oh really!'

'Spencer won't care but I bet James will be put out. He seems to think since we're still married, he has certain privileges.'

'But you split up ages ago. And anyway, *you* should do it,' Laura says.

'You're right! I *will!*'

She reaches for the big knife, which she hasn't used in an age.

'It's awfully blunt.'

Ray is the first to arrive and has brought a four-pack of beer with him. He usually lives in jeans and T-shirts but has put on a shirt for the meal.

'Good to see you again, Laura. Something smells good,' he says.

'Will you sharpen this knife?' Holly asks him.

He picks up the sharpening rod and moves the knife up and down it expertly.

'Want me to carve for you, Hol?'

'Thanks, but I'll do it. It would be great if you'd give us a progress report on the renovation.'

'Sorted.' He sits and Holly hands him a bottle opener and glass for his beer.

Spencer arrives next and Laura's let him in. They've only met a couple of times because his relationship with Holly pre-dated her friendship by years. They shake hands formally.

Spencer walks through to the kitchen and hands Holly a bottle of Malbec. 'This is so good of you, Holly.'

James joins them as Laura is pouring wine for Spencer.

'James, wine?'

'Thanks.'

The table looks good with the bowls of steaming vegetables and the chicken as the centrepiece. James sits in the chair at the head of the table. Laura notices and winks at Holly, who is looking stressed as she wields the carving knife.

'Food first and then we will talk house matters,' Holly says.

Ray spears a leg and several thick slices of chicken and pours a pool of gravy over his potatoes. James takes one slice of breast and large portions of the vegetables. Spencer, who is always ravenous, piles his plate high. Holly tries the chicken, relieved it tastes good.

'Great grub,' Ray says.

'So good,' Spencer agrees.

'Holly always did an excellent roast,' James says.

'Thanks. I thought I'd do us a roast once a month. Gives us an opportunity to discuss any issues about the house. And I'd like us to agree a few ground rules.'

'Ground rules?' James asks.

'Yes. I'm not going to get a cleaner. Grateful if each of you would clean your own floors and Spencer if you could keep the staircase up to the first floor swept, and James you sweep up to the second floor that would be great.'

'Good plan,' Spencer says.

She notices James says nothing. Hardly surprising, he hates having any terms and conditions dictated to him.

'I've found a gardener to tackle the wilderness out back and I'll pay him. Ray, will you update us on the works please?'

Ray sits back from the table. 'The roof repairs are

progressing. Slower than I hoped because of the rain. The old cast iron drainpipe is cracked. I've hired a specialist plumber and next week he'll replace it with a new pipe and inject a damp proof course.'

'Will the smell of damp go?' Holly asks.

'Yeah, it'll take a few weeks but it will dry out in time. The house should be weatherproof by mid-March.'

'That *is* good news,' she says.

'The electrician and plaster team are coming on Monday to scope the job. They'll work in tandem, and I reckon this phase will take six weeks. There'll be some disruption during the rewiring as they work through the house. Please clear your rooms as they reach your floor.'

James turns to Holly. 'Are you starting at the top or the bottom?'

Ray sighs. 'Oh, here it comes.'

James slaps the table. 'What's that supposed to mean?'

'I'm the one doing the job. Not Holly.'

'I know that.'

'So, talk to me.'

'So?' James eyes Ray coldly.

'So... what? You want us to start at the top. Am I right?'

'I want my rooms plastered and decorated as soon as possible. I need to get my treatment room up and running so I can treat a few people before my exams.'

'Course you do. Can't have James waiting his turn.'

The temperature around the table has dropped ten degrees.

Holly feels like a mother asking two children to play nicely. 'Ray, where do you plan to start?'

'We start in the basement and work our way up,' Ray says.

He leans over to pour himself a second beer, taking his time to fill the glass.

James's nostrils begin to flare, which Holly knows all too well is a sign he is about to blow.

'Your rooms will take longest, Hol,' Ray continues.

As if to take some of the sting out of a rapidly worsening stand-off, Spencer says, 'You know there's no rush to plaster my floor.'

Holly looks imploringly at Ray. He shrugs.

'OK. If it's all right with you, Spence, we'll do the top floor after the basement and ground floor.' Ray offers the compromise without even looking at James.

'Fine with me,' Spencer says.

Ray glances over at James with a sardonic smile. 'They let you loose on real customers then?'

'Patients not customers,' James corrects him. 'And I'll have completed one thousand direct hours with fifty new patients by the time I qualify.'

'Let's hope they won't all be covered in plaster dust then,' Ray says.

Holly gets to her feet. 'Anyone want fruit?'

There's no enthusiasm for fruit, and it's nearly nine.

'We need to take Cooper round the block for his lamp post walk,' Laura says.

Ray stands, goes to the sink, and scrapes and stacks the plates. Spencer runs hot soapy water and begins to wash the plates. James picks up the two empty wine bottles for the recycle box.

'And the beer bottles please,' Holly says.

He scoops these up. 'Thanks for the meal, Holly,' James says and leaves.

'Prat,' Ray mutters.

Holly and Laura wrap up as a sea fret is rolling in. The street lamps glimmer through the mist as they make a slow circuit of the neighbouring streets, giving Cooper plenty of time to sample the aroma of local dogs.

'That was most entertaining; James and Ray the two rutting stags locking horns,' Laura says.

'It was stupid and childish.'

'James hates Ray being in charge of the renovation. He's jealous you rely on Ray so much.'

'I don't think he's jealous. Not in that way. He just has to be the one in control.'

'He's always seen himself as an alpha male, hasn't he? The successful man who everyone defers to. But if it came to macho stakes my money would be on Ray winning.'

'Ray is skilled at all kinds of useful things.'

'And nice broad shoulders too,' Laura says.

'First thing that attracted me to him and his green eyes. But to be fair James has changed in some ways. I think he's genuinely trying to reinvent himself. He's far more frugal than he used to be, and he's got into meditation and vegetables. He used to throw things away all the time and now he hates waste of any kind.'

'I bet he's a composter.'

Holly laughs. 'He asked me to apply for a composting bin from the council.'

'Ugh. I hate those bins. You get clouds of horrible little flies. And I bet when James gets into something he has to do it one hundred per cent, so we'll all hear lots about his meditation and his commitment to recycling.' Holly smiles wryly.

'That's true. Did you notice Spencer doesn't get involved in these silly macho games?'

'Do you still have feelings for Spencer? He's nice looking

and not an ounce of fat on him. It's the male middle-aged paunch which turns me off.'

'I can't ignore how attractive he is. In fact, he's hardly changed, just a little bit of grey at the temples,' Holly says.

'I think James suspects you're still holding a candle for Spencer.'

'You think?'

'First love is very potent and anyway Spencer is the only grown-up male in the house,' Laura says as they head back.

———

Ray and Spencer have gone. The plates and pans are washed and dried and left on the table.

'They did all the pans too. That was good of them,' Holly says.

'Did you notice James cleared off before the dish washing started. Let's have a nightcap.'

Cooper flops at her feet and Holly pours the end of the red wine for them.

Laura takes her glass. 'You know, in spite of my initial reservations, I rather envy you your Commune of Exes. Lots of sexual energy swirling around.' She raises her glass to Holly.

Chapter Thirteen

MARCH

PENUMBRA HOUSE

L ast autumn, after receiving news of her legacy, Holly gave in her notice to Mr Bartholomew, the principal of the college where she worked. She had missed the whole term deadline needed for resignations and dressed in her navy suit, which she thinks of as her funeral suit, a white blouse and black court shoes, formal and conventional because she needed them as armour to face him.

They had never got along. She did not share her good news with him and when questioned on her reason for leaving merely said she was taking a sabbatical. He agreed she could leave in December, as she hoped. Indeed, she'd realised with a rush of surprise that Mr Bartholomew wanted to be shot of her as much as she wanted to see the back of him.

But this morning she finds she is missing her job and her students. The sixth form college was an important part of her life for eleven years. She started as a part-time teacher, after her second and devastating miscarriage. Her self-esteem was at its lowest. Going back to teaching had been her salvation. Her hours at the college increased until she became a full-time member of staff.

She has a gift for teaching sixth formers and enjoys their lively discussions. And she misses Gabriel, a favourite student of hers, who is studying English A-level. Some of his essays were outstanding. He is bright but a bit broken and Holly has maternal feelings towards him.

She tells herself she must accept she has walked away from the security of her career, to move to a new city where she has none of the networks she built up in London. Her task now is to build a new life for herself in Brighton and to make Penumbra House a beautiful place to live.

Nine thirty in the morning on the second of March and Barry Pumphrey the gardener turns up unannounced on her doorstep.

'*This* is the time to tackle a garden,' he says.

She takes him through the kitchen and down the steps and they walk the length of the garden, which is muddy, the path long gone. They push through waist-high nettles and brambles. The shed at the top is more ivy than wood and exudes a smell of rotting timber. Beyond, a blackberry bush has taken hold and spread.

'Worse than I expected. It's a job and a half. When's the scaffolding coming down?'

'End of next week,' she says.

They head back towards the fig tree, and she sees Spencer is watching them from the first floor. She waves to him.

'I can't take this tree on. You'd need a team of tree surgeons to cut this brute back,' Barry says.

'Oh, I guess that rather limits what we can do then.'

'There's *plenty* to do. Ivy and bindweed choking everything,' he says in disgust.

'What about those thorn bushes by the wall? They're ugly, like the thorns at Sleeping Beauty's castle,' Holly says with a small smile.

Barry shoots her a quizzical look. 'If you say so.'

Her smile wilts.

'I'll take my machete to them,' he says.

'Great. Shall we have some tea and discuss details?'

They return to the kitchen, and he watches her make a pot of tea.

'I like my tea strong,' he says.

She adds another tea bag to the pot. They agree Barry will come once a week through March, April, and May. They will reassess what the garden needs thereafter.

'It will be clearing and chopping back for months. Don't expect flowers,' he says.

'That's fine. I know it will take a while.'

'I do a three-hour shift, usually from nine. Can't say what day it will be, and you need to pay me cash,' he adds in a tone of voice which brooks no argument.

'Agreed.' She would have preferred to have a set day every week but does not think she has it in her to challenge Barry. He leaves by the kitchen door soon after. He's a die-hard curmudgeon, but also a man well-suited to tackling a wilderness.

She hears James in the hall, talking to someone on the doorstep, followed by the sound of two people going upstairs. About fifteen minutes later she hears them come down again and, intrigued, goes into the hall as James is closing the front door.

'This guy turned up, a painter and decorator. He saw the skip outside and asked if we need any decorating done. I've

JANE LYTHELL

shown him my rooms and he's doing me an estimate for painting them. Seemed a pleasant fellow.'

'OK, but I think Ray already has several local painters on his list.'

'We're each paying for our own decorating, right?'

'That's what we agreed.'

'So, the choice is mine and I'll wait and see what this guy wants to charge.'

Of course you will, Holly thinks.

That night she's woken by the creak of the scaffold outside her window. There it is again, a creak and a scrape as the structure takes the weight of someone or some*thing* climbing up from the garden level. She sits up in bed. It is well after midnight. She rubs her eyes and her throat tightens. No cat or a fox would be heavy enough to make the scaffolding creak like that.

It has to be a person climbing up. And the climber is trying to be stealthy, pausing to let the structure settle before moving on to the next level. The house has been empty for so long. Could it be a burglar? She wills herself to get up and creep to the window when the noise stops.

After five minutes of listening intently with no further noise evident her heart settles. She recalls her conversation with Ray. Why hadn't she paid the extra to have the scaffold alarmed? How stupid of her to economise on security. All she hears now is a light breeze making the fig tree rustle. She rolls onto her side and closes her eyes but it takes her an age to get back to sleep.

Holly wakes early. She's had an anxiety dream in which she's still working at the college, and has left an important task undone. She sits up and as the dream recedes, recalls an actual discussion she had with her student, Gabriel, about *Macbeth* and how the character's fatal flaw led him inexorably into betrayal and murder.

What remains with her from that discussion is a comment Gabriel made. He said brave people were people who lacked imagination. His classmates took offence at this, seeing courage as a virtue. But he had a point and Holly knows she isn't brave because she has too much imagination. Gabriel often said original things and she'll email him and ask him how he's getting on.

The sun makes Lillian's threadbare curtains almost transparent. Holly swings her legs out of bed and pulls the curtains apart. A dead seagull is lying on the plank right outside her room. A breeze lifts its beautiful white and grey plumage and its yellow beak with its telltale red dot is lolling over the edge of the plank. It looks like it has a broken neck.

She shudders, pulls on her tracksuit, and runs down to Ray's flat. He's shaving and his chin is covered with foam when he opens the door. He sees her face and puts up his hand.

'Give me five minutes.'

She's too agitated to sit down in his sitting room and paces around, the pungent aroma of marijuana permeating the room. He comes in.

'What's up?'

'Last night I heard something outside my bedroom window. Someone was climbing the scaffold.'

'When was this?'

'After midnight, it was the creaking which woke me. Then the sound stopped, and I went back to sleep, eventually. But there's a dead seagull on the plank just outside my window and *someone* put it there last night!'

'Show me,' he says.

Ray finds a shovel in the shed and buries the seagull at the top of the garden next to the blackberry bush. Is it the seagull she'd seen sitting on her wall looking noble? Poor dead bird. She's horrified at the thought of someone right outside her window last night holding the dead bird and placing it there for maximum effect.

'I was a fool not to get the scaffolding alarmed,' she says.

'It might have flown into the wall.'

'I heard someone climbing up, Ray. I didn't imagine it!'

'Look, the scaffold comes down next week so don't worry. Come back to mine and I'll make you a cuppa. We need to talk budgets.'

Seagulls do *not* fly into walls. Ray might be a townie, but surely he knows that.

Papers are spread out on his coffee table, and she drinks the tea he made her and watches as he adds up figures on a calculator. Ray writes down the sum he needs, in cash, to pay the men who worked that week, Friday being payday.

'A big one this week, Hol.'

She looks at the figure he's written with the hours of the workers itemised in columns.

'That's OK. And we're still on budget?'

'Slightly below so far.'

'That's good, thank you,' she says quietly.

She keeps thinking about how the seagull looked, its neck broken, its beautiful plumage lifted by the breeze. Someone put it there deliberately. To spook her. Why hasn't Ray reacted more to the dead seagull?

She gets the bus into town and walks up to the bank on the corner of North Street. A homeless man is sitting on a dirty sleeping bag on the pavement outside. The bitter weather of February has passed, but it's cold and damp, a damp which gets into your clothes.

As she queues for a teller her conscience pricks her, as it does every Friday, that she is avoiding VAT on the building works. She accepts this is how Ray does things and it's too late to change. Reaching the bank teller, she requests the amount in cash.

'Fifties or twenties?' the teller asks.

'Twenties please.'

He counts out a stack of notes and secures them with an elastic band. As she leaves the bank, she gives the homeless man a fiver and a two-pound coin. His hands are dirty, and his face is chapped.

'Bless you, pet,' he says.

She'd talked to James about the number of homeless people on the streets of Brighton, and he was hard-hearted saying they travel in from other places and any cash you give them goes straight on drink or drugs. She doesn't agree.

In the taxi back to Penumbra House she's conscious of how much money is zipped into her bag. Her mood is low and she tries to understand why. It isn't guilt about not paying VAT, though her father would have been very much against her paying cash under the counter for work done. It isn't the homeless man either. No, it's Ray's dismissal of the dead seagull which rankles.

She met Ray after a friend recommended him as a good builder. When she'd left James she'd moved into her one-bedroom flat and it had a horrible pink bathroom. Many months later Ray ripped it all out and installed a lovely new shower and they fell for each other. Their relationship was intense and short-lived. At first, she thought she was deeply in love but later accepted it was her neediness as well as lust and happy sex which had taken them over the bumps of their incompatibility for nearly a year.

It was Ray who ended their relationship, recognising their class differences were too wide a chasm to cross.

'We're too different, Hol. You like Shakespeare and I like westerns!'

She knows he refers to her as 'posh bird' to his mates. But he's also fundamentally a loner. Ray had married young and the marriage went sour quickly. He has a son who lives in Milton Keynes.

Too much intimacy makes Ray uncomfortable. He's like one of those cowboy heroes in westerns, sitting by a campfire with only his horse as his companion. He was so different from James, and she was attracted by Ray's kindness as well as his looks. Maybe it would not have worked long term, but she regretted their break-up when it came. Ray ending their relationship when she wanted it to go on gives him a power over her still.

When she gets back, he's in his bedroom sorting through his tackle box and the Dixie Chicks are blasting out of his sound system.

'I'm fishing tomorrow.'

'It's going to rain,' she says.

She's got into the habit of checking the weather forecast daily since the great storm of February.

'Rain won't stop me.'

She unzips the inner pocket of her bag and hands the wad over.

He thumbs through the notes. 'All present and correct.'

She turns to leave but knows she can't until she has said something about the seagull.

'Ray, *someone* was climbing on the scaffold last night and they left the dead seagull right outside my window.'

'Hol, let it go.'

'Don't make light of it. Please. It was left as a warning.'

They stare at each other.

'I try to support you as best I can,' he says at last.

'I know you do. And I appreciate it. Every day. But seagulls don't fly into walls.'

'OK, maybe I dismissed it too fast. I know you're a world champion worrier.'

'Someone put a dead bird right outside my window to threaten me.'

'I'll keep an eye out. Anyone getting into the garden has to walk past my windows,' he says.

'Thank you.'

She leaves him sorting his fishing equipment.

Chapter Fourteen

PENUMBRA HOUSE

Holly is thinking about her annual visits to see her aunt Lillian in April. She used to get the train from London and spend the night in the bedroom on the top floor of Penumbra House, in that narrow bed with its creaky iron bedstead. She would wash in the bathroom with its antiquated cabinet shower, cold because neither room had any heating. They would have an elaborate dinner in the evening and next day croissants for breakfast followed by a good lunch – her aunt liked to cook. Then Holly caught the train back to London in the late afternoon.

Lillian never encouraged her to stay a second night. And all that time, while Lillian prepared the food, they would talk about books or about Holly's plans or about Leo, Holly's father. Lillian never once mentioned Jacques Pichois or Emmanuel. What granite self-control she showed. At the end of April, her aunt returned to her small stone house in

Brittany. It has always been a mystery why Lillian held on to Penumbra House for so many years when she only used it for one month in twelve.

Holly comes out of her bedroom and sees the piece of paper lying on the mat and opens the front door before snatching it up. No one is on the street of course; the person doing this chooses the moments of delivery carefully. She feels a desire to hiccup build in her. Why does she have this physical reaction to these pages, this involuntary spasm of her diaphragm? She swallows hard and starts to scan the words. Hearing someone coming down the stairs, she hurries to her bedroom to read it properly, with her back pressed firmly against the door.

BRITTANY 1981

Over the years I have turned my garden into a meadow and planted wildflowers to attract bees and butterflies. At the top I created a small vegetable patch. It is not a true potager, yet I am growing lettuce, green beans, and tomatoes quite successfully.

Emmanuel was sitting crossed-legged watching me dig and my trowel unearthed a fat worm. He was excited and said he wanted to hold the worm. I placed it on his palm, and he stared intently as it wriggled. He is a watchful boy and maybe he has a bent towards the natural sciences.

I was thinking I could buy him a book about species when he lifted the worm to his mouth and bit it in half and flung the two body parts away. I told him it was a disgusting thing to do. He gave me a nasty grin.

When I told Jacques about it, he laughed, and this led to an argument. He said I was looking after Emmanuel's bodily needs well, but where was my joy in the boy? That felt like a slap.

I said Jacques came to see us twice a week at most. It is easier to experience joy when you can get away from a demanding child. Did he have any idea what it entailed looking after a young boy?

Jacques, who has been reading Rousseau's Emile, expounded some unrealistic theories about a child's interactions with the world; how learning should be less from books and more from nature. Hence his delight at Emmanuel biting the worm in half. Jacques calls him Manu and does not like the way I always refer to our son as Emmanuel.

I said I resented the way Jacques characterised me as a cold parent. Told him that I care deeply about the food I give Emmanuel and cook everything from scratch. I've tried to establish a soothing night-time routine and always read to him. All I wanted was two or three hours a day to do my translations.

Jacques said he is convinced I've been suffering from postnatal depression since Emmanuel's birth, and this is why I have never truly bonded with him.

I had to leave to fetch Emmanuel from school and we parted without a reconciliation or an embrace and this is rare for us.

I do not have postnatal depression. It is a convenient diagnosis for Jacques to invoke. The truth is I did not want a child, never wanted a child, knew this all my life. But Jacques wanted an heir. His face told me that so clearly when I shared the news of my pregnancy.

I am deeply bored with the job of being a mother. As someone once said: 'the pram in the hall, there is no more sombre enemy of good art'. Jacques and I used to have fascinating discussions on literature and history and politics over the fine lunches I cooked for him. Sometimes dinners too, when Severine was away.

Now we cannot get through more than a couple of sentences before Emmanuel interrupts us demanding our attention, and Jacques breaks off at once, always, to respond to his son and heir, his little Manu.

My work has suffered. My translations are not as good as they used to be.

This morning, as I packed a lunchbox for Emmanuel to take to school, I had to acknowledge Jacques's accusation from yesterday has some truth to it. I do not have maternal feelings towards my son. Most of the time I feel numb.

This afternoon I wrote to Mrs Pumphrey and asked her to spring clean Penumbra House, as usual. She is a young woman but is proving to be a thorough and reliable cleaner and when I arrive the house will be ready for me. I am not sure about her husband though. He strikes me as a surly man who likes to get his way. This year I will have to take Emmanuel with me.

Holly feels the hairs on her arm lift. The baby *had* lived. The baby had become a little boy and Lillian had brought him here to Penumbra House! How strange to think of them being here together, mother and son. Lillian claimed not to have had postnatal depression, but something was badly wrong. That poor child. Holly pities her aunt but feels she is in the wrong here. She didn't want a child, but once Emmanuel was born he had to be the priority. Lillian hates how the pram in the hall interferes with her work. How Holly would have welcomed the pram in the hall. Maybe it's her own former longing to be a mother which makes her judge Lillian harshly. *We're all too quick to judge mothers*, she thinks.

It is a sad tale and the sadder for Lillian keeping it all hidden with no one to give her the support she clearly needed. Surely Penumbra House should have come to her son, Emmanuel? Holly paces her bedroom, her mind unspooling various scenarios. Had Emmanuel died some years later? As a teenager or as a young adult? And there is the mention of Mrs Pumphrey, Barry's wife. Lillian approved of her and did not warm to Barry. Mrs Pumphrey would have known more, but Barry told Holly she is long dead.

Holly's sure there's more to come. This entry's dated 1981.

There are probably many more pages to this journal. She has no way of knowing when the next instalment will appear or who's doing this. Yet someone's carrying out a deliberate campaign against her. They're playing with her, revealing her aunt's private thoughts and troubles in these small, alarming, doses because she, the niece, should not have inherited Penumbra House.

Is it possible someone from *inside* the house found the journal and is doing this to her? No, that's stupid, paranoid thinking on her part. Yet she doesn't feel able to confide in the men. Ray wouldn't be much help as he doesn't like talking about emotional matters. He might think she was making a fuss about nothing.

James would be almost *too* interested, and she knows it would be laced with malice. He would enjoy speculating about Lillian's unhappy life because James enjoys indulging in schadenfreude. He might get some pleasure from Holly's discomfort too as she senses he feels she's had it too easy recently, what with her surprise and valuable legacy.

It's only Spencer she would like to confide in. He met Lillian and liked her, and he's not a gossip. But deep down Holly feels she must endure this on her own. She knows she's not going to be left in peace to enjoy her inheritance. But to what conceivable end?

Chapter Fifteen

PENUMBRA HOUSE

B arry arrives at nine sharp with a canvas sack of tools, and she watches him trudge to the top of the garden and wrench open the shed door. He clears it out, discarding rusty tools. Now and then she comes to the window to watch him at work. He has his machete out and is a ferocious chopper of brambles. She sees him pick up a shovel, and he is a demon digger too. She calls out to offer him a cup of tea. He stamps up the steps and wipes his feet on the mat for an age.

'A long garden like this needs a wheelbarrow,' he says.

Ray walks into the kitchen.

'Ray meet Barry. Barry, Ray is overseeing the renovation of the house,' she says.

The men nod at each other.

'Will you join us for tea?' Holly asks Ray.

'No ta. Got to get into town. I brought you these paint colours to look at.'

Ray hands her a sheaf of colour cards.

'See you later.'

He leaves, and Holly pours the tea which is a rich brown colour.

'Is he from London?' Barry asks.

'Yes, born and bred.'

'Thought so.'

Ray would have been amused to hear that comment, she thinks.

'The wheelbarrow,' Barry says.

'Oh yes.'

'You need one.'

'I better buy one then.'

'There's a lot of rubbish on the market. Don't go to the garden centre. Stupid prices there.'

'Maybe if you identify the model you want?'

'I'll drop the details off.'

Two electricians have started work and her sitting room is out of bounds with the furniture pushed into the centre and covered with dust sheets. The men are chiselling grooves in the walls where new wires will run. Holly heads up to the first floor and Spencer is standing by the back window with his sketch pad open, drawing with rapid strokes. When he draws and paints, he becomes deeply absorbed. After a minute he senses her presence and turns around.

'I'm making coffee. Do you want a mug?'

'I'd love one. I'll come down.'

'Can I see what you're working on?'

'I'll bring my pad.'

He follows her downstairs.

'You've got electricity down here,' he says.

'They said the kitchen circuit can stay on today.'

He washes his charcoal-blackened hands at her kitchen sink as she makes the coffee. Spencer was her first love. They met at university during their first term, an intoxicating experience of love and sex for them both. It ended when Spencer left his course to go to art school in Glasgow. They tried to stay together, but the distance defeated them. Their attachment was deep, and they've never lost touch.

What she admires most about Spencer is his refusal to give up. His art school friends have abandoned the struggle to paint full time, but Spencer sticks at it. When money gets tight, as it often does, he drives taxis through the night until he has enough to return to his art. Over the years, he has given her several of his paintings, including a portrait he did of her for her fortieth birthday.

He sits opposite her as she pushes down the plunger on the cafetière, pouring soya milk in hers and a heaped teaspoon of brown sugar. Spencer drinks his coffee strong, black, and unsweetened.

She opens the pad and turns the pages, and every sketch is of the fig tree.

'That tree is inspiring you.'

'It *is* inspiring me. I'm planning a series of paintings through the year, showing the changes.'

'There's something rapacious about it,' she says.

'That's what I like about it.'

'Your sketches have caught that. They're positively menacing.'

'Excellent, I want people to see the tree as a predator advancing across the garden.'

'I'll have to tackle it at some point. Barry says it would need tree surgeons to cut it back.'

'Please don't cut it. It may be a monster, but what a magnificent monster it is.'

'I won't cut it *down*. But Ray thinks the roots are cracking the drains and that's what causes the awful damp.'

'He's sorted that hasn't he?'

'For the moment. But we will have to dig down and explore at some point. And it would be nice to have somewhere to sit out in the summer.'

'Ask Barry to clear an area for you by the wall. I bet it's a suntrap; a lovely little patch of sunlight.'

She laughs.

'Oh, I'm allowed *a little patch*, am I? Thank you, kind sir.'

He smiles at her archness. 'You seem happy, Holly.'

'I'm feeling pretty good. The house is coming together.'

'It's your grand project.'

She thinks for the briefest moment about confiding in Spencer about the pages on her doormat but pushes the idea away. For some reason she's committed to keeping her secretive aunt's secret. Lillian approved of Spencer and he's the only one of Holly's boyfriends to have met her aunt. He came down to the house with her one April when they were students.

He explored every corner of the house and garden and asked Lillian lots of questions, which Holly had thought a bit intrusive at the time. But her aunt did not rebuff him, and they talked at length. He devoured Lillian's rich meaty dishes with gusto; Spencer is always hungry, and she offered him seconds, saying it was nice to cook for a man who liked to eat. Spencer and Lillian seemed to get each other.

'I was thinking about how Lillian liked you. I'm sure she'd be pleased you are making art here,' Holly says.

'I liked her too. She was an unusual person; clear-eyed and fearless.'

'And intimidating,' Holly adds.

'You think?'

'I mean, I admired her. You couldn't but. She was so clever

and brave and didn't care what other people thought. I was careful around her though.'

'Oh, I'm sure she loved you.'

'She didn't really show it. Wasn't touchy-feely. I saw her once a year and she would kiss me on each cheek, in a formal way. Never a hug.'

'She made those delicious meals for you.'

'True. I guess people demonstrate their love in different ways.'

'Cooking is often an act of love.'

Holly smiles. Could she describe her roast dinners for the men as an act of love?

'Dad said when they were growing up, she always had her nose in a book and fought with their mother because she kept the light on all night to read.'

'Maybe she liked books better than people.'

'I'm sure she did. They were her life. But she loved Dad and helped him a lot when my mother left us. And she thoroughly approved of you. Told me I should hang on to you because you were a serious man.'

Holly blushes after saying this. Why did she let that slip out? She changes the subject quickly. 'I'd like to learn a language. I've got the time now and there's a college up the road. I might sign up for Italian.'

'Italian? I thought you'd choose French.'

'Because of Lillian?'

'Yes, and didn't you have a French au pair for a while? When you were little.'

'Fancy you remembering Audrey. Lillian found Audrey for Dad, you know. It was such a sad time and maybe that's why I'm not drawn to French.'

'*Sì, è un buon piano,*' he says.

'Which means?'

'Yes, it's a good plan.'

Spencer learned Italian so he can talk with his daughter when they Skype, though she speaks English well.

'I can practise on you,' Holly says.

'With pleasure. *Grazie per il caffè*. Now I must get back to contemplation of my monster.'

'Can you check in with Ray when the electricians need to do your rooms.'

'Will do.'

Spencer has hit it off with Ray. Some evenings he goes down to his basement, and they sit up late sharing bottles of beer and listening to Ray's extensive music collection. Spencer told her that sometimes Ray cooks them a meal and they've all been good.

Holly knows Ray can cook. He'd learned when he was a kid because his mother worked long hours and it shocked her to learn that he wielded sharp kitchen knives from the age of eight. When they were dating Ray cooked Holly stews, steaks, and an excellent chilli con carne. She doesn't expect to be invited to join them, but wonders what they talk about.

Chapter Sixteen

PENUMBRA HOUSE

H olly hears the front door open, and James calls out to her. He is resting a single plank of wood against the wall.

'Do you have any tools?'

'Under the stairs in that cupboard. There's a hammer and pliers and a tin of nails.'

He switches on the light in the cupboard. 'I'll bring these back. I need a saw.'

'I don't have one. Ray probably does.'

'I'm not asking Ray.'

'Why not?'

'I'm fed up with waiting for him. I'll mend that hole myself!'

She watches him carry the plank of wood and the tools upstairs, intrigued at the idea of James doing carpentry. It was never his thing. If they ever bought a piece of furniture which required home assembly it was Holly, not James, who put it together.

The plasterers have started work on her sitting room, but the kitchen is still functional, and she intends to go ahead with the second of her Sunday roast dinners.

Laura has come down for it. She's only staying one night, and they will both have to sleep in Holly's bedroom as the sitting room is still off limits. The whole of the ground floor is dusty, and she warned Laura not to bring her good clothes. Holly is living in jeans and sweatshirts and having to wash her hair more often than usual.

They take Cooper for a walk in Preston Park talking about Charlie, Laura's son. He has asked his girlfriend, Iona, to marry him, and the wedding is scheduled for September, in Keswick. This has unleashed a storm of feelings in Laura.

'I'll be mother of the groom. Sitting at the top table. *Promise me* you'll come to the wedding.'

'I wouldn't miss it for the world.'

'We can stay in the same hotel, and you must keep me on the straight and narrow.'

'Yes, ma'am. The lakes are so lovely, and the house will be done by then.' Holly looks at her friend. 'It will be really nice, Laura; a celebration.'

'I know I should be happier about it, but it's another step on the path to losing him.'

'You'll never lose Charlie. He adores you.'

'Next Christmas it won't be the two of us, will it? He'll be a married man.'

She's right. From now on her ten days in Keswick with Charlie will have to be shared with Iona. Holly can see this will be a blow. They sit on a bench under a beech tree and fall silent. Holly looks up at the tiny buds uncurling and Cooper heads off towards a clump of bushes. Laura gives herself a little shake.

'Enough of my whingeing. Are the Three Stooges behaving themselves?'

'Most of the time. Ray and James hardly see each other, thankfully. James is studying hard for his exams. He still resents Spencer having the first floor. Spencer and Ray have become pals.'

'That's to be expected,' Laura says.

'Why do you say that?'

'They probably agree James can be a prat.'

Despite laughing, Holly says, 'I'd rather they didn't take sides. I want us all to get on.'

'It's inevitable. Two's company, three's a crowd.'

Laura enjoys conflict and drama and isn't above stirring things up for their entertainment value. It's for this reason Holly feels reluctant to confide in her about the pages from Lillian's journal. Laura already has ambivalent feelings about Holly's inheritance; seeing her project to renovate the house and live with the men as coming between them. Holly does not want her friend to say: 'I told you to sell it. I knew keeping the house was a mistake'.

THE SECOND ROAST DINNER

Holly and Laura are in the kitchen peeling potatoes and carrots. Cooper is stretched out on his towel, asleep with his face on his paws. Holly watches and feels tenderly towards him. She suggested Laura get a dog after Charlie left home, recalling how her own beloved puppy had helped her when her mother left them. Her father got her a cocker spaniel puppy which she named Plum.

She loved Plum with a deep and abiding ferocity. Plum lived for thirteen years and had to be put to sleep during Holly's first year at university. She got the train back from college, crying most of the way, and went with her father to the vets. The next day she saw her father's neighbour on the street.

'Sorry for your loss,' the neighbour said. 'She was pining for you.'

All these years later and she has not forgiven that woman for that remark.

She hasn't had a dog since Plum.

'That long walk tired him out,' Holly says. She puts the potatoes into the oven and checks the chicken. 'I'll sweep the floor, *again*. This plaster dust gets everywhere.'

Holly sprinkles water on the boards, sweeps the floor and closes the kitchen door.

The men arrive. Ray's carrying his four pack of beer and sits himself down at the top of the table. Spencer's next, and he hands Holly a bottle of Malbec. James walks in and sees Ray is already seated at the head of the table. He sits at the other end.

'That gardener, where did you find him, central casting?' James asks Holly.

'He turned up on my doorstep. His wife used to work for Lillian. Came in March and spring cleaned the house from top to bottom.'

'And he looked after the garden?'

'No. He offered his services, but Lillian declined.'

'I wonder why?' Laura says.

'Lillian only employed his wife for those few weeks. Maybe she thought it wasn't worth him touching the garden. She didn't get much use out of it did she. He was critical of Lillian, before he found out I was her niece. Told me she wasn't good for this house.'

'Aha, he resents the fact your aunt employed his wife but not him,' Laura says.

'I hope not. Resentment is bad for the soul,' Holly replies.

'Ohmmm,' Ray says.

'OK, can you give us the latest on the works, Ray?'

'The rewiring is nearly done, and the new fuse box is in.'

'Hurrah, a new fuse box,' Holly says. 'And the plastering?'

'The big job is your sitting room, Hol, but I reckon all the rooms will be done by end of April. It dries fast and we can paint the rooms soon after.'

'Great. I want to have my floor decorated as soon as possible,' James says. 'This guy I've found has offered to paint my rooms at a very good price.'

'What's a good price?' It sounds more like a challenge than a question from Ray.

James takes out a sheet of paper and reads out the estimate. It's clear he brought it with him to the lunch to make a point.

'That's for all the rooms, *including* painting the floors.' He is almost triumphant.

'Too low,' is all Ray says.

James mocks him. 'Too low. That's it?'

'What else do you want me to say?'

'The guy's new to the area. He's trying to get work. Of course his prices are low.'

'You be careful you don't get what you pay for,' Ray says.

'And that's the point. We're all paying for the painting ourselves, so I get to choose who does my rooms.' James turns to the others. 'His name is Max. He's willing to quote for the rest of the house.'

'Is he now?' The thickness of Ray's voice makes this a threat.

Holly and Laura exchange glances.

Spencer is in quickly to lighten the rapidly darkening mood. 'I won't be needing a painter. I'll slap some paint on my walls when I get the time.'

'Let me guess, brilliant white?' Holly says, doing her bit to ease the tension.

'What else,' Spencer replies and smiles.

'So, apart from mine, there's only Holly's floor which needs doing,' James says.

'If we overlook the small matter of the hall, stairs and landings,' Ray is still simmering.

'All the more reason for Holly to use my guy to save herself some money.'

True to form, James will not let it go. It's another dumb power struggle, Holly thinks. Ray is managing the renovation and has secured her good deals on everything. She doesn't need him and James fighting over a painter. But, of course, they aren't. This is all about stupid male pride.

'I want my sitting room to be beautiful and we don't know what this guy's work is like, do we? Ray has a list of tried and trusted painters,' she says diplomatically.

There is a moment of tense silence. Laura picks up her glass and drinks, moving her eyes between Ray and James.

'Tell you what,' Ray says to James, 'you get this what's his name? Max? You get this Max to do your floor and when he's finished, I'll check his work. See if his standards are as low as his prices.'

'Like we don't already know what the verdict will be.'

'OK. OK. If his work *is* good, Holly should go with him. He's undercutting rates, but why turn down a good deal.'

'Thank you.' James reacts with overdone politeness, if only to ensure that, yet again, he has the last word.

'An excellent suggestion.' Laura smiles wickedly.

Holly stands, fuming at the pair of them. She hadn't bargained on this simmering antagonism in her house. 'I bought us an apple pie for pudding,' she says in a tight voice.

They eat the pie in silence. Holly's phone rings and it's her friend, Nikki. Holly goes into the empty sitting room to take the call, glad to get away from them all.

A few minutes later, as she hangs up, she hears movement in the hall outside and then Laura's voice.

'You're not being very Zen, James.'

'What's that supposed to mean?'

'I thought you were trying to leave your previous persona behind but you're still being competitive with Ray.'

'You've never liked me.'

'It's not about liking or disliking. It's about knowing that Holly wants a harmonious household. She's been very generous to you and Spencer and Ray.'

'I suggest you butt out. You don't live here.'

'I know that Holly cooks you a roast dinner and wants you all to get on. Why can't we enjoy the meal without you and Ray locking horns?'

'Get off your soap box, Laura. You make a lot of emotional demands on Holly. Always have. I'm not taking any lecture from you.'

James stomps up the stairs.

Holly comes out of the sitting room and Laura looks flushed. 'Oh God, did you hear that?'

'I did.'

'All of it?'

'All of it.' Holly smiles wryly.

'He hates to be told anything, doesn't he. He hates to be told the truth. A leopard can't change his spots.'

Holly nods while thinking that Laura isn't so keen on being told the truth about herself either. That last comment from

James probably hit home. But then again Laura enjoys a good argument and has been itching to tell James what she thinks of his behaviour at the roast dinners.

'Thanks for supporting me,' she says.

———

Holly and Laura lie under their respective duvets in the bedroom. Cooper has settled on the floor next to Laura's sofa bed.

'Is it even worth carrying on with my roast dinners? They're turning rancid,' Holly says.

'Don't let James stop you doing them. Have to say Ray went up in my estimation tonight. It was smart the way he dealt with that; offered a compromise but he keeps the power. He'll decide if the work is up to scratch and James couldn't really argue against that,' Laura says.

'James has always underestimated Ray's intelligence.'

Holly switches off the light. Big surprise her commune isn't turning out to be The Waltons! Had she, albeit unconsciously, tried to create an alternative family for herself at Penumbra House? She isn't in a relationship, but her three exes are now very much in her life. Had that been her motivation?

Chapter Seventeen

EARLY APRIL

PENUMBRA HOUSE

Holly joins James on the top floor. He plans to use the front room for his patients and has positioned his treatment table in the exact centre of the room. He's covered the single bed she gave him with a woven orange throw and matching cushions, so it looks more like a consulting couch than a bed. In pride of place on the shelves is the figure of the stone Buddha.

'It's looking good, James.'

'It will work well as a treatment space.'

'You must qualify soon?'

'In June.'

'And you're still enjoying it?'

'Very much. I find it fascinating what the body will tell you about a person. I worked on a woman last week who suffered a traumatic childbirth twenty years ago. I'm telling you there were *still* traces of that trauma in the muscles of her pelvis and back. Remarkable.'

She notices she and James can talk about childbirth without it having the massive weight of expectation and disappointment it carried for them for years. There is a small kitchen on this floor which was once used by servants in the heyday of the house. She has an urge to peep in and see how James has arranged things in there. It is bound to be spick and span and clutter-free.

She stops herself because he is paying rent and she should respect his privacy. The back room overlooking the garden is his personal space. This is also dust-free and tidy, his clothes packed away in a high chest of drawers. He opens a long wooden box by the wall and takes out two cushions. James likes everything to have its designated place.

It's a bright spring day, and they place their cushions in a pool of light. He turns on the meditation tape and they reach the end without interruption. Holly is getting better at blocking out distracting thoughts, her 'monkey mind' as the gurus describe it. She stretches her arms above her head. 'That was good. Thank you.'

'Gets better the more you do it. I'll have to clear the front room tonight. Max starts work here tomorrow.'

'I hope he works out.'

'No reason why he shouldn't. It's absurd the way Ray feels he has to be in control.'

'He was just suspicious at how low the estimate was,' she says, thinking this was as clear a case of the pot calling the kettle black as she can recall.

'Ray smokes too many joints and has paranoid leanings.'

She sighs. 'This thing between you two is tiresome.'

'What thing?'

'The constant carping. I'd like this to be a happy household. Can't you try to get on?'

'I take it you're not bothered by his habit then?'

'If you mean the odd joint it's not a problem.' She walks towards the door, energised by a rush of irritation.

'It smells strong. I bet it's that skunk stuff. People have been known to hallucinate on that,' James says almost with relish.

'Stop it. Don't be petty about Ray. He's a good builder and a good man.'

James shrugs and spread his palms, the picture of innocence. 'Like you say, no big deal.'

'Then why did you raise it?'

'Maybe because you let Ray have too much influence and he's not the steadiest of men.'

'That's rubbish. He's totally reliable. You just always have to be in control.'

She stomps down to her floor. Her irritation with James has completely cancelled out the calming effects of the meditation.

Holly stands in her sitting room and surveys the newly plastered walls and ceiling. It is such a large and lovely room. On her walk through Preston Park yesterday she spotted a small purple tent pitched in the shelter of a hedge and realised that small tent was someone's home. And here she is with all this space.

As she walks to the window, she treads on the loose floorboard which cracks loudly. She must remember to tell Ray about it. Outside a battered blue car draws up and a man gets out, opens his boot, struggles with an old computer, and chucks it into her skip.

She runs from the room, pulls the front door open and reaches the end of the path as the blue car disappears round the corner. Hazel, her neighbour, is walking by.

'Did you see that? He chucked his rubbish in my skip,' Holly says.

'I did. Some people are shameless. I wish I'd got his registration number.'

'That skip was only delivered three days ago and it's nearly full.'

'People want something for nothing. But how nice to see Penumbra House being restored at last.'

'Thank you, we're getting there. We're knee-deep in plaster dust at the moment. You must come over and take a look when it's in better shape.'

'I'd love to. Now, Holly, would you be interested in joining our Neighbourhood Watch group. We meet once a month and it's the best way to find out what's happening round here.'

Holly's heart sinks. She wants to reach out to Hazel, who's been friendly in their several chance encounters. But the thought of attending meetings to discuss street lighting and parking permits shrivels her soul.

'When do you meet?'

'8pm, the last Thursday of every month. The next meeting is at mine, on Thursday week. Do come along and I can introduce you to the gang.'

'I think I'm in London that day. Can I let you know,' Holly says, deciding on the spot she'll go to London and stay with Laura that evening.

Hazel nods. 'Give me your email and I'll add you to our mailing list. We're keen to get more people from this end of the street.'

Chapter Eighteen

PENUMBRA HOUSE

There are signs of new life everywhere. Shadows thrown by the giant fig tree cut dark swathes across the garden and as Holly pushes the kitchen window open, she hears a chorus of birdsong and smells clean air with maybe a touch of sea salt. How she wishes she could enjoy living in Penumbra House, living in Brighton, but the journal pages are derailing her new beginning and she is anxious most of the time. James comes into the kitchen with the painter he hired.

'Holly, please meet Max.'

The man is wearing overalls yet manages to look well turned out.

'Hello. Would you like some coffee,' she asks.

'Thank you.'

James sits at the table and Max joins him as she busies herself with the cafetière.

'This will be a remarkable house when it's finished,' Max says.

'I hope so. Do you take milk, Max?'

'Yes, please.'

She hands him the carton of dairy and pours soya milk into her coffee. 'James tells me you're new to Brighton too?'

'I am and it's a good place to start again,' he says.

She wonders what he is starting again from, a marriage break-up most probably. He looks to be in his mid-forties and is slim and dark-haired.

'I've chosen light green for my treatment room and Jasmine White for my bedroom,' James says.

'Nice. I'm leaning towards a pale yellow for the sitting room. I take an age to choose colours,' she says to Max.

'We once had our kitchen in London painted and when it was done Holly *hated* the colour.'

Holly laughs. 'It was horrible.'

Max blinks slowly, and she feels slightly awkward because she senses an air of expectation about him. He looks up at the ceiling, tracing the cracks which run from the central light fitting to the edge, and is probably calculating the work it will take to fill and paint the ceiling. Looking down he catches her eyes and smiles. He seems pleasant enough, yet she is determined to wait for Ray's verdict on his work.

THREE DAYS LATER

Holly is slicing onions and her eyes are watering furiously. She blows her nose and runs her fingers under the cold water tap and sees Barry outside wielding his machete with brutal force against the thorns by the wall. Barry's approach to life reminds her of a student she taught and grew fond of.

Usain was an awkward young man who found it difficult to mix with the other students and who sat at the back of her class. On more than one occasion Usain offered an intriguing angle during class discussions and she grew to look forward to his insights.

In a similar way the men in the house take Barry at face value, dismissing him as gruff and uncooperative. She feels there is more to it. Barry may be on the autism spectrum and, like Usain, has had to forge his path with people thinking unkindly of him, not seeing his strengths and virtues. She transfers the onions to the stockpot as James comes into her kitchen.

'Hi, what are you making?'

'Pea and pesto soup, but everything begins with onions.' She stirs them with a wooden spoon as they sizzle gently.

'I like your pea and pesto.'

'You're welcome to have some later.'

'Thanks. I want to put in a good word for Max. He's doing a terrific job on my treatment room. Would you like to see what he's done so far?'

'Yes, OK, in a bit.'

'You've met him now. Will you hire him?'

'I'll wait for Ray's opinion.'

An expression flits across James's face. 'Ray has got quite a hold over you, hasn't he?'

Not again! She's stung into replying more sharply than she intended. 'He's a builder and I trust him on building matters just as I'd trust you if my back was bad. It's not personal, it's professional.'

Is this true or does her trust in Ray spring from some other source, from their former intimacy and because he makes her feel safe?

'Max is a decent guy, and the poor devil needs a break,' James says. 'We went out for a meal last night, to a Thai café in Hove. He told me his story and he's had it bloody hard.'

'What happened?'

'A bad marriage and an even worse divorce. His wife took everything. Left him high and dry and virtually homeless.'

'But how could that happen?'

The onions are turning transparent. She stirs them and puts on a kettle to make the bouillon stock.

'The mortgage was in her name when he moved in with her. He helped pay the mortgage, but when they split up, he had no legal standing, and she was vindictive. He couldn't afford to appeal and was left without a bean.'

'Any children?'

'No, thankfully. I treated him to the Pad Thai last night. The café does an excellent Pad Thai.'

'It's nice of you to help him, James, but I'll wait for Ray's opinion,' she says firmly.

'Max is trying to rebuild his life.'

She wishes he would let it go. Does James think he can wear her down?

'The soup will be ready in about thirty minutes.'

'Right,' he says and leaves the kitchen.

James has taken up Max's case because he identifies with him, and she knows why. Both men have experienced severe financial setbacks and are trying to rebuild their fortunes in their mid-forties.

She adds the stock and a bag of frozen petit pois and stirs the mixture, enjoying having the time to focus on domestic tasks. It is owning the house that's made such a difference to her life. Yet underneath her calm front she worries most of the time about her legacy. Should the house be hers?

She takes a mug of strong tea out to Barry. He's standing by the wheelbarrow he told her to get, brandishing his shovel. He makes a run at a seagull strutting round the garden. The seagull launches himself into the air with a squawk and lands on the roof of the shed.

Barry bangs his shovel furiously against the shed door. 'Get off there!'

The seagull takes flight and wheels above the garden. Holly watches its elegant flight path as it circles higher and higher.

'I *hate* seagulls. They're the blight of Brighton,' Barry says.

She hands him the mug, not telling him she thinks they are handsome birds.

'I meant to ask you, Barry, how many years did your wife work for Aunt Lillian?'

'Rita started work here when she was in her twenties.'

'So, a long time then.'

'Yup, many years.'

'And only during March?' she presses.

'She helped Miss Hilborne close up the house at the end of April too.'

'Did my aunt ever have guests staying here?'

Holly is keen to know if Jacques Pichois has ever visited. She hadn't begun her own annual visits to Brighton until she was at university and her aunt was always on her own.

'One year there was a little boy with her. Rita hadn't been working here very long.'

Holly stands very still. 'A little boy?'

'She told Rita he was her godson. A strange quiet boy, Rita said. He never came again.' Barry hands her his empty mug. 'I need to get on.'

He walks away and she is frustrated Barry is a man of so few words. That poor little boy. Lillian lied to Rita about her own son! She claimed Emmanuel was her godson. How cruel to disown him like that. It was unhinged behaviour, wasn't it? Does Barry know more than he is saying. The notion she might not be the rightful owner of Penumbra House is growing stronger, making her deeply uneasy.

Before Holly moved into the house, she'd booked a firm of clearance men to take away the pieces of Lillian's furniture she did not want, the dark wardrobes and sagging armchairs and desperate beds.

There was something so forlorn about Lillian's furniture. Maybe it was because her aunt had never lived fully and happily in the house. Holly had kept a few pieces though, the splendid kitchen dresser, a pretty corner cupboard, the table and six chairs in the kitchen and a bedroom chair upholstered in pale green velvet. It was torn and faded but was a pretty shape. It's time to re-upholster this bedroom chair. She needs to do something productive to take her mind off Lillian and poor little rejected Emmanuel.

Holly lays out the rich blue velvet she bought and her stapler, rubber mallet and pliers. She unwraps the upholstery needles she found at a wonderful ironmongery shop in the centre of Brighton, where she also bought new brass rivets to replace the rusted ones.

It's thanks to Laura she knows how to upholster a chair. Several years ago, Laura met an attractive man at a drink's reception, and he told her over the canapés that he ran courses in upholstery, in Covent Garden. Laura asked Holly to sign up for the course with her, hoping to get to know the man better. Holly took some persuading, but Laura was persistent, said the course would be fun and they could go for drinks afterwards.

In fact, the course *was* enjoyable, and Holly showed an aptitude for upholstery. Laura's potential romance came to nothing as the man was married and faithful. But he was an excellent instructor and Holly learned a useful skill which Penumbra House gives her an opportunity to use.

She's careful as she pulls out the rivets and detaches the faded velvet cover from the frame of the chair. It needs to be in one piece, to act as her pattern for the new velvet. As she works on the chair, she grows calmer.

Chapter Nineteen

PENUMBRA HOUSE

olly is in the kitchen, flicking through a recipe book and thinking about what to cook for her next roast dinner for the men. They need a change from chicken. She'll buy a joint of beef from the butcher shop in Fiveways; a good-sized joint to serve them. The radio is on and the kitchen fills with the rich tone of Kenneth McKellar singing 'My Love Is Like a Red, Red Rose'. She stands to turn the radio off but pauses as the familiar romantic words wash over her.

How she aches to have a love like that. It amazes her to notice tears are rolling down her cheeks. She is being soppy and tells herself to get a grip! And at that moment she hears the letter box clatter, and she runs out of the kitchen. Paper is lying on the mat. By the time Holly flings open the front door, her path is empty, and she can only see two elderly women ambling down the street with their shopping baskets on wheels.

Who is leaving these pages? How can they disappear into thin air?

Her hands tremble as she carries the pages into her bedroom. What will she learn today? The paper has been cut out with its usual precision and her diaphragm spasms as she reads.

BRITTANY 1986

Emmanuel is becoming a secretive, indeed a dishonest child. I have caught him in several outright lies and when I challenge him, he gives me this strange, almost vacant look.

Jacques of course cannot see his faults.

For his twelfth birthday, Jacques bought Emmanuel a rabbit and a sturdy wooden hutch. He drove to our house in the afternoon and presented his gift with something of a fanfare. We found a spot for the hutch near the top of the garden. I covered the floor with hay, and we moved the young rabbit into his new home.

We had cake in the kitchen and when Jacques rose to leave at five Emmanuel made a fuss saying why couldn't Papa stay longer on his birthday.

I followed Jacques out to his car. He spoke to me again about the Brighton house, urging me to sell it so I could buy a larger place here. He thinks Emmanuel needs more room, though he did not say that was the reason. And I did not tell him why I am keeping Penumbra House. One day I hope Jacques and I will live and work there in freedom and harmony once Emmanuel is grown up and gone. It would be a relief to get away from the prying eyes of the village. And it will be my turn to choose where we live.

Emmanuel has not given his new pet a name; he calls him Rabbit. He never feeds Rabbit or cleans out his hutch, though he does sit cross-legged and watches him a lot.

I am becoming fond of Rabbit. I select nice leaves and carrots for him, little treats he will enjoy. I give him fresh water every day and clean out his hutch on Sundays. At night I put a blanket over the hutch.

BRITTANY 1987

I was walking back from the boulangerie in the village with Emmanuel.

On the outskirts, next to the pétanque court, was a handwritten poster tied to a tree. It was headlined RECENT CAT STABBINGS and Emmanuel stopped to read it.

I read it too, over his shoulder. It said there had been three recent incidents of fatal cat stabbings in the village, causing deep distress to the owners. It warned all cat owners to be especially vigilant, to put a collar with a bell around the neck of their beloved cats and to report any sightings of suspicious behaviour at once to the village council.

Emmanuel was clearly stirred by the words on the poster. He asked me what 'fatal' meant, and I said it meant causing death. He asked what 'vigilant' meant, and I explained it meant to be especially watchful for harmful behaviour or situations. He seemed more than stirred, the words excited him, and he repeated them out loud with relish.

Clemence joined us at the tree. She is a thoughtful girl, a couple of years younger than Emmanuel. I am not keen on children, but I like Clemence. She flinched as she read the poster.

'Fatal means causing death,' Emmanuel said to her almost triumphantly.

'I'm going to keep my cat in the house,' Clemence said.

'You can't do that. That's cruel,' Emmanuel said.

Clemence looked upset. 'It's not cruel.'

'It is. You can't keep a cat locked up.'

'I don't want anyone to stab her.' She was on the verge of tears.

'Talk to your maman, Clemence. I am sure you can keep your cat

safe. And we will all be on the lookout and catch the bad person who is doing this,' I said.

I wondered at the wisdom of highlighting these incidents in such a public way. The children would be able to read the poster. Who could walk past it with such a headline? It was the stuff of nightmares. The village had a monthly newsletter, which covered local events and news. It would have been a more appropriate channel of communication as it was aimed at adults.

I had to pull Emmanuel away from the poster, so deep was his fascination. Clemence was crying, and I suggested we walk her back to her house.

Holly sits at her desk and chews on her thumbnail. The content of the latest instalment makes her as uneasy as the strange appearance of these pages on her doormat. Emmanuel has grown into a weird child. His excitement about the cat stabbing poster is unnatural and disturbing. The little girl's reaction is far more normal.

Lillian does not like her son, describing him as secretive and dishonest and having a strange, almost vacant, look. These are not the words of a loving mother! And Lillian resents that Jacques cannot see the boy's faults. How awful the atmosphere must have been between mother and child. Dislike and distrust on both sides. On balance, she feels more sorry for Emmanuel than for Lillian. A child cannot choose its parents and a child *knows* when he is not loved.

Here too is the explanation for Lillian hanging on to Penumbra House for all these years. She saw it as the place she and Jacques would live in as a couple one day, when life allowed them to do that. It was her great wish, her fantasy for decades. Her dream never came true. The house has always felt melancholy to Holly. It is a place of broken dreams.

How is she going to find out who is leaving these pages? Someone must have found Lillian's journal, presumably after her death. Where had the journal been left? At Lillian's house in Brittany no doubt, but who cleared the house? Would the solicitor in Rennes know? Could it be Emmanuel watching Penumbra House, waiting for the moment to post the pages? This is fanciful. Emmanuel lives in France if he still lives at all.

Holly must not let her imagination run away with itself. But someone's playing with her, and she needs to understand why. She's developing an almost morbid fascination into her aunt's state of mind. She did not understand Lillian's bequest to her when it happened in October and these pages are giving her an insight. She hates the feeling of being at the mercy of events while also being deeply curious to know more about Lillian's life and motivation, her unknown and secretive aunt.

Spencer enters the kitchen carrying two used mugs which he washes up.

'I love the way you do that,' she says.

He turns and she sees at once how happy he looks.

'Holly, I'm so chuffed. I've just had the best news, five minutes ago. I've been offered one day a week teaching at Brighton University; on their Fine Art Painting BA.'

'That's fantastic news!'

'I've been trying to get in there for years.'

'It's so well deserved.'

'You're the first person I've told.'

She hugs him.

'I think we should celebrate with more than coffee, Spencer.'

'You're right. You up for an evening in the pub later?'

'I am. Ray says The Wounded Hart is the only proper pub round here.'

The Wounded Hart is a short walk from the house and a favourite with the locals. Holly orders the best bottle of wine on the list.

'*I'm* getting this,' she says.

They clink glasses.

'Well done you.'

'I'm looking forward to working with the students.'

'I learned so much from my students and sometimes they surprised me.'

A woman and a teenage girl come in and sit down at the table next to them. The woman is tidy in a blouse and pleated skirt and the girl wears cut-off frayed jeans, and her T-shirt hangs off one shoulder. The woman brings a gin and tonic and a Coke to the table.

'Where are my crisps?' the girl asks.

'You just had supper, and say thank you when I buy you a drink,' the woman snaps.

They start to hiss nasty things at each other, and it's difficult to ignore.

'Let's take our drinks outside,' Spencer suggests.

They settle at an outside table.

'Did you see how those two were with each other, pretty toxic?' Holly says.

'Teenagers can be hard work. How do you feel about your mum these days?'

When they were first together they talked about her mother's desertion at length. It still felt raw then.

'You remember I thought I must have done something really bad to make her leave,' Holly says.

'Yes, and I said children are nearly always blameless.'

'I don't feel I am to blame anymore. It was her life choice to leave us. I've been feeling angry with her for so long, and I'd like to let it go but I can't seem to forgive her.' She feels her throat start to heat up but carries on speaking. 'It must have been *so awful* for Dad. Humiliating. He had to face his friends and colleagues afterwards, and carry on. He was a hero.'

'I hope Raffy doesn't blame herself for our split,' Spencer says after a moment.

'She was a baby when you and Sofia parted.'

'One year old.'

'Even more blameless. How's she doing now?'

'Growing into a right heartbreaker. She was over for two weeks last August and wanted me to buy her a bikini of all things.'

'And did you?'

'Yes! I had to brave the Brighton shops with her and that was hellish.'

'She's… thirteen?'

'Fifteen.' He scrolls through his phone and shows Holly a picture of his daughter, her face in profile, standing on a clifftop, her dark curly hair caught by the wind.

'I took this when she wasn't looking. Otherwise, she does this silly pout thing.'

'She's lovely.'

'She takes after her mum,' he says.

Holly and Spencer's eyes meet. Spencer never married, but he lived with Sofia for seven years. He was painting full time and received a few commissions, but after Raffaella was born Sofia wanted him to get a proper job, as she put it. He refused, they fought and a year later she went back to Turin, taking their infant daughter with her. An unspoken question hangs in the silence between Holly and Spencer.

'It couldn't have worked,' he says.

When they've finished the bottle they stroll back to the house and he gets on his bike.

'You sure you're OK to ride?'

'I'll be careful, I promise.'

She wonders if she should suggest he stay over, but before she can say anything he leans forward and kisses her goodbye. It makes her tingle. It doesn't feel like a kiss between friends.

Chapter Twenty

PENUMBRA HOUSE

Three in the morning a crash shatters the peace of the house, slicing through Holly's dreams. She sits up in bed feeling dazed. Her mouth is dry. There's a tinkling after-sound of glass falling. Fumbling for her kimono she follows the sound coming from the sitting room at the front of the house.

As she switches on the light she sees a large hole in the centre of the main window, cracks fanning out from it and shards of glass still falling. Fragments are scattered all over the floor, even in the farthest corner of the room. A breeze is coming through the broken pane.

There's a brick on the floor and she gasps and steps back. Someone is hammering on the front door, and she pulls it open. Ray looks half asleep, and his sweatshirt is inside out.

'Someone threw a brick through the window.' Her voice shakes.

He moves past her and surveys the room. 'Bloody hell.'

She is shivering on the threshold.

'Put some slippers on, Hol, or you'll cut your feet.'

He goes outside and runs up the road. When he returns Holly is in the sitting room, slippers on, and holding a broom. She needs the broom to lean on as she surveys the damage.

'Didn't see anyone on the street,' he says.

'Who would do this? In the middle of the night…'

'Some drunk arsehole probably who's scarpered. Tell you what, whoever it was they hurled the brick with a lot of force. See how far the glass has scattered.'

'I noticed that.'

He takes the broom from her. 'You look white. Go sit in the kitchen and I'll sweep up here.'

Ten minutes later James joins them in the kitchen as Ray is emptying the dustpan onto a newspaper he's spread on the floor. He rolls up the glass fragments and pushes them into a bin bag.

'I only just realised something was wrong,' James says.

'Didn't you hear the crash?' Ray asks. 'It was enough to wake the dead.'

'I heard something, but I wear earplugs at night,' James says.

'Go look in the sitting room.' Ray puts on a kettle and reaches for Holly's teapot, adding three tea bags. James comes back, and they sit at the table. Holly pours the tea and her hands are shaking.

'That's the biggest window in the house so whoever did it went for maximum damage,' James says.

'You think it was deliberate? You think it was someone getting at me?' Holly asks, grasping her mug.

'Course not. It was a random act of vandalism by some lowlife,' Ray says, giving James a look.

'What else could it be? You've got no enemies here, have you,' James says.

'It's such a horrible thing to do. They must have come right up the front path to throw the brick,' Holly says.

'There are arseholes everywhere, Hol. Don't let it get to you. I'm a hundred per cent sure it was random,' Ray repeats.

She looks at him. 'But what do we do now?'

'We can't board up the window tonight. We'll get a glazier in later today. It's an enormous pane. They might have to order it in, but we cross that bridge if we have to. There's a lock on the sitting room door, isn't there?'

'Yes.'

'OK. James and I will move your furniture into the hall. Then we lock the room and go back to bed,' Ray says.

She washes up the cups as she hears Ray and James manoeuvring her sofa bed, coffee table and other bits out into the hall. Ray locks the sitting room door and gives her the key.

'Thank you both for doing that,' she says.

Ray and James have gone to their respective beds. Will she be able to get back to sleep because someone could climb into her house through the hole with only the sitting room door to keep them out? She's being silly. Why would anyone risk doing that? But she lays her phone on her pillow ready if needed.

Eventually, around 5am, she falls into sleep.

At eight thirty someone banging on the front door wakes her. She drags herself out of bed, pulls on her kimono and, feeling very weary and almost liverish, with lack of sleep, opens the door to Max. Max looks aghast.

'What happened?'

'Someone hurled a brick through the window just after three this morning.'

'What! But who would do that?'

'We have no idea.'

'Morons! Can I see the damage?'

'I've locked the room,' she says.

'Odd that they targeted your house.'

She shakes her head. 'I don't understand it at all.'

'You look exhausted.'

'I am. I need to get back to bed.'

Max moves around the furniture in the hall. As she heads for her bedroom and the comfort of her pillows and duvet, she hears him walking up the stairs to James's floor.

At eleven o'clock Hazel, her neighbour, comes round with a tin of home-made flapjacks which she presents to Holly.

'Oh, my dear, what happened?'

'A brick thrown from outside at three in the morning,' Holly says.

'What a *ghastly* thing. Ian, that's my husband – I must introduce you, thought he heard something. Can we do anything to help?'

'You've already helped with these flapjacks. Will you stay for a coffee?'

They move to the kitchen and Holly, who has only just showered and dressed, fills the kettle and spoons coffee into the cafetière. She still feels dazed by her broken night.

'It was the loudest crash. I was asleep and–'

'Horrible! Have you got onto the glaziers yet?' Hazel asks.

'Yes, my friend Ray has measured the window. He's at the supplier on London Road now.'

'They're a reliable company.'

Holly places the mugs, cafetière, sugar and cartons of milk on the table and slumps in her chair, recalls Hazel's involvement in the Neighbourhood Watch Group.

'Have a flapjack,' Hazel says in a soothing voice, opening the tin.

Holly takes one and nibbles on it. 'This is good.'

She feels close to tears because Hazel is being kind. 'Has anything like this happened on the street before?'

Hazel takes a flapjack from the tin. 'I can't recall there ever being a brick through a window. There was an accident with a scaffold pole once, at Mrs Thompson's house. Now Ian, my husband, said he could smell marijuana strongly on the street last week. Do you think there could be a connection?'

Holly blushes and hides her cheeks behind her mug. She suspects the smell is coming from Ray's basement and hopes Hazel won't make the connection to Penumbra House. She caught a whiff of it herself when she was in the garden with Barry, and whatever Ray smokes, it certainly has a pungent woody aroma.

'Probably local kids experimenting, don't you think,' Holly says.

Hazel lifts her mug. 'Could be. But it's a worry isn't it, hurling a brick like that is *so* aggressive.'

'That's what upset me.'

'To cause so much damage. It's an *enormous* window. I recommend you report it to the police. I'm not suggesting they'll be able to find the perpetrator, but best they know it happened.'

'I'll do that,' Holly says, wondering if she will. After all, what's the point. They won't catch the perpetrator and she does not want to draw attention to Penumbra House, particularly with Ray's smoking habit.

'Would you mind if I include the incident in my next

newsletter? We like to keep a record of crime on the road because it makes everyone more vigilant,' Hazel says.

Holly looks doubtful. 'I guess that's OK.'

'And it happened around 3am?'

'Yes, 3am.'

'I'll write a brief report and share with you before I send out. We've also got a petition on the go, Holly. We want the council to chop down the larger elms on the road, the ones causing so much damage.'

'Chop them down? But I love the trees on this road. It's what makes this road special.'

'You must have seen how the roots are pushing up the tarmac. It's positively hazardous. And some roots are getting into our inspection chambers,' Hazel says firmly.

'Inspection chambers?'

'In our drains. The roots work their way in and cause cracks. Then you get sewage leakages.' Hazel wrinkles her nose.

'But don't we need to preserve the trees?' Holly says, her voice tentative because Hazel is a woman of certainties and someone, she suspects, who has no room for sentiment. Holly hears footsteps coming down the stairs and is glad when Spencer walks into the kitchen.

'Hazel, this is my friend, Spencer.'

Hazel looks at Spencer with interest. She picks up the tin and offers him a flapjack.

'Lovely, thank you,' he says.

Holly stands. 'I'll make more coffee.'

'Are you from Brighton, Spencer?' Hazel asks.

'No, I pitched up here after art college. I'm based in Saltdean, near the lido.'

'Ah, Saltdean.'

'What Spencer hasn't told you is that he's a fine artist and is working from a studio upstairs,' Holly says.

'An artist. How exciting.' Hazel gazes at Spencer, clearly intrigued as to where he fits into the household and what his relationship is to Holly.

After Hazel has gone, Spencer suggests he and Holly go for a walk in Preston Park.

'Come on, it's a lovely day and far too good to spend cooped up inside.'

It's unusual for Spencer to leave his easel in the morning, and Holly guesses he is doing it to give her support. She appreciates the offer.

'Hazel asked to include the incident in her newsletter, and I suppose it will be the talk of the street now,' Holly says wryly as they head to Preston Park.

She and Spencer walk the perimeter of the park towards the Preston Twins; two ancient elm trees over four hundred years old and the pride of Brighton. Today they see only one giant elm and are shocked to see the stump of the second one. An old man walking by stops at their side.

'Went a few months ago. Heard about it on the radio and came down to watch. There was a team of them and the lads from the TV. Needed a big crane to take it away.'

'But why?'

'Elm Disease. Those council men were as upset as I was. Been here since the reign of James the First and now gone forever.'

Holly walks over to the remaining ancient elm and touches its rough bark. It has a hollow cave at its centre, yet new leaves still grow every spring and a circle of aconites bloom at its base.

'Will this one be OK?'

'They won't know till the spring.'

'It's such a shame. My aunt told me about these elms. She'd have been sad to know one had gone.'

The old man walks away. Beyond the elm there's a walled garden, and Holly and Spencer sit on the bench by the pond. She reflects how nothing stays the same. Her father is gone, her aunt is gone, and now one of the historic elms is gone too. They thought she didn't remember, because she was so young, but Holly can recall vividly the day her life was turned upside down.

As if it was yesterday, she sees her mother packing a large suitcase lying open on the bed. Her mother is folding her best dresses and blouses into it.

'What are you doing, Mummy?'

'Clearing things away and I need to get on.' Her mother's voice is sharp, impatient.

Later, Holly sees her mother push the suitcase into the spare bedroom when her father opens the front door. Holly runs down to him, and he lifts her into a bear hug. She says nothing about the suitcase; she is nearly five and doesn't understand what it means. But she has picked up on the unhappy atmosphere between her parents because children can read non-verbal communication.

That evening at supper her mother eats nothing and makes Holly go to bed early. She lies on her side gazing at her creamy nightlight with its circle of china mice at its base. Before she falls asleep their voices come up through the floor of her bedroom but make no sense to her.

The next morning her mother is gone, never to return. Her father's eyelids are red, and he hasn't shaved. He does not go to work that day or for the next week. Her mother has run off with her American tennis instructor and her father fights for and gains sole custody of Holly.

Aunt Lillian helps her father find a French au pair, Audrey, to look after her. When she arrives Audrey isn't very interested in Holly. From that point on her father focuses even more love and attention on her and she could not have had a better dad. The evening of the day her mother leaves Holly swallows soup which is too hot, and it burns her throat. Ever since, whenever she thinks of her mother, she gets a burning sensation in her throat.

She feels the heat there now and pushes herself up and off the bench.

'Let's head back.'

It never does her any good to think about that time of misery and upheaval. Somehow seeing the ancient tree gone has triggered memories of the first huge loss of her life. She was so young, and wonders if this is why she still finds it hard to deal with loss.

They have to wait three days for the glaziers to source a pane of glass large enough to fit the window. Two men put it in place and the bill for the glass and the labour is substantial.

Holly has swept the sitting room three times and yet is still finding tiny fragments of glass on the floor. She can see herself doing this again and again until she is content there are no further traces.

Whoever hurled the brick has succeeded in leaving damage in more ways than one.

Chapter Twenty-One

PENUMBRA HOUSE

Holly unlocks the front door noticing her kitchen door is closed and as she approaches, she's met by a nice smell of something cooking. She opens the door to see James standing over a pan on her hob.

'I'm glad you're back. I thought I might have got the timings wrong,' he says, glancing at her.

She looks at him in puzzlement and then sees he has laid the table with plates and cutlery and wine glasses for two. There's a bowl of green salad and purple tulips in a vase.

'What's this?' she asks.

'My turn to do some cooking for you, Holly. I'm making us a classic risotto. Hope you don't mind me commandeering your kitchen and pans but I'm thin on utensils upstairs.'

'I love a risotto,' she says.

He smiles at her. 'There's a bottle of Sauvignon Blanc in

the fridge. Can you open it and pour? The risotto needs my full attention for the next few minutes.'

Holly opens the fridge door and takes out the wine. She pours them each a glass. 'This is a lovely surprise. Thank you, James.'

They don't talk much as they eat. James's risotto is a good one and Holly raises her glass to him.

'That was delicious. I'd love some more,' she says.

'Onion, garlic, celery and, a key ingredient, two glasses of vermouth.'

James occasionally cooked for Holly when they lived together but she is surprised by his gesture this evening.

'My risottos can be hit or miss,' she says as she finishes her second helping. 'I enjoyed that so much.'

James has finished too and pours them both more wine and pushes his chair back from the table. 'I felt you were due an apology.'

'An apology?'

'I wasn't there for you when you miscarried the second time.'

Holly winces at the memory and the direct way he has brought it up.

'I didn't know how to cope with your misery,' he says.

'I didn't know how to cope either,' she says quietly. 'You were never at home.'

'I buried myself in my work. It felt like you were unreachable. That there was *nothing* I could do to fix it.'

She nods at the truth of this. Her inability to carry a pregnancy to term could not be fixed by her husband. But his withdrawal, his leaving her alone until late most evenings, had felt so personal.

'It felt like you blamed me,' she says.

'I was out of my depth.'

It's rare for James to admit to being out of his depth and she feels he is waiting for her to absolve him. What can she say? She does not think any words uttered now can erase what happened then.

'I appreciate the apology, James, and thanks again for making supper. It's such a treat to be cooked for.'

She stands. 'Now I'll do the clearing up as you did the cooking.'

As Holly washes the dishes and pan, she doesn't know how to read what James has said and done this evening. They had started out so hopefully and a year into the marriage agreed to try for a baby. It took some years, but she got pregnant, twice. She miscarried at two months the first time and at four and a half months the second. The second time was traumatic. Thinking she was out of the danger period she told her dad and her friends the happy news at three months. It was the hope which got you. Hope followed by loss and wretchedness.

It had not made them grow closer. Quite the opposite. James worked even longer hours in the city, and Holly retreated into sadness. Their marriage limped on for a while, but their bond was destroyed. It took Holly too long to leave James but eventually she found the strength to do so. It's an aspect of her character she dislikes; her tendency to put up with things for too long. She thinks she would have been a good mother. It would have helped heal the hurt inner child who still lurks inside her. And the person who was there for her in those deeply painful months after her second miscarriage was Laura.

Holly is on the train to London, to stay with Laura so she can miss Hazel's Neighbourhood Watch meeting. She looks out of the window, enjoying the landscape, and thinks again about the clandestine love affair between Lillian and Jacques. They were lovers for decades and seem to have been soulmates. They had a child. But having a child did not bring them closer together, rather the reverse.

Holly can think about her childlessness without the deep ache she suffered in her thirties, yet still laments the lack of a partner. She thinks of the misunderstandings she's had with her men over the years. Maybe finding a soulmate is an impossible dream.

———

When she arrives at Laura's flat, after first making a big fuss of Cooper, Holly tells her friend about James's surprise risotto.

'I came home to find the table all laid out in my kitchen, a bunch of tulips in a vase and his risotto and salad.'

Laura is quick to respond. 'What's he after?'

'It could just have been a kind gesture.'

'You think that? Honestly?'

'I agree it's out of character. I wondered if your Zen comment hit home and got him thinking. Because, well, he said sorry for how he treated me before we separated.'

'Oh, he's *definitely* after something.'

'It was an excellent risotto.'

'You know what I think.'

'Tell me.'

'Well, it seems to me you're getting especially fond of Spencer.'

'I guess I am. He thinks about other people's feelings. *And* he washes his dirty mugs.' Holly grins at Laura who has a theory that men do not notice dirty cups or plates.

'Once you've been physically intimate with a man something always remains, doesn't it?'

'I suppose it does.'

'There's always the possibility of a rekindling,' Laura persists. 'So, my theory is James has noticed the spark between you and Spencer. He doesn't like it at all and he's trying to court you!'

Holly shakes her head. 'I don't *think* that's what was going on. He wasn't exactly courting me. But he behaves as though he has special privileges with me. I mean we *are* still married.'

'It was a mistake to delay your divorce, Holly.'

'Maybe. And he doesn't like that I won't eject Spencer from the first floor and make him paint in a garret.'

'My point exactly. James has noticed your growing attachment to Spencer.'

Holly knows her friend is digging. She isn't ready to talk about how Spencer makes her feel. Sometimes she is delighted and sometimes confused by her reactions to him.

'Spencer is lovely, but any woman who was with him would have to take second place to a canvas.'

'Ask yourself how you'd feel if he took up with a new woman.'

'Hmmm, I wouldn't like that,' Holly admits.

Laura stands. 'This is all very fascinating, but I need to get cooking.'

Holly watches her friend at work and feels guilty about the secrets she's keeping from her. She hasn't told Laura *or* Spencer about the pages on the doormat. Keeping secrets creates a distance between you and your nearest and dearest.

Laura cooks them salmon fillets and roasted vegetables and gone is her usual lavish use of olive oil. This evening she squirts a low-calorie cooking spray over the asparagus, courgettes, and red onions.

'I'm on a diet because of the wedding. No potatoes and no rice. Sorry, sweetie, but I have to shift a stone by September.'

'You really don't. You look great.'

'Please back me up on this. I plan to wear a trouser suit, a fitted evening one. And no bloody hat! I want to look very London.' Laura sighs. 'The most difficult thing is the not drinking.'

'I shouldn't have brought wine.' Holly's surprised at the level of anxiety Laura is showing over the wedding, still five months away. They sit down to eat.

'I got to meet Iona's parents when I was in Lancaster last week. They drove down, and we had an engagement dinner in the hotel. Iona's a bright girl and Charlie's clearly happy to be with her.'

'I'm so glad. Did you like her parents?'

'They were nice, long-term married, very settled and conventional. They made me feel a failure, actually.'

'Why would you feel that?'

'Because I'm on my own. The Single Mother. I wish I had a fella to accompany me on the Big Day.'

'Stop this at once. You're an amazing, brave and gorgeous woman and Charlie is dead proud of you.'

Laura is rueful. 'You're my best friend and see me through rose-tinted glasses.'

'You brought Charlie up on your own and he's a terrific young man. Be proud of that. I know I would be.'

'I *am* proud of him. But I'm nearly fifty and on my own. It won't do, so I'm taking the plunge with internet dating again, on our old friend Match.com.'

'Really?'

Laura had urged Holly to sign up to Match.com after she and Ray split up. She helped her write her profile and took ages choosing which photos to upload to the site. Laura said most men only took notice of the pics, so the trick was to keep the words short and the photos alluring.

Holly's profile was posted and there was a flurry of interest. She recalls those excruciating first dates. Not once had she wanted to meet any of the men again, and she gave up after six months.

'I know what you're thinking but it can work out. Christabel met a nice man on Match.com and they're living together now. He's a widower and I think maybe widowers are the best option. The long-term singles are usually mad, sad or bad, and the divorced ones are often bitter,' Laura says.

'You're a braver woman than me.'

'It would be ideal if I could find a personable male to accompany me to the wedding.'

Holly thinks this is a misguided notion, but who is she to be critical of her friend when only hours before on the train she was lamenting her lack of a soulmate!

Laura pushes her plate away and pours herself a glass of wine raising it with a sigh. 'Only the one glass tonight.'

Holly wishes she could shift her friend from this mood. Usually, Laura is confident and fun, but when the glooms descend, she becomes overly self-critical.

'I'm feeling uneasy about my inheritance,' she says to shift the focus.

'Really? What's brought this on?'

'It feels like the house doesn't want me there. There was the dead seagull and the brick through my window. It's like I'm an unwanted guest.'

'A great big house like that, such a change from your flat, it's bound to take getting used to.'

It is time for Cooper's evening lamp post walk around Camden Square.

'I won't be able to get to your roast dinner this month,' Laura says. 'I'm disappointed as it's fun watching your soap opera unfolding, the drama of the rutting stags and now the added spice of watching James watching you and Spencer.'

Holly smiles affectionately. 'You're wicked, and you'll be missed. James hired that painter Max. I've had coffees with them and it's awkward. He looks at me expectantly, waiting for me to hire him.'

'James would like you to hire him. It would get one over on Ray.'

'True, but James wants to help this guy too. His ex-wife cleaned him out and he's trying to rebuild his life. I think James identifies with him.'

'God, we're all having mid-life crises, aren't we!'

'I guess we are.'

Cooper has found a bush and explores its roots with much energetic snuffling.

Holly continues. 'Barry's been working on the garden. He's a grafter. We'll have a nice spot to sunbathe in this summer.'

'Great.'

'And Spencer is keeping a close eye, making sure Barry doesn't go near his beloved fig tree with the machete!'

'How's big bad Ray?'

'He's the best. Checks the work and won't let me make any final payments till all the snagging is done. I'd hate having to do that. None of it would be happening without Ray.'

'He's your knight in rusty armour.'

'He really is.'

'Shame you can't loan me one of your men for the wedding,' Laura says archly as they head back to her flat.

Chapter Twenty-Two

LATE APRIL

PENUMBRA HOUSE
THE THIRD ROAST DINNER

Holly lays the table placing yellow tulips in a vase in the centre. The beef is resting and, as the men arrive, she is spooning horseradish sauce into a bowl. She pours the rich gravy into a warmed jug and the men sit down.

Ray and Spencer compliment her on the beef and both ask for second helpings. James takes the thinnest slice of meat, and Holly asks if he would like more.

'No thanks. I'm trying to swerve red meat.'

She sees Ray raise his eyebrows ironically at Spencer.

James continues. 'Max has finished my rooms and I'm delighted with the job he's done. You've taken a look, Ray.'

'Yes, he's slow, but he's done a good job, I'll give him that,' Ray says.

'He's got your seal of approval then?' James says with an edge of sarcasm.

'I just said he's done a good job.'

There's an edge to Ray's tone and Holly is in quickly to defuse another standoff. 'I'm glad he worked out. An odd thing though; I looked Max up on Google this week, to see if there were examples of his work, and there's nothing about him. No Facebook, no Instagram, no LinkedIn. Why would that be? I mean, usually you can find everyone on Google.'

'I know the reason for that. I asked him the same question,' James says.

Holly is surprised. Although people do it all the time, it is vaguely stalkerish to Google people you know. 'You told him you looked him up on Google?'

'Not like that. I'm setting up my work Facebook account and looked Max up to see if he could be a friend. I asked him why he wasn't on Facebook as it would be a good way to get his name as a decorator out there.'

The three of them are looking at James, intrigued by this.

'He wiped everything about himself off the internet, because of the vindictive ex. He doesn't want her to know where he's living or what he's doing. Max really is starting out with a blank sheet of paper.'

Holly is vaguely ashamed of her suspicions about Max, but it *is* unusual for a person to have no footprint on the internet.

'There's a vindictive ex?' Ray asks.

'Oh yes, an ex-wife who took *everything* and is still bitter against him. He's told me about her and she's one of those dominant shrewish types.'

'You've only heard his side of the story,' Holly points out.

'Ah, cue Holly-the-Feminist,' James retorts.

'I'm just saying his version might be one-sided.'

'There are plenty of vindictive women out there. I know of two cases of women who made false allegations and ruined men's lives.'

'That was when you worked in the city,' Holly says at once.

'What's that got to do with it? Those guys were making big bucks, but they didn't deserve to be ruined.'

Holly shakes her head crossly. 'They were both awful men.'

'And the women were gold diggers. Sorry, guys, this is a retread of an argument Holly and I used to have. Turns out the men are *always* in the wrong.'

Ray winks at Spencer. 'Don't mind us.'

Holly gets up with a scrape of her chair to fetch the apple crumble she's made. She hands each man a bowl, and they eat the pudding in silence, passing the jug of custard between them.

'Nice pud, Hol,' Ray says at last.

'Thanks for making us custard when you can't eat it,' Spencer says.

'Yes, very good, Holly. Shall I tell Max you want him to do your rooms?' James asks in a friendlier voice.

She glances over at Ray, who nods his assent.

'Please do.'

'And maybe he can do the hall, stairs and landings?' James adds.

Ray shakes his head. 'Too big a job. He'd need an assistant if he took that on.'

'You *know* he hasn't got an assistant. I just told you why he's new to Brighton,' James retorts.

'Not our problem,' Ray snaps.

James throws his spoon into the bowl with a clatter. Ray smirks. Holly clenches her fists under the table. Why can't they get through one meal without this macho bullshit? Spencer is not macho, but sometimes she wishes he would intervene when James and Ray argue. He's so even-handed it sometimes grates on her.

Chapter Twenty-Three

PENUMBRA HOUSE

Holly stands in the lumber room on the first floor and looks at the large cardboard box in the corner with its French postage. Lillian's solicitor had told her back in December that he was sending her a box with Lillian's work papers and the original manuscripts of her translations.

Holly has neglected to open it all this time thinking once open she'll have to decide what to do with the manuscripts because Lillian is considered an important translator. Holly closes the door and sits on the floor cross-legged and pulls the box towards her. Strangely it looks as if the box might have been opened and clumsily resealed.

She spends the next hour taking out the manuscripts and arranging them in chronological order all over the floor. Lillian was prolific. So much work and so many words. She dedicated her life to creating the best possible translation, and her father told her Lillian's desire to be true to each writer was her obsession. No, she can't throw these away. She'll have to find a university language department which might want them.

The papers have made her dusty and she comes down from the first floor to wash her hands. She hears the crack of the loose floorboard in her sitting room. She hurries in to find Max standing in the centre of her room.

'Sorry, I was gasping for a drink and James has got someone in with him so I couldn't get to his kitchen. Hope you don't mind, but I helped myself to a glass of water.'

'That's fine, just startled me.'

He blinks and looks down at the floor, then he treads on the board deliberately and makes it crack again. Their eyes meet.

'You need to get that fixed,' he says.

'It's on the list, the ever-growing list.'

'I'm so pleased you want me to paint your rooms. Thank you, Holly. I won't let you down.'

James must have told Max the job was his. He looks like he wants to chat, but she has a lot of things to do and glances at her phone.

'My pleasure, Max. I must get on. Let me fill your glass again.'

He follows her into the kitchen, and she takes a bottle of iced water from her fridge and refills his glass.

'Thank you, Holly. James is immensely focused, isn't he?'

'I think he has to be, what with starting a new career.'

'I admire him and I'm sure he'll make a success of it. A big change for him, isn't it?'

Her mind is full of Lillian's manuscripts, and she doesn't want to prolong their conversation or discuss James's life change with Max.

'It is a big change. I really must get on.' She smiles at him to soften her words.

'Don't mind me; I'm a chronic chatterbox. A few final

touches needed on James's floor, and I can start work on your rooms as soon as you want.'

'Great. I've got it down to three shades of yellow for the sitting room. I'll decide very soon.'

After he's gone, she reflects Max and James have become friends and have been out for meals together, returning to the Thai café in Hove. She isn't sure this is such a good thing because she feels like she may be being manoeuvred.

THREE DAYS LATER

Barry and Holly are working in the garden. He told her the bindweed is out of control. She offers to help and wonders if she is slightly afraid of Barry. He's so blunt and surly and seems to bring out the people-pleaser in her.

'You have to grasp the bindweed low down and pull it out from its roots. Like this.' He wraps his hand around the base of the plant and gives it a powerful tug. It comes out roots and all.

'I'll do my best.'

A branch has grown out horizontally from the trunk of the fig tree. It nearly reaches the wall, is as thick as a small trunk, and divides the garden in two. She and Barry are standing on either side of it.

'Could we cut this one branch off, Barry? It would free up a lot of space.'

'Leave it be. I told you I'm no tree surgeon.' Barry heaps more weeds into the wheelbarrow.

'Ray thinks it was the roots which damaged the drains before and we'll have to dig down sometime and check.'

'Folk always want to go digging where they don't need to.'

He turns and pushes the wheelbarrow up to a compost heap he's created at the top of the garden. She carries on weeding, glad he can't see how often the bindweed snaps in her hand, leaving the roots under the soil to live to see another day. She tugs hard at one near the wall and catches her hand on a thorn bush.

'Ouch!'

Holly sucks at the beads of blood which ooze from her knuckles. The bindweed is a real pain, and she recalls with nostalgia her small well-kept patio in London with its potted plants of geraniums and pansies. It was beautifully low maintenance. She gave her pots to Laura when she moved. Max is watching her from the kitchen window, and she waves at him as Barry comes back brandishing his shovel.

'I need to talk paint colours with Max,' she says.

Barry attacks a withered bush with the shovel. 'This is coming out.' He digs at its base, making small grunting noises.

She joins Max in the kitchen and runs her hand under cold water. She has circled two colours on the paint chart and hands this to Max.

'Pale Primrose for the sitting room and Duck Egg Blue for my bedroom please.'

He studies the chart. 'OK. I'll get these mixed at the paint shop today. What's the story with the garden? It looks like it's not been touched in years.'

'It was left to run wild. My aunt lived in France and hardly ever came here.'

'So you're going to transform it?'

'I couldn't leave it as it was.'

'Will you leave the fig tree?'

'Oh yes, that's a fixture. Spencer would never speak to me again if I cut it down! But someone will have to inspect the roots if we're not to have another problem with the drains.'

Max turns to go.

'Max, I realise I don't have your mobile number.'

He stops and pulls a small black Nokia out of his back

pocket. 'I can't afford a smartphone. I bought myself this Pay-As-You-Go. I don't know my number off by heart yet.'

He scrolls down and reads out the number. She writes it on the kitchen pad, and he gives a sardonic laugh.

'I've been told people call these drug dealer phones.'

After he's left with the paint colour chart she doesn't want to return to the bindweed and tidies the kitchen instead. She has decided not to get it painted yet because she needs a functioning kitchen. Truth is, she spends more time in here than in any of the other grander rooms.

Barry stomps up the steps from the garden. 'I won't come in today, I'm mucky.'

She hands him an envelope she's prepared. She doesn't like to count notes into his hand, which is somehow demeaning. As he takes the envelope, she sees beneath the dirt a white scar which runs across his palm from his thumb to his little finger. He looks in the envelope and nods.

'See you next week. Can't say what day it will be.'

She follows him down the steps into the garden. He has made good progress on clearing the thorn bushes.

'I'm glad we can see some of the garden wall now. I like those old bricks. Thank you, Barry.'

Barry trudges away by the side of the house.

Ray is standing on his doorstep and calls out to him. 'Hello, Bazza.'

'The name's Barry,' he says shortly.

In the evenings Holly has got into the habit of taking a glass of wine and sitting on the steps which lead down to the garden. She put up a tube feeder and likes to watch the little birds flying in to perch and peck at the birdseed, marvelling at their agility. She also bought a low feeding table for the larger birds.

Most evenings seagulls, magpies and pigeons fly down to eat. Barry would disapprove. A squirrel comes too and plants himself on the table. He gorges on the birdseed, is getting plump, and she's named him Bunter. There is a definite pecking order. The seagulls take precedence, followed by the magpies, then the wood pigeons while the street pigeons wait, knowing their place as the underclass.

Tonight, she feels slightly nauseous and puts her glass of wine down. The sky above the trees is turning pink. Her head feels strange too, heavy and muffled. She leaves the steps and returns to the kitchen. The sky is deepening in colour, layers of pink and gold, beautiful. This is a good spot to watch a sunset, but she feels unpleasantly dizzy. She steadies herself against the sink and pours the wine down the plughole. Maybe the bottle was off.

Chapter Twenty-Four

EARLY MAY

PENUMBRA HOUSE

It rained during the night and when Holly goes out to fill the bird tube feeder, she sees her laptop power lead lying on the ground. She picks it up and it's covered in wet soil. How did that happen? The last time she used her laptop was in the kitchen, yesterday morning. She examines it more closely and the cable looks badly bent. It won't work again she is sure.

One of the men must have borrowed it. But surely they have their own equipment. James came down to her kitchen yesterday, to borrow tea bags – again. Thinking about it, she isn't sure if Ray has a laptop. He has a desktop computer, an old model. Spencer is in the clear because his equipment is in Saltdean.

She goes inside and leaves the lead on the table, lying on a piece of kitchen roll, like an exhibit, and washes the soil off her hands. She hears James coming down the stairs, heading for the front door.

'James,' she calls out.

'What is it? I've got a train to catch.'

'I want to show you something.'

Max is at work in her sitting room and as James stands at the kitchen threshold, she beckons him in.

'My laptop power lead,' she says.

He sees it lying on the table. 'That looks a mess.'

'It's ruined. It was left in the garden overnight and I didn't put it there. Did you borrow it?'

'Of course not.'

'You were in the kitchen last.'

It comes out as more of an accusation than she intended and he's quick to curl his lip.

'Why would I take *your lead*? I have a Mac.'

He stomps out of the kitchen and bangs the front door behind him. Max chooses that moment to come out of the sitting room. He must have heard their sharp exchange.

'Those cupboards, Holly, the ones on either side of the fireplace?'

'Yes?'

'Do you want me to paint them in primrose yellow or white gloss?'

'Let me think about that,' she says, feeling irritated he came out just after she and James had words. Max has a curious look on his face and no doubt he would take James's side. Truth is she had sounded more critical than she intended.

'Sure thing. I'll hang fire,' he says.

She shuts the kitchen door, cross that she'll have to go down to Churchill Square and buy a new laptop lead. Shopping malls are one of her least favourite things. Far from being the temples of delight where your every desire is satisfied, the moment she steps into Churchill Square she is wearied by the recycled air and the febrile atmosphere. She puts the ruined lead into a plastic bag.

'I have to go out, Max. Help yourself to tea and coffee.'

Churchill Square is as trying as ever, and she is glad to get home. She unwraps her new lead and plugs it into her laptop. Her mobile rings. Laura. She rarely calls Holly during working hours, so something must be up.

'Hello, is everything OK?'

'I'm having a *shit* time at work; Julie undermines me at every opportunity. She's so sly.'

'What's she up to now?'

'Only making out she landed the latest contract when it was ninety per cent down to me.'

'I hate it when people do that. But you're brilliant at your job. Your boss sees that.'

'Not enough, is it? Julie's pals with the boss's wife, goes round to their house after work. It only takes a few barbed comments over the gin and tonics to get my stock to fall.'

'Horrible woman. I'm sorry you're having such an awful time.'

She'd read an article which said when your friends complain to you, just listen, acknowledge their difficulties, and *don't* offer advice.

'I can't stand even looking at her. I've got a new nickname; she's Julie Face-Ache.'

'Good one.' Holly steps onto the footstool to reach the upper shelf where she keeps her fancy teas.

'What are you doing?' Laura asks.

'Looking for camomile tea bags. Wine made me feel sick last night, so I thought I'd have herbal tea instead.'

'Very abstemious of you.'

'Oh no!' Holly exclaims.

'What is it?'

'Hell!'

'Holly?'

'I just found my laptop lead on the shelf with the herbal teas!'

The lead is tucked behind the boxes of tea. She takes hold of it and steps down from the footstool.

'So what?'

'This morning I accused James of taking my lead and he took huge umbrage.'

'Oops.'

'I found it in the garden. Wet and ruined, and I had to buy a new one. It must have been here all along.'

'And you accused James?'

'Yes.'

Laura chuckles. 'Oh, that's brilliant. You've actually managed to cheer me up.'

Holly takes her camomile tea and sits on the top step to watch the birds. She's agitated and even seeing Bunter the squirrel trip over to the feeding table, his tail like a question mark, does not lift her spirits. She rarely drinks herbal tea, so how did her laptop lead end up on *that* shelf? And who does the ruined lead belong to? She'd thrown it in the kitchen bin when she got home.

She goes back inside, puts on rubber gloves, and rummages through the used tea bags and coffee grounds to find it. It's exactly the same model as her lead. Hardly surprising she made a mistake. It can't have been in the garden for long because she fills the bird tube feeder regularly and only spotted it this morning. Now she'll have to apologise to James. Even though he's in and out of her kitchen more than she likes, *she* is in the wrong. She has noticed that when a day begins badly, it often carries on like that.

Max arrives every day at eight thirty sharp to work on Holly's sitting room. He is a meticulous if slow worker. If she is in Holly makes a pot of coffee around eleven and invites him to join her in the kitchen.

Today, over their coffee, he tells her that at the end of the day he plans to deliver several hundred business cards which James has had printed to promote his osteopathy business.

'I want to cover all the streets round here. James says it's a good catchment area. Plenty of people with bad backs and enough money to pay for treatment.'

He hands her one of the business cards.

'It probably is,' she says, looking at the card with interest. James has called his business *Penumbra Osteopathy.* Does this mean James plans to stay longer than he first suggested? The card is purple and has a slight Victorian vibe to it. The address and his mobile number are printed under his name in white in a classic font.

'I want to thank James for his support,' Max says.

He'll be delivering for free and she can't stop herself from commenting.

'You know when James is fired up about a project it's like everything else has to make way for it. It's good of you, but don't let him take advantage. He doesn't mean to but–'

'I'm happy to do it, Holly,' Max interrupts. 'I really am. I don't know anyone in Brighton, except for you and James, and you've both been so supportive.'

He's probably lonely in the evenings, having fled his past life. Maybe doing this for James makes him feel more connected to life in Brighton, she thinks.

Holly calls Laura for their Sunday evening catch-up chat.
Theirs is a friendship built on knowing the minutiae of each
other's life. They discuss Charlie's wedding and move on to
Laura's latest Match.com disasters.

'Enough about me. How's life at the house?'

'It's OK, though I'm surrounded by testosterone, and I
miss you.'

'Ditto, sweetie.'

'Men don't talk about stuff like we do. Max is here every
day working on my sitting room. He offered to work Saturdays,
but I said weekdays were enough. I mean, he's nice, but I like
to have my rooms to myself at the weekend.'

'Have you found out any more about his situation?'

'Not really. He doesn't mention his ex and I haven't asked. I
told you about his internet blackout, didn't I? He joins me for a
coffee sometimes and I sense he's trying to get to know me. I
guess he's lonely, but I'm holding back from saying too much.'

'That doesn't sound like you. I thought you had a soft spot
for working men?'

It's one of Laura's theories that Holly prefers working-class
men to privileged men. This is entirely based on her having
fallen for Ray.

Holly laughs. 'Oh, I'm not attracted to him. I guess he's
nice looking, but he's not my type.'

'I look forward to meeting the mysterious Max.'

'James has become pals with him. And he's getting him to
deliver his new business cards all over Brighton.'

'James never overlooks an opportunity to get something for
nothing,' Laura says crisply.

Laura has never liked James and since his split with Holly
she gives free rein to her barbed comments. The feeling of
dislike is mutual. James often made negative comments about

Laura saying she might be a lot of fun, but she was also brittle and demanding and expected Holly to drop everything when she needed company.

Holly dismissed his criticism as the resentment a spouse feels for his wife's best friend. She leans on Laura and Laura leans on her. But Holly concedes that sometimes Laura is brittle and possessive. Strange how you can see a friend's faults and yet still love them dearly.

'When are you coming to London for a weekend at mine?' Laura asks.

'Soon, darling, I promise. I've been feeling wiped out this week. Yesterday afternoon I fell asleep for a couple hours – that's not like me at all.'

———

Back from her seafront walk on Monday Holly enters the house and hears a loud crashing noise coming from Lillian's former bedroom. The plasterers are back to work on it. She hurries upstairs and stands on the threshold as Ray wields a mallet against the ancient gas stove. He's breaking it into pieces in front of her eyes.

'What are you doing?'

Ray turns and exhales in frustration. 'Couldn't unscrew the stove. Having to break it up. Don't worry, I've capped the gas tube, and I'll get a gas engineer to check it.'

'You're destroying it,' she says.

'What…?'

'It was rather lovely; I mean the carved metal surround and–'

'It was a hazard. Your aunt should have taken it out years ago.'

'I'm just saying…'

'What?'

'I wish you'd asked me.'

Ray's expression darkens. 'Max said you were out,' he snaps.

'Only for a walk. I had my phone with me.'

'Christ's sake. I thought we'd established I was the expert. I don't say these things for the good of my health, I do them for yours! The plaster team needs it out *today*.'

She hovers on the threshold as he glares at her, holding the mallet across his body. It is their first real row about the renovation and Holly, knowing what a proud man Ray is, knows she is teetering on the edge of a major bust-up.

'I just thought it was a nice period feature, like the radiators,' she says.

'And that bloody wallpaper. I'm not an interior designer. I'm a builder!'

He pushes past her and leaves the room. She hears his steps vibrate on the staircase down to the front door which he doesn't actually slam but closes firmly.

James chooses this moment to walk downstairs and raises his eyebrows at Holly. 'Oh dear, a clash of aesthetics?'

'You can't wait to stick your oar in, can you?' she says with some venom because he is loving her discomfort. How she wishes she could talk to Spencer about the row, but he's staying away while his rooms are being plastered. She looks at the mess of twisted metal and shattered ceramic on the floor and feels like banging her head against the wall. Restoring Penumbra House and living with competitive men and those bloody sheets of paper appearing on her doormat are testing her to the limit.

In the evening she feels thoroughly miserable about her fight with Ray and knows she won't feel better until they patch up their differences. She goes down to his flat and knocks gently.

When he opens the door, he looks at her severely. 'Yeah?'

'May I come in?'

He jerks his head towards his sitting room, and she follows him in there. He doesn't ask her to sit down.

'Maybe I overreacted,' she says.

'Maybe you did!'

She takes a deep breath. 'I'm sorry, Ray.'

'You leave the decisions about what's safe and what's unsafe to me.'

'I will, of course I will.'

'I'm about to have my dinner,' he says.

'I'll leave you to it then.'

At the door, she feels they haven't cleared the air enough. He is still simmering.

She stops and looks back at him. 'Ray, I really appreciate everything you are doing in the house.' She flees before he can say anything else.

Chapter Twenty-Five

MAY

PENUMBRA HOUSE

H olly stands in the hall her head in her hands. Her chest has gone into violent spasm. She tries to hold her breath and count to twenty to stop the insistent hiccups. The latest instalment was on the doormat first thing, and her mind is reeling from its content.

BRITTANY NOVEMBER 1987

I smelled the smoke before I saw it. I had been in the village to see the cheese man who brings his van on Wednesdays and parks by the church. I had bought Pont l'Eveque and a slab of Beaufort which Jacques and Emmanuel both like. As I got nearer, I saw smoke and flames rising from the top of my garden. I ran up the garden and Rabbit's hutch was engulfed in flames. Emmanuel was sitting cross-legged and watching as if in a trance.

'Where's Rabbit?' I screamed at him.

'Rabbit was a prisoner. I let him go,' he said calmly.

'He's a pet, you stupid boy. He won't survive in the wild.'

I scanned the garden frantically. I saw Emmanuel's hands were sooty.

'How did the fire start?'

He didn't answer; he was watching the flames intently, fascinated, trance-like. I felt the heat on my face. It was too late to put out the fire. I shouted at him to go inside and wash his hands. I hunted for Rabbit everywhere, along the brambles at the top of the garden and into the field which lay beyond. I walked all the way to the copse beyond the field. I prayed Rabbit had broken for freedom and was hiding where no bird of prey could swoop down and kill him.

I returned home feeling sick and shaken and more distraught by Rabbit's disappearance than I would have imagined possible. Emmanuel was sitting in the kitchen and had helped himself to the cheese. There were black finger marks on the slab of Beaufort. He looked up at me with that same strange light in his eyes. He wasn't upset at all; his look was defiance.

'I told you to wash your hands. Do it at once.'

He scraped his chair back from the table and I had to resist the urge to smack him. I have never smacked him.

In the evening I was raking out the embers when I found the bones of a rabbit in the ashes. I vomited in the garden. Emmanuel is a monster.

I passed a sleepless night. There is only one option. Emmanuel must go to boarding school at once. I phoned Jacques at his house, something I rarely do in case Severine answers. He sounded tense and I told him I will not wait till the new term begins. Emmanuel goes away now. I did not add how I can hardly bear to look at the boy's face.

This child, Emmanuel, burned his rabbit to death; trapped in a locked hutch. It is unspeakable, unbelievably cruel, the worst. Holly's heart hurts. She wants to tear all the pages up and never look at them again. Is it possible for a child be a psychopath?

Holly paces through the house and says to herself, *I must accept that I inherited Penumbra House because Lillian hated her son.* She looks at the cupboards on either side of the fireplace and shivers. It's as if the house holds some of the pain and sadness of Lillian's life. Her aunt had good reason to fear Emmanuel. He was a child who liked to hurt animals and that *is* the sign of a psychopath.

Holly looks at the pages in her hand. The way the pages are being cut out with deliberation and posted through her door also seems weirdly obsessive, the work of a person who is unhinged but also on a mission, someone who has calculated that the drip, drip, drip of this awful information will destabilise her and make her want to get as far away from Penumbra House as possible.

Her need to confide in someone about this tortured family drama is getting stronger by the day. Usually she shares her troubles with Laura but can't seem to do it this time. Is it because of the shame Holly feels that she has a weird cousin who does the most hateful things?

She is the beneficiary because of a buried secret in her family; mental illness. Emmanuel's warped personality.

Somehow to reveal all this to Laura would be too painful. Her friend knows how much she's staked on her new life in the house; her great project that promised so much. Maybe there is some pride mixed in there too. It's hard to admit she's made a mistake.

What more is there to come from Lillian's journal? This

was written in 1987, thirty-two years ago. What kind of a man has Emmanuel grown into? If he still lives, he'll be a dangerous man who will want to punish the person who got his inheritance.

It is Spencer she would like to confide in. Maybe he could help her make sense of these awful revelations. But should she take the leap? Or must she carry on keeping Lillian's awful torment a secret?

———————————

Barry is peering down at the soil when she brings him his mug of tea.

'Nature never wastes anything,' he says.

She follows his gaze.

'Slugs eating fox shit.'

Two long slugs are grazing on a mound of wet excrement. He raises his eyes and catches her disgusted but fascinated expression. She cannot drag her eyes away. The slugs are feasting!

'I'll get more slug pellets,' he says.

He shovels up the shit and the slugs and deposits them on the compost heap at the top of the garden. She hands him the mug of strong tea and a plate with two digestive biscuits. He takes off his gloves and sits on the bottom kitchen step. He's told her he prefers to take his tea break outside. The first time he came she had put four biscuits on a plate, and he had eaten two. The next time she put three biscuits out for him, and he had eaten two. So now this is what she gives him.

'This means we have a fox in the garden?' she asks.

'More than one, I'd say. Can't mistake that smell.'

He dunks a digestive in his mug. 'Ever hear any screaming in the garden at night?'

She looks at him and remembers. 'The first week I moved in I did. The most awful blood-curdling cries. It woke me up.'

'Foxes mate in January and the female will scream. Males do too, to mark their territory. And we have rats in the garden.'

'What charming wildlife we are blessed with,' Holly quips.

She sees how Barry's dogged ferocity against the thorns is proving ever more effective, and a larger space is emerging by the wall. She walks over and places her hand against the old bricks which are warmed by the sun.

'It catches the sun here. I'll buy a sun lounger; in fact, I think I'll treat myself to two.'

'That blackberry bush at the top of the garden doesn't fruit anymore,' he says.

'That's a shame.'

'I'll pull it up.'

'OK.'

He's eaten his two biscuits and finished his tea. He puts his mug down and pulls on his gloves.

'It used to fruit well,' he says, and he trudges up the garden.

She thinks about his comment about the blackberries as she rolls the recycling bin onto the street. Rita, his wife, only came to Penumbra House in March and April. How did Barry know the bush fruited unless he came to the garden in the autumn?

All the houses on the street have tall side gates leading to their gardens, all except Penumbra House. It's possible to access the garden at any time so maybe Lillian told Rita she should help herself to the blackberries? But should she put up a gate with a lock? The house stood empty for eleven months a year for decades. Anyone could wander into the garden. Someone might have got into the house too. Then again, with Hazel and her husband on watch, was that likely? Holly will talk to Ray about installing a side gate.

On the street she sees Hazel with Trisha, her neighbour from the other side. Trisha is a woman who favours ethnic prints and is keen on crafts. Today she is clad in a full-length colourful kaftan with wooden beads around her neck. Hazel and Trisha are close friends, and they walk over to Holly as she positions her bin for collection.

'How's it all going?' Hazel asks.

'Good, on the whole. We've had a few setbacks.'

'That's to be expected,' Hazel says.

'The house was so neglected. I hope my aunt would like what I'm doing.'

'I'm sure she would, and I would *love* to see how it's coming along,' Trisha says.

'You'd both be welcome to pop over and take a look. Maybe next week? How about Monday evening? Come for a glass of wine and see for yourselves the progress we're making.'

They're pleased and agree to come on Monday. Max comes out of the house and throws an empty paint tin into the skip.

'Have you met Max? He's painting my rooms,' Holly says.

Hazel and Trisha greet him, and Holly watches him turn on the charm.

'We're looking forward to seeing what you've achieved on Monday,' Trisha says to him.

'Holly's rooms are a challenge because of their height, but I'm happy with how the sitting room is turning out,' he says.

He is giving both women the full blaze of his attention and Trisha begins to play with her wooden beads. Fair enough, Holly thinks, he needs to meet people to get more work.

'See you on Monday,' she says, and leaves them chatting with Max on the street. She had invited Hazel and Trisha over as the least she could do after their having to put up with living next door to an abandoned house for decades. She knows her aunt was not a good neighbour.

Chapter Twenty-Six

PENUMBRA HOUSE

H olly sees Ray standing on the front path smoking a roll-up. He is surveying the house. She still regrets their run-in, isn't sure he has completely forgiven her yet and joins him outside.

'Penny for your thoughts,' she says.

'Some of the brickwork needs repointing. See those patches under the ground floor windows.'

'Let's do it.'

'The brickwork is worth looking after.'

'The façade is fine, isn't it? I don't like how the name looks though.'

Several houses in the road have their names painted in gold on the fanlight, and these look elegant. The letters here are painted thickly and '**P e n u m b r a**' is inscribed in a semi-circle above the word '**H o u s e**'. It isn't elegant at all. It is just emphatic.

Ray shrugs. 'It's only a name, Hol.'

'I don't like the way the letters are painted so thickly in black.'

He glances at her, and she guesses he's struggling to understand why she finds this a problem. She recalls his comment that he is no interior designer. 'If we scraped the black paint off and repainted in gold letters it would look nicer.'

'We can, but that will have to wait.'

'Of course, not a problem, just a thought,' she says.

Ray is key to achieving the renovation and she very much wants them to be friends again.

Her huge and gracious sitting room is nearly finished. The room looks as lovely and elegant as Holly hoped, but her pleasure in the room is dimmed. She hasn't been feeling well for a while and suffers headaches, bouts of dizziness and an exhaustion she can't shake off. It doesn't matter how much she sleeps; she's tired most of the time. This beautiful room deserves to be shown off and Hazel and Trisha are coming on Monday.

Holly heads down to Ray's flat, and he makes mugs of tea for them. His leather three-seater sofa fits the back wall, and his sound system dominates the alcove. Ray still plays CDs, and these are stacked in two towers. He has unpacked all his boxes and painted his sitting room cream and the room is almost an exact replica of the sitting room at his London flat. She sinks onto his sofa, yawns and, leaning her head back, fights the desire to stretch out and close her eyes.

'What's up, Hol?'

'I'm feeling tired *all the time*. It's been a few weeks. Could it be the paint?'

'Unlikely, unless you're super-sensitive.'

'I've never been sensitive to paint before. You painted my bathroom in London. It was tiny and yet I had no ill effects.'

He grins at her. 'You couldn't swing a cat in there.'

Is he remembering their getting together at that time? She recalls how she longed for his daily visits and tried to think up other decorating jobs to keep him near her.

'Did Max get the paint from the supplier on London Road?' Ray asks.

'Yes, he had it mixed there.'

'They're reputable. Are you keeping the windows open during the day?'

'There's plenty of air circulating in the rooms and I wedge the sitting room door open at night. It doesn't even smell much.'

'Must be something else making you poorly. Are you stressing about the renovation?'

'I *wasn't*. I've been happy how well it's going. All thanks to you. But the dead seagull and the brick through the window has stressed me.'

'Stop brooding on that. Some people are just plain envious.'

'You think someone's targeting me?'

'No, not *personally*. It's a case of spite against a big house. House envy. When I bought my new van, some arsehole keyed it all down one side. Ruined my pleasure in it.'

'Some people are so poisonous.'

Should she tell Ray about the pages on her doormat? They're the *true* source of her stress and unease. Or would telling Ray make her feel even more strongly she is losing control of her life and her dream project is slipping away from her.

'Maybe you need a change of scene. I'm off fishing this

weekend and that's the best tonic. Are you getting down to the seafront?'

'I haven't left the house much for the last few days,' she admits.

'Get yourself down there and blow away the cobwebs. I'd join you, but I'm in the middle of doing the figures.'

He is getting local jobs as well as overseeing the house, and his coffee table is littered with invoices and receipts.

'Good advice, kind sir,' she says.

She'll follow Ray's advice and get a bus to the seafront and walk from the functioning pier to the ruined one.

The bus stop at the bottom of her road shows a bus coming in four minutes. A bus pulls up on the other side of the road and Max gets out. He crosses to her side.

'Hi, Holly, I'm ready to start on your bedroom,' he says cheerily. 'Shall we move the furniture into the sitting room? I assume you'll be sleeping in there?'

She wavers. She doesn't feel like walking back to the house and missing her bus. She has a powerful urge to walk along the beach and experience sea breezes on her face.

'Sorry, Max. I'm getting the next bus. Can it wait?'

'I'd like to prepare your bedroom for painting, you know. Tell you what, give me your key and I'll shift the furniture and set the room up ready for tomorrow. I'll leave your key with James or Ray when I'm done.'

She hesitates, fighting her reluctance to part with her keys. But Max wants to get on and it's not fair to waste his time. She unzips the pocket in her bag and takes out the keys.

'I'll be gone for a few hours. Maybe text me when you're leaving.'

JANE LYTHELL

'Will do.'

On the bus they pass the pound shops and nail bars of London Road, before reaching the Old Steine Garden with its ornate fountain. She gets off and watches seagulls bathing in the fountain's spray. They look joyful as they swoop and splash in the water; almost like they're playing.

It is a weekday and yet there's a crowd of day-trippers at Brighton Pier stopping to watch the street artists doing their acts. She heads away from the noise and crowds towards the Hove end of the beach which she prefers. Here the promenade widens and there's plenty of room for the dog walkers and rollerbladers.

She slows down as she approaches the ruined West Pier and sits on the pebbles. Watching the waves roll in and out induces a meditative state in her. She lies down, managing to get comfortable on the pebbles, her bag as her pillow. The clouds drift slowly above, their shapes reminiscent of landforms. As a child she would lie on her back in her dad's garden and watch the clouds change shape and wonder how it would feel to lie on a cloud.

She falls asleep and when she wakes it is early evening. Hundreds of starlings are flying in spinning cones above the West Pier. They move as a single harmonious entity, and she watches in awe. *I should come here for a walk every day*, she thinks. *I haven't been making the most of living by the sea. Penumbra House may be my grand project, but I am allowed time away from it.*

When she gets back Max has gone, and James lets her in. Her keys are on the kitchen table.

'He's only just left,' James says.

Max has moved all her bedroom furniture into the sitting room. He has put her double bed right under the large window. She knows she won't be able to sleep under the glass where the brick was hurled and asks James to help her move the bed to the other side of the room.

'Max did a great job in here,' James says.

'He did. Isn't the colour lovely.'

'It's very *you*.'

'He's starting on my bedroom tomorrow. Duck Egg Blue.'

'What about your kitchen?'

'I'm leaving it for now. I need the kitchen every day.'

'Will you ask him to do the hall and landings?'

'Ray's clear that's a job for two men.'

James shakes his head. 'Not necessarily.'

'Ray's the expert and I want the painting over with as soon as possible.'

'I was only going to say—'

'James, drop it please,' she says, tired of the never-ending rivalry.

'OK. OK. I'll get back to my books.' He turns to leave then stops. 'I meant to ask you: Ray gives every impression he's here for the long term?'

She recalls she didn't tell James the arrangement she'd made with Ray.

'I mean, beyond when the renovation is finished,' James adds.

'He can stay as long as he likes.' Holly stares back at James, defiant.

It's *her* house, and she's not going to justify her decisions to James.

'Got himself a really good deal, didn't he,' James says, and he turns and climbs the stairs to his floor.

And your deal is pretty good too because you're paying less than the market rate for this area, she feels like shouting up after him but keeps her peace.

She recalls her lunch with him in December when she first told him about her inheritance and shared with him that Ray and Spencer were joining her in the house. She and James had got into the habit of meeting twice a year for lunch at a cheap and cheerful Thai café in Kentish Town. You could bring your own bottle of wine.

They exchanged gifts; books wrapped in Christmas paper. It was a tradition when they were together to give each other the book they'd most enjoyed during the year. James always chose non-fiction and she picked novels and she doubted if either of them ever read the books they were given.

'I have some interesting news,' she had said.

He had been amazed when she told him about her inheritance.

'But I didn't think you were close to Lillian.'

'I wasn't especially. I'm stunned she left me her house.'

'What a turn-up. She didn't have children, did she? I guess blood is thicker than water.'

'She would have left the house to Dad if he'd lived.'

She had felt the prick of tears and James shot her a look. He hated any shows of emotion.

'How's your mum doing?' she'd asked swallowing hard.

'Her dementia's getting worse, and my sister has found a *very expensive* nursing home. I reckon all Mum's money will go on paying for that bloody place,' he said looking grim.

Their lunches were their attempt at reconciliation but as they parted outside, she was aware of how separate they were. He hadn't congratulated her on the legacy. James had things on his mind. Financial pressures. He looked drawn when he mentioned his mother's illness and how much money would be needed to care for her.

And Holly hasn't grown any closer to James since he

moved into Penumbra House. Seeing him twice a year for their lunches had been enough. She hasn't told him she's feeling unwell and is worried about her symptoms. And no way is she going to confide in him about the pages appearing on her doormat.

Chapter Twenty-Seven

It's Saturday morning and Holly double locks the house. James is visiting his mother in London, and she's catching an early train to meet Laura. It's a good time to get away because she's not sleeping well with her bed stationed in the sitting room. In fact, her sleep has been troubled over the last few weeks and she has to take a nap most afternoons. This makes her feel very feeble. Yet at night she lies awake fretting about what's wrong with her. She tells James, Ray, and Spencer she is postponing their end-of-the-month roast dinner.

Laura's at the barrier at Victoria station and Holly's touched to see she's come to meet her. Laura is in high spirits.

'It's been a trial, but the pounds are coming off at last. And I've seen the trouser suit that's perfect for the wedding.'

They catch the tube to South Kensington and head straight to the Victoria and Albert Museum for an exhibition of film costumes. They take their time gazing at the glass cases of evening dresses made from the most glorious and extravagant of fabrics – velvet, satin, brocade and silk.

'So glamorous. When did you last wear velvet or satin?' Holly asks.

'Not for years. I had a vintage dress in my twenties. It was velvet and old rose colour. God, I loved that dress!'

'I had these purple velvet trousers I thought were so cool. I wore them till the nap wore away,' Holly says.

'We've lost our glamour, haven't we? It's all jeans and T-shirts these days.'

They move on to the museum shop and browse its delights. Laura loves museum shops and often buys an umbrella or a scarf based on an Old Master. Holly buys postcards of her favourite dresses from the exhibition.

'What do you fancy tonight? Do we go out or eat in?' Laura asks when they are on the tube heading back to Camden Town.

'Eat out, and dinner's on me,' Holly says. 'But I'll need a siesta before we go.'

'You're still not back to normal?'

'Not completely. I've been walking by the sea most days and that's helped. But I can't shift this tiredness.'

'Sounds to me like you're suffering from post-viral exhaustion, or even ME.'

'But I didn't get a virus. This tiredness came on almost overnight. That's the odd thing about it.'

'Get it checked up, please. There's this GP at my practice and he'll *not* accept ME exists. He thinks it's been dreamed up by neurotic North London women to get attention! I gave him a piece of my mind. Of course ME exists. My friend, Saskia, you remember Saskia, red curly hair…'

'Who works in publishing?'

'Yes, well she has ME and has been poorly for ages.'

They reach Laura's flat, and Cooper is ecstatic at their

175

return. Holly takes off her shoes and stretches out on Laura's pretty sofa with a cushion under her head. Within minutes her eyelids are drooping.

'Sleep now,' her friend says, putting a pashmina over her.

When Holly wakes, Laura and Cooper have gone and there's a note on the floor by the sofa.

So sorry I had to go out. Work crisis! I've booked us a table at The Lady Miranda at 8pm. Can you join me there as I'll be tied up till then. I've got Cooper. XX

The Lady Miranda near the canal is their favourite gastropub and it's also dog friendly. They'd celebrated the news of Holly's inheritance there last autumn. Laura bought champagne and they discussed whether Holly should sell Penumbra House.

Holly sets off and shivers as she walks through the first of a series of dark tunnels by the canal. She wishes she'd brought a thicker jacket with her. It's unseasonably cold for May. As well as shivering with the cold, she feels uneasy about the route she is taking along the canal path. Should she have come this way? On a sunny day this is an attractive shortcut. But not tonight. Tonight, there are no cyclists or dog-walkers about, indeed no sign of life in either direction.

The brutal murder of a young woman three weeks ago has been leading the headlines for days. The young woman took a seven-minute walk through a park to meet a friend, just as Holly is doing. It was reported today that the man who struck and killed her was a complete stranger. Holly cannot get that out of her head.

The oily water of the canal slaps against the brickwork and condensation drips from above. What a melancholy sight the stained canal path makes in the fading light. She must not scare herself with these thoughts. But is it wise to enter that long dark tunnel ahead? She's only five minutes from the exit stairs which lead up to The Lady Miranda. But five minutes is long enough. If she turns round and walks back and along the upper lighted streets, she'll be late.

She stops walking as her fear rises. Is there a stranger lurking in the tunnel ahead? Is that dark shape someone standing there, watching her? The hairs on her arms and neck lift and her throat tightens. Sometimes men kill women. Sometimes strangers kill women. Better late than dead. She takes two steps towards the tunnel. Then, gasping, she turns and runs away from the aperture she cannot bring herself to enter.

Laura's bagged a corner seat and Cooper's at her feet when Holly hurries in slightly breathless. She sits, glad to be in the cheerful pub.

'Sorry I'm late. I bottled out of the canal walk. It felt scary tonight. I think I'm developing a morbid imagination.'

'Not a problem. I'm going to have steak and salad. Why don't you have steak too. You may be low on iron.'

They order a bottle of red wine to go with their steaks.

'I should write a blog about the trials of internet dating,' Laura says. 'Take last Friday, I knew after five minutes this guy was the most boring person on earth and I was thinking *what is the shortest time I can decently stay*. He'd bought me a glass of wine and was droning on about his hobbies. I got my phone out, looked at it with great concern and said I'd had a text from a friend who was having a meltdown. I was so sorry, but I had to go to her at once.'

Laura shakes her head before continuing. 'So, Mr Boring wants to travel back on the Northern Line with me. He knew I lived in Camden Town you see. I lied and said I was getting the District Line to see my friend. We parted at the top of the escalators and walked off in different directions. I doubled back to get the Northern Line. As I was walking towards my platform, I saw him straight ahead and he turned and saw me and looked puzzled and waved. He started to walk towards me, and I panicked. I turned and *ran away* from him.'

Holly laughs. 'That poor man. You've probably given him a complex.'

'Terribly rude, I know. But I have to grit my teeth and carry on with the dates. I need to find my plus-one for the wedding.'

'I'll be your plus-one. Speaking of which, show me the trouser suit.'

Laura spools through shots of a sharply cut evening trouser suit with satin lapels in a shade of deepest red.

'Very chic and very *you*,' Holly says.

Holly takes out her phone to show Laura shots of the renovation of the house. She has taken a series of photos of the sitting room and in one has caught Max at the edge of the frame.

'Let me take a closer look at your mysterious Max.'

Laura uses her fingers to enlarge the photo. Max is dressed in his usual overalls. Holly's shot has caught him in profile staring at something out of frame.

'Can't really see too much. He's nice and slim,' Laura notes.

'He paints all day, and he and James go running in the park.'

'Ah, a bromance.'

Holly nods. 'I think it may be.'

Holly's been hesitating all day, but she has brought the two photos and Lillian's draft letter in a plastic folder to show to Laura. She can't bring herself to share the journal pages, but she wants to hear Laura's assessment of Lillian's disturbing draft letter. Holly pulls the plastic folder out of her bag.

'Remember the small dusty box I found in Lillian's bedroom? When we were making the video?'

'I think so. I'm sorry the video came to nothing. I did chase them once, but they said no joy.'

'It was worth a try. Anyway, that box contained this draft letter written by Lillian and two photos, and I want you to see them.'

Laura reads the letter.

> *September 1996*
> *My darling,*
> *I met her mother in the village. She is broken, has aged ten years, and says their future has been taken from them. I have hardly slept since so deep is my dread. I am consumed with the thought I have not done the right thing and should have reported my suspicions.*
> *He was in the area, and I know he is capable of killing. Remember Rabbit.*
> *I am frightened of him. I have decided I cannot and will not see him anymore. I urge you to seek professional help for him.*
> *My love as always,*
> *L.*

Holly leans over the table and for some reason she doesn't fully understand, she lowers her voice. 'What do you make of that?'

'It's weird. Disturbing, isn't it? Who is this man she's frightened of?'

Holly evades the question. 'It's out of character because

Lillian was such a fearless person. She lived alone and Dad said her house was in an isolated spot,' she says.

'Well, she was scared of someone this time. And *Remember Rabbit*. What does that mean?'

Holly shrugs guiltily. She now knows what the words mean but cannot bring herself to explain.

Laura reads the words out loud. *'I met her mother in the village. She is broken, has aged ten years, and says their future has been taken from them.'*

'Someone has died or been killed.'

'Sounds like it,' Holly says.

'Who was Lillian writing to?'

'I think I know the answer to that. She was involved with this man.'

Holly places the two photographs on the table side by side.

'These were in the box with the letter. A younger Lillian and the same man in both.'

Laura studies the first photograph. 'She's got your hair!'

It's true, in the photo Lillian has the same curly dark hair yet Holly had never noticed that before. She only remembers seeing her aunt with strong grey hair, tamed by clips, and looking severe, though she was always a handsome woman.

'She's stylish, isn't she? Great sandals. You've always described her as a blue-stocking recluse,' Laura says.

'I thought she was. I think she was writing to him, Jacques Pichois.'

Laura examines the photo again. 'He's attractive. Do you know anything about him?'

Laura picks up the second photo and, as Holly had done, turns the photo on its side to read the name on the book.

'It's the same man, years later. He's dead, died three years before Lillian. I googled him. He was an academic and wrote books about the French Revolution. But all I found on Google were his dates and a list of publications, and it said he was married to a Severine Pichois.'

'You think they were lovers?'

'They look like lovers in this one,' Holly says.

'They do.'

'Long-time lovers.'

'A married man.'

'Yes, that old story.'

Laura picks up the letter again. 'She's frightened of someone related to him, to Jacques. She says he must get him help. Maybe he had a son?'

Holly's guilt deepens at the details she is holding back from Laura. Why is she doing this partial sharing of information? She shakes her head but says nothing.

'Seems your aunt Lillian had a more exciting life than you thought.'

'More troubling than exciting. It explains why she was hardly ever here. Jacques Pichois was the reason Lillian stayed in Brittany. I'm going to frame the black-and-white photograph and hang it in the sitting room as a tribute to Lillian.'

'She's getting a hold over you,' Laura says as their steaks arrive.

SUNDAY EVENING

Holly packs her overnight bag.

'Are you *sure* you want to go back tonight?' Laura asks. 'I've got an early start tomorrow, but I've got a spare set of keys and you could have a lie-in and lock up later. Post my keys through the letter box when you go.'

'I have to go because my new fridge/freezer arrives tomorrow, and it might come any time after nine.'

'Can't one of your men take delivery?'

'James is with his mum, and I can't be sure what time Spencer will arrive. Ray said he was working off site tomorrow.' Holly zips up her bag. 'I'm feeling a bit better; less wiped out. Must be your good influence.'

'Eat more steak!'

'Yes, ma'am.'

She has enjoyed her time with Laura but does not miss living in London. Hazel and Trisha are coming for a tour tomorrow evening, and she'll buy a good wine and some olives and crisps. Maybe she'll buy some cheese too. She can't eat it, but most people like cheese with their wine.

It's well after ten when the taxi stops outside the house and Holly gets out with her overnight bag. She opens the front door and is hit by the most horrible smell. It's coming from the cupboard under the stairs. She wishes James was upstairs to help her investigate.

Pulling the cupboard door open she sees the rotting carcass of a rat. It is crawling with maggots, is alive with maggots and its eyes have been eaten. She retches and runs to the bathroom. She empties her stomach into the toilet bowl. Then sits back on her knees, trembling.

Struggling to her feet she flushes the toilet, runs the cold tap, and sluices water around her mouth until the bitterness of her vomit has gone. She washes her hands for an age before emerging back into the hall, glancing at the cupboard with fear and revulsion. She slams the cupboard door shut and runs outside and downstairs to knock on Ray's door. The sound of music is coming faintly from his flat.

Ray must have been asleep on his sofa. He comes to the

door looking drowsy and out of sorts. 'What's up? I was asleep.'

'A dead rat, rotting, upstairs, stinking the place out.' She gasps as another wave of nausea hits her and she closes her eyes. She reaches for his door frame to steady herself.

He rubs his hand over his face and yawns widely. 'Shit! I'm knackered.'

'Sorry. I was sick.'

'You better show me then,' he grumbles.

She stands several steps behind him in the hall, her hand pinching her nose, as he opens the cupboard door.

He exhales loudly. 'Very dead. Fetch me a brush and dustpan and a bin bag.'

She hurries to the kitchen and gets him what he's asked for.

'You look green. Go sit in the kitchen, Hol.'

She hears him bending and scraping at the floor and the rustle of the bin bag. There is a draught as he opens the front door. He returns a few minutes later and runs hot soapy water into a bowl. She hears him scrubbing the floor of the cupboard. Thank heavens for Ray. He washes his hands for an age at the kitchen sink. She sits watching him, incredibly grateful but unable to say anything as queasiness washes over her again.

Finally, he sits opposite her. 'The rat might have been disturbed when we dug up the drains.'

'That was months ago.'

'Yeah.'

'But how did it get into the cupboard?'

'That *is* odd.'

'It's been dead for a while.'

'I noticed,' he says wryly.

'I looked in that cupboard a couple of days ago. There was no rat then. Is there *any way* it could have got to my floor from the basement? Is there a passageway or something connecting the floors?'

'I haven't found anything like that.'

'Or pipes it might have come along?'

'I guess it might have crawled in from the garden in its death throes,' Ray says without much conviction.

'Barry said we had rats in the garden. But the house has been locked up all weekend and the cupboard door was shut when I left.'

'It's a mystery and a damned nuisance.'

He thinks she should have cleared it up herself instead of her turning to him to deal with the mess and the stink.

'Thank you for dealing with it and washing the floor. I couldn't bear to go near it. I'm sure it was horrid for you.'

'Don't read too much into it. I know what a worrier you are,' he says.

'And I woke you up.'

'Yeah, you did. See you tomorrow.'

He stands and goes back to his flat. It's late but she has to do something to neutralise the image of the rotting rat and those hideous writhing maggots. The smell is still stuck in her nostrils. She runs a deep bath, squirting scented bath oil under the hot water tap. As she strips, she recalls Laura gave her a Moisture Bomb Face Mask. You position the mask so you look out of the eyeholes. It's covered with a gluey gel which sticks to her cheeks.

She steps into the hot scented water. 'Keep it on for fifteen minutes,' Laura said, so Holly stretches out in the bath and rests her head on the edge.

Later, she plays a sleep meditation on her phone, which James recommended. She puts her phone on the pillow and presses start. Usually, she is asleep before the meditation ends. Not this time.

The bath, the face mask, the meditation; nothing helps and she passes a deeply unsettled night. There's something so malignant about the dead rat turning up right inside her house, in her cupboard, on her floor. The house has been empty all weekend. Even Ray, who is the epitome of common sense, cannot account for it.

Chapter Twenty-Eight

PENUMBRA HOUSE

The next day Max raps on the door at eight thirty. Holly plods along the hall, in her pyjamas, her back and neck aching after her bad night.

Max is in a conspicuously cheerful mood. 'You OK, Holly? You look tired.'

'I'm OK.'

It never helps when people say you looked tired, she thinks. She has a full day ahead with Hazel and Trisha coming for drinks in the evening. She won't tell Max about the rat and get drawn into a conversation about it.

'Funny smell in the hall,' Max says.

She ignores this. 'I've got a delivery this morning; a fridge/freezer. I don't know when they're coming. If I'm in the garden, will you open the door?'

'Sure thing.'

'Thanks,' she says listlessly.

As she gets dressed, she ponders how nice it'll be when the painting's over and she can lie in bed as long as she wants. She's not sure why Max is irritating her this morning. Maybe it's because he's so buoyant. This isn't his fault. Time to get the house ready for the neighbours' tour, which she now regrets. It's a good thing Spencer will be joining her.

The delivery men bring the new fridge/freezer and install it. They take the old fridge away and Holly follows them out, worrying about the smell in the hall. She walks down to a flower shop and buys a bunch of freesias and narcissi to put in the sitting room. Breathing in their sweet fragrance she arranges the flowers in one of Lillian's vases, yet the image of the rat keeps coming into her mind.

Holly polishes the two liqueur glasses she found in the cardboard box and holds one up to catch the light and reveal its engraving. She places them at the centre of the mantelpiece. Her bedroom furniture is pushed against the walls, yet the size and beauty of the sitting room is still evident.

Hazel and Trisha are due to come at six thirty. Is there still a whiff of rat in the hall? She lights a scented candle and pops it in the cupboard, looking away fast. Max packs up and leaves at six and as the front door clicks behind him, she hurries to get the wine glasses polished and the snacks onto plates. She hasn't invited him to join them and is struck at her ungenerous behaviour. After all, it is his work which helped make the sitting room look so splendid. Spencer comes down the stairs.

'Does it smell bad in the hall?' she asks him.

'No, it smells fine; slightly scented actually.'

She blows out the candle, Sandalwood her favourite, and the wax is a hot liquid pool around the wick. She resists the temptation to stick her fingers in and roll the melted wax into a ball.

'Can I do anything to help?'

'Just be Mr Charming. I think Hazel is intrigued I share my house with *three* men. She may start digging for information. She likes to talk.'

'Is that a polite way for saying she's a gossip?'

Hazel and Trisha arrive together just before six thirty, and both are bearing gifts.

'Flowers from my allotment.' Trisha hands her a bunch of daisies and ranunculus tied with twine.

Hazel gives her a jar with a handwritten label. 'And my green tomato chutney.'

'Lovely treats. Thank you, both. Come into the kitchen and we'll get a drink before our tour.'

Spencer is waiting for them.

'We met before,' Hazel says.

'We did. And hello, Trisha.'

He opens the wine and pours four glasses. Holly puts the flowers into water, and they walk to the top of the house. James is still away so Holly only shows them his treatment room and hands them his *Penumbra Osteopathy* cards.

Trisha is taken with the stone Buddha. 'What a fine piece.'

They take longer in Spencer's studio. He lays out his series of sketches and paintings on the floor in the front room.

'I like your portrait of Raffaella,' Holly says.

'Do you? I'm not sure. I don't like working from a photograph.'

'I think it's lovely.'

'So do I,' Hazel says.

'It's for her sixteenth birthday, though she'd prefer a

voucher from Zara,' he says.

Holly smiles warmly at him. With his daughter in another country he does his best to be a good father, spending every Christmas in Turin in a budget hotel and skypeing every week. Hazel wants to know more about his beautiful daughter and gradually winkles out the story of Spencer and Sofia and their parting of the ways.

They walk down to the sitting room.

'This is the loveliest room in the house,' Trisha says.

'I'm very lucky. My London flat would almost have fitted in here,' Holly says. 'I'd like a giant mirror for the wall opposite the windows. My mirrors are dwarfed in here.'

'I know some places you could try,' Hazel says. 'I meant to ask, what's your gardener called?'

Holly is handing round the dishes of crisps and olives and Hazel takes a handful of crisps. 'Barry, Barry Pumphrey.'

'My husband, Ian, often used to see him on the street, standing there and staring at your house. Years before you came here, Holly. Ian is very observant, you know. He's Chair of our Neighbourhood Watch Group, and he's spotted your gardener a few times.'

'Barry has an attachment to the house. His wife used to work here, for my aunt Lillian, as a cleaner. Rita. She's dead now, and I think he's lonely.'

'I've been thinking I should get someone in to do the heavy work in my garden,' Trisha says.

'Barry's a hard worker and he's made a real impact. Though one of his quirks is he won't let me know what day he's coming. He just turns up once a week.'

'Really? I'd want a set day and time,' Trisha says.

'Me too,' Hazel agrees.

Holly shrugs. 'It's not a big deal. I go along with it.'

The women gaze at her and she guesses they think she's letting Barry take liberties.

'He's very good at chopping back and he's a demon with the shovel,' Spencer adds.

After they've gone, Holly and Spencer sit at the kitchen table. He eats cheese and biscuits with lashings of Hazel's chutney, and Holly has toast with hummus.

'A successful visit,' Spencer says.

'They're both nice.'

'Hazel seemed to have a bit of a down on Barry though.'

'She's super-cautious. James calls her a curtain-twitcher. I mean she's on the lookout for crime. In this street? It's hardly inner city, is it?' Even as she says this she wonders if she is trying to speak certainty into existence. An image of the neatly sliced white pages arriving on her doormat intrudes on her mind.

TWO DAYS LATER

Since ten o'clock that morning five strangers, four women and one man, have rung the bell and asked to be shown up to James's floor. Holly has walked each of them up two flights of stairs. James greets his 'patients' cheerfully at the top and ushers them through to his treatment room, without giving Holly a glance. James is so arrogant sometimes.

She wants to ignore the next door-ringer. But on the third long ring Holly succumbs and wrenches open the front door with a scowl to find a middle-aged woman on the doorstep.

'I've come to see James Hadfield.'

Holly points up the stairs. 'Second floor,' she barks.

The woman looks startled and heads up the stairs

nervously, looking back over her shoulder at Holly who regrets her rudeness to this stranger.

Sometime later Holly hears someone leave the house. She peers out from the sitting room window and it's the last woman she let in walking away. Holly takes the stairs two at a time to James's floor, her anger well and truly stoked.

'This isn't right. I can't be opening the door and up and down the stairs all day. I'm not your bloody assistant!'

James's face is one of hurt innocence. 'I thought you'd understand. I'm doing a last push before my exams. They're *not paying* me.'

'So what?'

'I'm happy to give you free treatments too.'

'I don't need any treatments. You want to use my house as your practice you plan ahead. You know when these people are coming, don't you? Why can't you wait downstairs to let them in?'

'Not the best use of my time, Holly.'

'What about *my* time!' She hears the shrill squeak in her voice. James has always been like this. Whatever he's doing is somehow more important than anything she has to do.

'Stop shouting,' he says.

'I'm not shouting.' She lowers her voice. 'Come to think of it, didn't you say you'd install your own doorbell when we discussed this last December?'

'I did and I will.'

'Oh yes? When?'

'Soon. It's been a busy few months.'

'Soon needs to be *this week*, James. If more people come tomorrow, I'll ignore the doorbell.'

As she marches down the stairs, his voice floats down after

her, calm and patronising. 'You know we should be able to discuss this rationally, without raised voices.'

It's like all the rows they had before. James would take up the cool-headed rational stance and accuse her of being the emotional unreasonable one, no matter what he had done to trigger her anger. She stretches out on the sofa in her sitting room, suddenly weary. As so often happens her anger is turning to sadness.

———

That evening she calls Laura.

'It's not working with James.'

'What's the latest?'

'He said he'd get a doorbell installed, for his business. He hasn't done it of course. Today I was up and down those bloody stairs directing his patients.'

'Did you confront him?'

'We had a row. I don't know why I agreed to let him move in. He said it would be temporary, but he's had cards printed and it's looking a lot more permanent.'

'Put the rent up,' Laura says tartly.

Holly notices the sharpness in her tone. 'Are you OK, Laura?'

'No, I'm not. Why does it always have to be about you? Your problems, your feelings. I have troubles too!'

Holly is taken aback at Laura's hostility. 'What is it? Tell me.'

'Julie just got promoted.'

'No!'

'Oh yes. Being best friends with the boss's wife paid off. She'll be on £7,000 a year more than me from next month. *And* she gets to order me around.'

'That's so unfair!'

'I can't do a damn thing about it, can I?'

'I don't know, I mean…'

'I have to suck it up,' she says bitterly.

'I'm so sorry.'

'Charlie's getting married, and you've moved to Brighton. You're both getting on with your shiny new lives and I feel so *damned stuck and alone*.' She starts to cry.

'Oh, Laura, sweetheart. Come down this weekend. Please. I miss you.'

She has been here before. When Laura suffers a setback, she lashes out. Holly recalls the time Laura was shortlisted for an award for event organisers. Holly couldn't get to the award ceremony because she had booked a dinner for her dad on a steam train through Sussex; her birthday gift to him. The award ceremony was a big thing in Laura's life, and she took Holly's absence badly.

The next morning, having heard nothing, Holly googled the results and saw Laura had won the award. She sent a huge bouquet to Laura's flat with a card saying: *I salute you my brilliant friend. So sorry I couldn't be there to see it. XXX*

In the evening she received Laura's response by text:

> Thanks for the flowers but I don't need a
> bouquet. I needed you to be there.

That wrinkle in their friendship took weeks to iron out. As for the shiny new life Laura thinks she is having – nothing could be further from the truth. Holly wakes most mornings with dread in her heart at where the next setback will come from. But Laura made it clear tonight she does not want to hear about Holly's problems.

As she gets ready for bed, she reminds herself that Laura feels able to lash out at her because she is one of her nearest and dearest and is sure Holly will forgive her. She does forgive her, but it still stings.

Chapter Twenty-Nine

PENUMBRA HOUSE

Holly reads the latest pages in her sitting room and her temples throb. Whoever's leaving the pages is now doing it at night, after everyone is in bed. This is his pattern, and she is convinced it is a man, is convinced it must be Emmanuel Pichois.

> *BRITTANY 1991*
>
> *Severine Pichois is dead. Her suffering is over. Her diagnosis was terminal, yet she lasted far longer than the doctors predicted, and this must testify to her strength of spirit.*
>
> *Over the years, I often thought how I would feel when I heard she had died. She was not an intellectual woman. She put her energies into homemaking, loved to cook and to craft, and by all accounts was a kind person. Jacques met her when he was young, and they married in their early twenties.*

We never met, but our love for Jacques connected us.

I waited until a month after the funeral, which I did not attend of course, before I told Jacques that from now on Emmanuel would have to live with him. It was not a request but a statement.

Jacques argued with me, saying a boy should be with his mother. I told him this was exactly the time when he needed the influence of his father. I would not be moved from my resolve. He has lived with me for seventeen years. Let Jacques see for himself how unreachable the boy is.

During the Easter holiday we moved Emmanuel into Jacques's house. I do not know how Jacques will explain the sudden appearance of a teenage boy bearing a striking resemblance to him to his neighbours. However, Jacques does not worry about such things. It was always Severine he wished to spare. I continue to pay half of Emmanuel's school fees.

After Emmanuel had left, I walked round my house and was glad all his things were gone. I painted the room he used to sleep in pale yellow and bought a good upright armchair. It is now my reading room. It is a joy to have my house returned to me after all these years. My hope is I will be able to create great translations again.

Jacques has been everything to me since we met during that life-changing summer. I fear our disagreements about Emmanuel are eating away at our love and perfect trust. He is blind to Emmanuel's malignant energy. Maybe because the boy takes after him in looks so much. He has the same striking eyebrows as his father. His son and heir. And he turns on the charm for Jacques.

My good times with Jacques are when Emmanuel is away at boarding school. Then we can go days without mentioning him.

In spite of my best efforts to rise above it, I see bitterness is infusing my thoughts. All those years Jacques and I hoped one day we would be able to live together openly and in perfect harmony. We planned to spend half the year in England. Jacques wanted to do

some research in the British Library. With Severine dead our time
had come. It is not to be. Emmanuel stands in our way. I had
harboured such dreams of making Penumbra House a beautiful home
for the two of us.

Holly sits for a long time thinking. How must Emmanuel
have felt when he found this journal and read his mother's
bitter thoughts about him? Lillian has totally rejected and
disinherited him. He must be a very damaged and angry man,
her cousin.

Holly scratches her left arm which has started to itch
fiendishly.

***

As Holly comes back from the post office, after sending a
paperback she's just finished and enjoyed to Laura, she sees a
young guy in brown council uniform standing by the elm tree
on the street right outside Penumbra House. He pulls a piece
of the bark away from the trunk with ease, as if he is pulling a
sheet of paper off a pad. She approaches him as he examines
the bark closely.

'Is the tree OK?'

'We're checking it. Looks like it might have Elm Disease.'

'Oh no, I hope not. I love having the tree right in front of
my house.'

He looks gratified that she cares about the tree.

'Most people don't get what's at stake. Brighton has around
17,000 elm trees and that's special. But they buy these
wretched logs for their wood burning stoves and the logs are
infested with beetles which carry the disease. There's so much
ignorance around.'

She likes his passion. 'I was sorry the ancient elm in the
park had to be cut down.'

'The twin. Losing the twin was a major blow.'

'Will the other twin survive?'

'We hope so. We dug a trench to sever any link of interconnected roots with the diseased one.'

'Oh, I hope it works. Fingers crossed.'

'And we'll try to save this one,' he says.

They nod at each other, and she goes into the house.

———

James is late with his rent. Holly has waited a week, then ten days. Now it is three weeks past its due date. It's not a lot of money but she doesn't want to set a precedent with him. She heads up the stairs.

Spencer has gone for the day, and she peeks into his studio and as always, he has left it tidy with his brushes cleaned and lined up. She rehearses what she'll say to James. Why is talking about money so uncomfortable?

Reaching the top floor, she taps gently on the door.

'Come in,' he calls out.

He is sitting cross-legged on a cushion, his feet bare.

'Sorry, are you meditating?'

'I just finished. What's up?'

She hovers on the threshold, losing confidence and wishing she hadn't come up.

'I was wondering… well um… the thing is, your rent hasn't arrived in my account this month.'

'Oh yes, I meant to ask you, Holly. Can I pay you two months' worth in June? I'm waiting on a cheque,' he says airily.

'I see.'

'It's not a problem, is it? You're hardly strapped for cash.'

It's amazing how he knows how to press her buttons and make her cross in an instant.

'What's that supposed to mean?'

He shrugs. 'Nothing.'

She goes on looking at him.

'Just saying I can't believe it makes such a difference to your bank balance. You'll get double in June.'

She bites back what she wants to say and walks over to his window and looks down at the garden. 'OK,' she says with her back to him.

He has made her feel petty. The silence stretches out between them uncomfortably. She searches for something neutral to say so she can get out of his room and away from this atmosphere between them.

'Barry is doing a good job on the garden,' she says. It sounds lame but is all she could think of.

James gets to his feet and puts the cushion away in the linen chest by the wall. He turns to face her. 'You know, Holly, I can't help noticing you've got us all in one place, in your palace, so you can play your games with us. It must make you feel powerful.'

She's so taken aback by his accusation that she turns and hurries out of his room without another word.

Holly heads for her kitchen and she's angry. Very angry. James thinks she's on a power trip with her exes and is playing games with them. That really stings. She hadn't known what to say at that moment. But what she should have said was 'but it was you who invited yourself into my house. It wasn't my idea, and I went against my judgement when I said yes. You are twisting things to put me in a bad light'.

How familiar this feels to her. James putting her in the wrong. She paces the kitchen resisting the urge to go back upstairs and put the record straight. It would escalate their row still further. More conflict. She pushes her feelings down.

She has a craving for comfort food and will cook herself a big bowl of tagliatelle with tomato and basil sauce. She bought a bag of fresh pasta and fresh pasta is such a treat. When she opens the fridge, she can't find it. Did she put it in the cupboard? Unlikely, but she searches for the next few minutes without success. She knows she hasn't eaten the pasta.

This is ridiculous. Is someone taking her food? They aren't students anymore. She resents how everyone thinks they can come into her kitchen whenever they want and help themselves to her things. Then she stops herself from the spiral of her negative thoughts. She must not let herself sink into resentment of the men. It will make her unhappy.

She makes herself toast with her butter substitute and marmite and eats the hot greasy slices too quickly, standing up, looking out at the garden, angry thoughts still churning in her head despite her best intentions to let it go. You shouldn't eat when you are angry.

Her left arm has started to itch again. She boils a kettle, makes a mug of tea, and goes to fetch her laptop. Her life was simpler and more peaceful in London and being honest she was happier then. Penumbra House is such a mixed blessing.

She misses her teaching job, misses Gabriel, and Usain, her two surprising and original students. Teaching made her feel she was doing something worthwhile. Their exams are soon and she wants to wish them luck. Turning on her laptop, she writes a personal message to each of them, and doing this calms her a bit. She should try to get a teaching job in Brighton next year.

But she can't get James's accusation out of her head. Does he resent her good fortune in inheriting Penumbra House? That snide use of the word 'palace'. It signifies a complete reversal in their fortunes.

When she met James, he had been the one with the money. Now he has to pay rent to her.

Her father used to say good intentions often go punished, because we want the best for people and never learn they won't change. That is her and James in a nutshell.

Chapter Thirty

PENUMBRA HOUSE

It's Friday and Laura is coming for the weekend, arriving that afternoon, staying three nights. It's a nice gesture, and is probably to make up for her sharp words to Holly when the horrible Julie got promoted.

Holly waits for her, thinking she needs her friend. It's as if Penumbra House is coming together and she is falling apart. Her tiredness has been worse this week, and she has a dry mouth and a near-permanent headache. She feels physically and emotionally fragile and the itchiness in her left arm keeps flaring up. Why is she getting these mysterious symptoms? Yet she is determined not to complain to Laura about her health or about the other things going on in the house. This weekend she'll be upbeat.

The taxi draws up outside, and the women embrace on the street. Cooper runs around them in excited circles.

'I'm *so* glad you're here. Now, come see what we've done to my sitting room.'

'Oh, I love this colour, it really works,' Laura says.

Holly's bed is now next to the sofa bed. 'We're both in here this time. Max is still painting my bedroom.'

They sink onto the sofa and Laura leans in.

'Is Max still here?' she asks in a low voice.

'Yes.'

'Will you introduce me? You know I'm keen to meet the mysterious Max.'

There is a febrile air about Laura and Holly recalls her questions about Max over the last few months. Her friend tends to fixate on things and get what she wants, but she also has the fatal flaw of making what is in front of her fit what she wants it to be.

Holly takes Laura through to her bedroom. Max always wears an overall over his jeans when he's painting and as they walk in he is disrobing from it. He laughs nervously, and they wait for him to recover himself. Cooper pads behind the women and plonks himself down at the threshold, not moving into the bedroom.

'Max, this is my very dear friend, Laura.'

They shake hands quite formally.

'You've done a fantastic job on the sitting room,' Laura says.

'Thank you, you don't come across many rooms like that.'

'Absolutely stunning. Looking good in here too. I love the pale blue. When I think of Holly's tiny flat in London and now she's living in this palace. Happy days.'

'I've enjoyed painting these rooms,' he says.

'I've brought two bottles of red. Will you join us in a glass of wine, Max?' Laura asks.

He smiles. 'I'd love to, thanks.'

They move to the kitchen. Holly takes down three glasses

and polishes them to a shine before putting them on the table. Laura uncorks the red and pours three generous portions. They clink glasses.

'To Holly's palace,' Laura says brightly.

It's another of Laura's nicknames, 'the palace', and it's starting to grate on Holly. James used it the other day too. Maybe he heard Laura using it. It points to an element of envy from them both about her legacy. For most of the years of their friendship Laura has lived in her beautiful spacious flat on Camden Square while Holly perched in her pretty shoebox up the road.

Laura's flat is way beyond what she could afford on her salary as an event organiser. Her father is a judge, and although he disapproves of his daughter having a child out of wedlock and of her continuing status as an unwed mother, he helped her to buy the large flat on the desirable square. Now Holly has the bigger residence. Is it possible Laura resents this?

Holly sips her wine. She has been drinking much less alcohol recently, thinking it might be contributing to her dizziness. Laura is generous with her gifts, and this is an excellent wine. *Focus on the good things*, Holly tells herself, *and shake yourself out of these stupid negative thoughts*.

'This is very good, thanks, Laura,' she says.

'Holly tells me you're new to Brighton, Max?' Laura leans towards him.

'Indeed I am.'

'How are you finding it?'

'It's a nice town, but you get the feeling it's seen better days.'

'I thought the same,' Holly says. 'It looks shabby. I'm sure it looked smarter when I used to visit Lillian.'

Cooper has not settled and is skittering around the perimeter of the kitchen.

'Are you nearly finished here?' Laura asks Max.

'The bedroom needs more work. The cornicing takes time.' He glances at Holly. 'I'd love to be considered for the job of painting the hall and landings once it's done.'

Holly's cheeks heat up. She goes over to the sink and runs water into a bowl for Cooper.

'Ray thinks it might be too big a job for one person, and I don't like to go against Ray,' she says as she kneels and strokes Cooper.

Max has made her feel awkward. He has been working for her for weeks and couldn't have been more helpful, but two men would get the job done in half the time. Laura leans over and pours more wine into Max's glass.

'Shall I let Cooper into the garden?' Holly asks.

'Please.'

Laura flicks her hair back in a way Holly has seen her do before, unabashedly flirting with Max.

'I better fold the loungers up too. Heard it might rain tonight,' Holly says.

Laura and Max are looking at each other, not at her. Holly opens the door and Cooper bounds down the steps.

As Holly goes out, she hears Max saying, 'I need to build up more contacts, so if you have friends who need any decorating, please tell them about me. I'd be happy to work in London.'

Holly walks over to her new sun loungers, folds them up and leans them against the wall. She breathes in and out slowly to ease the tension she's feeling at watching the way Laura is being with Max. Cooper is digging by the fig tree. Again.

She heads to the top of the garden and sees Barry has uprooted the blackberry bush leaving a large bare area. They should put a flowering plant in there, something pretty and fragrant. Maybe white lilac.

She fights her reluctance to go back to the kitchen. Cooper

refuses to leave the tree and as she reaches the bottom step, she hears Max mention her name. She stops.

'Holly was lucky to inherit this great big house,' he says.

'Yes, but it's odd, when she got the news, she didn't seem especially happy, not at first. I would have been *thrilled*. She deserves good things. She's such a dear.'

Laura's voice is warm, and Holly takes the first step, but Max's next comment stops her.

'I'm surprised Holly and James split up. They're both so nice and have both been supportive to me.'

'Well, James used to be super successful and he's intolerant of anything he perceives as failure. Holly had a few health issues and I think that derailed their marriage.'

'Health issues?'

Holly recoils. Surely Laura isn't going to tell Max about her miscarriages.

'Just take it from me that Holly's had some tough stuff to deal with and she deserves all the breaks. And who knows why a marriage fails really?'

'As well I know!' Max says. 'Did you know Holly's aunt? Was she an eccentric woman?'

'I never met her. Lillian Hilborne. I'm told she was very intellectual and formidable.'

Holly cannot stand outside any longer, eavesdropping on these two, and she stamps up the steps so they will hear her.

'What is it with the fig tree? Spencer is obsessed with it and Cooper can't keep away either!' Holly is falsely bright.

Laura looks up and is flushed and excited.

The wine bottle is empty. Neither woman moves to open the second and Max gets to his feet and says his goodbyes.

'You were flirting with him,' Holly says as soon as she hears the front door close behind him.

Laura giggles. 'I was a bit. I mean he is attractive, isn't he?'

'I guess he is.'

'Will you let him do the hallways?'

'I don't know what to do about that. He's always helpful; almost too helpful.'

'Really?'

'I know I'm being mean.' Holly sighs.

Laura is holding a piece of paper with Max's name and number written on it.

'Max Clancy,' she says thoughtfully. 'He asked me to see if any friends need decorating done. Said it would be worth his while to do the short hop to London. It's slightly odd, isn't it? What is a man in his mid-forties who seems well educated doing scrapping around for decorating jobs?'

'He's starting out again.'

'Maybe, but I noticed his jeans and trainers are expensive.'

Laura knows about brands and can tell the price tag at a glance. 'I liked him. He's easy to talk to,' she adds.

Holly pushes herself up from the table, takes a ready-made meal out of the fridge and turns on the oven. 'I've been lazy and bought us this for supper. Sorry. I haven't planned a roast dinner for the guys either.'

'Why's that?'

Holly hesitates. She planned to be upbeat with Laura but, hell, she feels bone tired. 'I've lost my mojo.'

'I thought you seemed subdued.'

'Guess I am. I'm still feeling tired all the time.'

She feels guilty about being a misery, but Laura gets up at once and takes the foil box from her.

'You sit down, and I'll pop this in the oven. And I'll help you cook for the guys on Sunday if you want.'

'OK. We'll do the meal. It's more of an occasion when you're here.'

'You know how I love to participate in your soap opera.'

SATURDAY MORNING

Holly and Laura walk up to the parade of shops at Fiveways with Cooper on his lead. Laura stands outside the butcher's while Holly buys two chickens. They cross the road to Fiveways Fruits.

'Salad as well as vegetables,' Holly says.

They drop the bags of shopping at the house and head into town with Cooper. Holly is carrying the black-and-white photograph of Lillian and Jacques Pichois, which she first thought of as The Lovers' Picture and now thinks of as The Doomed Lovers' Picture. There is a framing shop in the North Laine and Laura helps her choose a simple black wooden frame. Afterwards they go in search of a coffee.

'Even more coffee shops here than in Camden Town,' Laura says.

She watches as Holly adds a heaped teaspoon of sugar to her oat milk cappuccino and stirs the chocolate topping into the froth.

'I've been thinking about your aunt and her lifelong attachment to the man in the photographs,' Laura says.

'Jacques Pichois.'

'He stayed married so she would have missed out on a lot, Christmases and weekends without him, the whole lonely mistress thing.'

Is this the moment to tell Laura all she now knows about Lillian's and Jacques's relationship? Her aunt was such a private person and kept the existence of her son a secret, at great cost to herself and her child. She does not want Laura to judge Lillian, and she may question why Holly has not confided in her before.

'Maybe she preferred it that way. Lillian liked her own company and moved away from her family to be with him.'

'You said she was never big on family reunions and wanted you gone after one night.'

'She was distant with me, but she loved my dad.'

'Now what I'd like to know is did *the wife* know about Lillian,' Laura says.

'The wife was called Severine.'

'Was there ever a showdown between them, do you think?' Laura raises her eyebrows.

'Oh, you and your love of drama.'

'That draft letter, your aunt felt guilty about something. And she took her secret to the grave,' Laura intones in a dramatic voice like the narration for a B movie.

Holly smiles at her affectionately. 'Lillian wasn't always the nicest person you know.'

'What makes you say that?'

'She liked to stir things up. Dad told me she had a thing about Winston Churchill, hated him and thought he was a warmonger. So, she would go out of her way to make disparaging comments about him to relatives who saw him as a Great Briton who saved the country at its lowest point. She wanted to puncture their rhetoric and loved to have an argument.'

'Is that so bad?'

'She was clever and could shred their arguments, Dad said. Not a very kind thing to do to elderly relatives.' Holly yawns hugely and covers her mouth with both hands. 'Sorry, I'm feeling tired again. It hits me every afternoon and not even a double shot of coffee can keep me awake.'

On their return, Holly leaves Laura and Cooper in the kitchen. Laura has a weakness for high-end magazines and has brought the latest *Vogue* and *Harper's Bazaar* with her. Holly goes into the sitting room, looking forward to lying down for an hour or two. She can't find her eye mask. Did she drop it in her bedroom?

Her bedroom is empty except for Max's cans of paint and the window is open. She sees Spencer in the garden, using a camera with a large lens to take close-ups of the fig tree. Laura and Cooper come down the kitchen steps and Cooper is straight over to the fig tree to dig at its base, his tail wagging in excitement.

'What's there? You looking for a buried bone?' she hears Spencer say.

Laura folds open the two sun loungers which fit the space by the wall that Barry has excavated. 'This is a nice if compact spot.' She stretches out on one of the loungers with her magazines.

Spencer puts his camera down and sits on the edge of the other one.

'Do you paint from photographs?' she asks.

'Not usually. These will be part of a portfolio I'm putting together on the fig tree. How are things with you?'

Holly hesitates. They can't see her from where she's standing, and she knows she should leave but something keeps her there, listening in to her closest friends.

'All fine and dandy, thanks. But I'm worried about Holly. She seems stressed and has been complaining of tiredness for weeks now.'

'She has been a bit down recently.'

'She was so hopeful and full of energy when she first moved in. It was her big project, and she was happy about how it was coming together. I noticed straight away how the atmosphere in the house has changed. How her mood has changed.'

Holly stands very still. This is the second time she has listened in to the conversation of others, and she hates herself for doing it. Yet she stays rooted there, eavesdropping.

'The brick through the window and the dead rat didn't help. They upset her a lot,' Spencer says.

'She's always been a worrier and she needs a break from Penumbra House. I mean she doesn't have to be here all the time, does she? Ray's overseeing the works. I suggested we book a week away in early August, a proper do-nothing beach holiday. I'm fully committed at work till then.'

'And *is* she going?'

'She said she'll think about it but isn't up to travelling at the moment. I've *never* known Holly turn down a holiday before. Ray and James are so caught up in their stupid rivalry they don't notice what's happening right under their noses. Will you keep an eye on her? She's not right.'

'I will. I should have noticed. Thanks for the kick up the arse.'

Holly creeps out of her bedroom, enters the sitting room, shuts the door, and is close to tears. You should never listen to what others say about you in your absence. It puts a distance between you and them. It puts a distance between you and life. They were both loving in their comments and showed how much they care about her.

But what is she turning into? She's weak and useless, like one of those fainting dames from Victorian literature who feared they were suffering from something sinister and brought it on through their imaginings and inertia. But she *isn't* imagining the dizziness, the headaches, and the tiredness. The dizziness is the worst.

There are moments when she loses her balance and must stagger to stop herself from falling. She is terrified a tumour is growing in her brain. There she has admitted it to herself, her deepest fear. Her beloved father died suddenly and without warning. Struck down.

And she is afraid.

Chapter Thirty-One

PENUMBRA HOUSE
THE FOURTH ROAST DINNER

At four thirty the doorbell rings and Laura goes to answer it. Max is standing on the doorstep.

'Hello, Laura.'

'Hello again.' She sounds pleased.

'I've popped round to have a word with James. Gosh, something smells delicious,' Max says and walks up the stairs.

Laura heads back to the kitchen where Holly is dressing a large bowl of salad. 'That was Max.'

'Really? I wonder why he came round today?'

'Said he was here to see James about something. Can we invite him to join our meal?'

'It's awkward. I'm not sure we have enough food for an extra place.'

'Oh, I think we do, with the vegetables and the salad. And we'll put bread on the table.'

'OK, I'll ask him,' Holly says, feeling Laura is forcing her hand.

Laura takes out her mirror and does a quick check on her make-up, licks her finger, and shapes her eyebrows.

Max accepts the invitation and Holly lays a place for him as Laura polishes his wine glass. Ray arrived early and bagged the seat at the head of the table. He watches as Max seats himself next to James. Laura sits opposite him, offering to fill his glass. They've opened her second bottle of good red.

'Two chickens today. Ray, would you do the carving?'

'Sure thing.'

Holly hands him the carving knife, recalling her earlier concern about putting James out if she asked Ray to carve. What was the point of that. Her earlier efforts to stop the rivalry between the two men has proved fruitless.

Ray slices expertly into the first chicken. 'How's good old Bazza doing?'

'You *know* he hates you calling him that.'

'I know. He called me Raymond the other day.' He laughs.

'He is brusque sometimes,' Holly says.

'*Brusque!* He's a misanthrope,' James says. 'And he doesn't like dogs. I was talking to him last week. He told me working dogs were one thing, but dogs nowadays are spoilt rotten, and their owners have more money than sense.'

'What nonsense,' Laura says.

Holly thinks James shared this comment to get at Laura, and she bends down and strokes Cooper's head. 'That's not right. You deserve to be the most loved dog ever.'

'Holly, when do you plan to get the front path restored?' James asks. 'It really spoils the look of the place when you approach the house. It's like a mouth full of broken teeth.'

'I'll get someone in to replace the missing tiles. There's more pressing stuff to do first.'

James is thinking about his patients and the impression the

missing tiles will make on them and she thinks again about the non-existent second doorbell as Max leans towards her.

'Talking about the renovation, Holly, I hope you don't mind me raising it, but I could manage the hall, stairs and landings on my own.'

'I don't think–' Ray begins to speak but Max holds up his hand.

'Please hear me out. It's the papering which requires two men. You need an assistant to help on the big drops. Right?'

'Right,' Ray agrees.

'But this is all *new* plaster. The walls don't need papering. So, I would be able to do it on my own.'

Holly looks over at Ray, who shrugs his agreement.

'It's a point, but it'll take longer. Use two men and it's done in half the time,' he says.

'Surely it's the finish that matters. What's a couple of weeks in the great scheme of things?' James says superciliously.

Ray looks at Max. 'I'll talk it over with Holly. We'll let you know.'

James is pointedly ignored.

At the end of the meal Spencer suggests Holly put her feet up in the sitting room and they will clear away and wash up. He stacks the plates. Max pitches in on the washing up. Ray joins Holly and Laura in the sitting room and closes the door behind him, standing with his back against the door, his arms folded.

'That wasn't on. Max pitching to you for work over our meal,' he says.

'It *was* awkward.'

'You want the painting done and dusted. Use Max and it goes on longer.'

'I know that's the issue, but I feel mean.'

'Hol, mean doesn't come into it,' Ray says.

'Max is competent, isn't he?' Laura asks Ray.

'Oh yes, he's perfectly competent. But he takes a long time on each room. I couldn't manage on what he earns.'

The men have gone, and Holly and Laura are getting ready for bed in the sitting room. Cooper is lying on a towel between them. Laura gets out her mirror and embarks on her complex night-time beauty routine.

'There was more than enough food to go round,' she says, which Holly can't help but feel is to reprove her for her earlier reticence.

'You know, thinking about it I'm sure James put Max up to coming round today. I bet he told him about the meal and suggested he time his visit to secure an invitation,' Holly says.

'Would he do that?'

'I think he would.'

Laura giggles. 'The Machiavelli of the house. There's nothing more annoying than someone saying *I told you so*, but...'

'You told me so,' Holly says, smiling at her thinly, because there *is* nothing more annoying. She sighs with resignation as well as weariness. 'And I should have listened to you.'

'Will you let Max do it?'

Holly sighs again. Will nobody let it *rest*?

'The whole thing is petty, isn't it?' she says at last.

'All their fights have been petty.' Laura smooths cream into her neck with upward strokes. 'And it's clear he's desperate for work.'

'I don't like being manipulated, and it feels like I was this evening.' Holly wonders if Laura will realise she's included in this statement.

Apparently not because she continues blithely. 'I'll ask

around for him. Saskia was talking about redecorating her ground floor.'

'Saskia who's got ME?'

'Yes. She's spending a lot of time at home and thinks some new colours will buck her up.' Laura packs away her expensive creams in a velvet wash bag. 'Have *you* been to the doctor about your exhaustion?'

'Not yet.'

'Holly, you said you would!'

'I'll get round to it. I promise.' Holly suppresses the irritation she feels at this – is she being nagged now too? – then reminds herself Laura only has her best interests at heart. 'Thanks for your help today. It's always a tonic having you here.'

'I enjoyed it.'

Holly switches off the light. 'Pleasant dreams.'

As she lies in the darkness Holly accepts the inevitable. With Laura, as well as James, championing Max she has no option but to go along with it and let him have the work. Laura's keenness to help Max points in one direction; she was already drawn to the idea of him before she met him.

The reality has only confirmed her expectation that Max is an attractive man. Holly recognises the signs only too well, having seen her friend through several impulsive romantic attachments. Which have all ended badly.

Chapter Thirty-Two

PENUMBRA HOUSE

S pencer has gone to Turin to be with Raffaella for her sixteenth birthday. He's taken his painting of her and told Holly he'll be away for ten days. Raffaella will then come back with him for a week in Saltdean, and he is keen for Holly to meet her.

Holly misses Spencer. They'd got into the habit of having coffee together most mornings and this was often the best part of her day. She's still sleeping in the sitting room although thankfully her bedroom is nearly finished. Soon, Max will start work on the hall, stairs and landings.

Before she climbs into bed, she thumbs through the prospectus for the college where she thought about doing an evening class in Italian. The prospectus has been lying around for weeks and the beginners' course is due to start in September. She is so weary these days. Can she be bothered to apply for it? She drops the prospectus on the floor.

2am and Holly wakes with a start. Are those footsteps in the hall? She listens intently. Is it the creak of body weight moving stealthily on the bare floorboards outside the sitting room? She has learned Penumbra House is a place of unexplained noises, especially at night. Big houses move and shift and creak.

It's not James. He came back hours ago and she heard him walking upstairs. Ray will be asleep in the basement because he goes to bed early and gets up at six thirty on weekday mornings. The creaking in the hall stops and silence engulfs the sitting room. Holly rolls over, closes her eyes, and sinks back into sleep.

She opens her eyes again wide to the sound of water running, gushing somewhere in the house. She sits up in bed, still half asleep. Is that noise rain? There are no raindrops pelting the window. As her head slowly clears, she identifies the sound is coming from *inside* the house.

Wrapping herself in her kimono she steps out into the hall. The noise is coming from the other side of the staircase. She crosses the hall and stops in terror at the light in her bathroom, shining brightly under the door. And the noise is a tap turned on full and gushing into the bath. Someone's in her bathroom running a bath. In the middle of the night!

She stands frozen for a full minute. Strange how sinister it sounds, bath water splashing against the enamel, usually an innocent sound. But it's impossible. How can anyone have got into the house and why run a bath?

There has to be a rational explanation for this and she must be sensible and push the bathroom door open and investigate. She waits, trying to build her resolve to act knowing she turned the bathroom light off before bed. Her nightly ritual is to lock up the house and turn off all the lights. She puts her hand on the doorknob but cannot bring herself to twist it and open the door.

How she hates her weakness as she creeps up to James's floor, wincing at every creak of the stairs. He sleeps in the room overlooking the garden and his door is shut. She taps lightly and tiptoes in.

'James,' she whispers. 'James wake up.'

He sleeps on, rolled on his side, his duvet rumpled.

'James!'

No response. She has to lean over and shake him awake.

'Whaaat...'

He opens his eyes, sees her, and sits up. 'What the hell? Why did you–'

He takes out his earplugs. Rubs his eyes.

'There's someone in my bathroom!'

'Your bathroom?'

'I need you to come down with me now. And investigate.'

'Christ's sake, Holly.'

'Please!'

James exhales in irritation, swings his legs out of bed and slides his feet into felt slippers. He's wearing a T-shirt and boxers and gets to his feet. 'But, Holly–'

'Shhh, keep your voice down,' she whispers. 'I don't want them to hear us.'

'Them...?'

He gives her a strange look as she puts a finger to her lips but follows her down the two flights of stairs as she goes ahead, taking every tread gingerly.

They reach the ground floor and stand outside the closed bathroom door. The bath tap is still gushing. Holly points to the door handle and nods. James wrenches open the door. The bathroom's full of steam and there's no one in there. Hot water is pouring out, and the plug is not in the plughole. He turns off the tap tightly.

'False alarm,' he says.

'But I didn't leave the tap on.'

'You sure?'

'One hundred per cent sure.'

'You had a bath before bed?'

'Yes. And I turned the tap off. Of course I did.' Why is she having to convince him? 'That tap *wasn't* running when I went to bed.'

He gives a huge yawn. 'Maybe the washer's gone.'

'And the light. Who put the light on?' She hears the tremor in her voice. It doesn't make any sense.

'I don't know. I'm tired. Can I go back to bed now?'

He turns to head up the stairs but she's far from feeling reassured or safe, and she follows him.

'We need to check Spencer's floor,' she says.

'Why would we do that?'

'In case whoever was in the bathroom is hiding there now.'

He stops and looks at her with incredulity.

'Are you serious? There was no one in the bathroom! There's no one in the house except you and me and Ray tucked away in the basement. What's got into you, Holly?'

'Taps and lights don't just turn themselves on in the middle of the night.'

He puts his hands up in mock defeat. 'OK. OK. We'll check Spencer's floor.'

The two rooms of Spencer's studio are empty. They cross to the other side and look into Lillian's bedroom, which is bare of furniture and newly plastered. The light from the street lamp glimmers on the floorboards.

'Nowhere for anyone to hide. This is a good room and it's wasted,' he says.

'We'd better check the lumber room too, just in case.'

James checks the lumber room where Holly has got round to sorting Lillian's manuscripts chronologically into four piles, one for each decade. 'Nowhere to hide here either. You want me to look under your bed now?'

'Shut up, James.'

'Don't bother thanking me for getting up in the middle of the night!'

He stomps up to his floor and she stomps downstairs, goes into her kitchen, and puts the kettle on. If she had called on Ray, he would have stayed for a cup of tea. So would Spencer.

The incident has disturbed her. The washer may have gone, but the tap was on full blast. And it doesn't explain the light being on. James is sure she left it on. But she hadn't, she knows she hadn't. And those footsteps she thought she heard in the hall?

Chapter Thirty-Three

PENUMBRA HOUSE

Holly's bedroom is finished at last, and her furniture has been moved back into place. She is glad to be back in there, away from the huge window of the sitting room. Max arrives promptly every morning to paint the hall on the ground floor. James is about to qualify and will start his practice on a professional footing any day. Spencer is still in Turin.

Another anonymous delivery waits for her on the mat. As she sees the white pages glimmering, she catches her breath and swallows hard while dread, but also a fierce curiosity, envelops her. What more is there to come? Snatching the pages up she makes herself wait until she is back in her bedroom, sitting on the floor with her back pressed against the door before she starts to read.

BRITTANY 1996

A lovely young woman in my village, Clemence, has been murdered. She was strangled. I am shaken to my core and heart sick.

I have known Clemence since she was a child, an intelligent girl who liked to read. Her family were farm labourers and had no funds to send her to college and she was destined for a dreary job and one well beneath her capabilities.

I went to see her parents and offered to coach Clemence for a scholarship. They were initially reluctant, but I explained that Clemence was gifted, and it would be my pleasure to teach her. Her mother was able to persuade her father that this would be a good thing for Clemence.

I have been working with her for the last year and she responded well to my teaching. We talked about books and ideas in many a long session and we had grown close. I looked forward to her visits and was confident she would get into college and achieve much. Now her short life is over. What did she have to endure in her last hours? It must have been so dreadful an ending.

Her body was found in the copse which lies beyond the field bordering my house. She had been buried in a shallow grave and was discovered by a man out hunting with his dog.

We have all been questioned by the Officiers de la Police Judiciaire about our whereabouts on the night she was murdered. To date, no one has been arrested. A profound gloom and cloud of suspicion has settled over our village. People fear the killer is living amongst us.

Her parents are broken. Her mother is religious, and I saw her standing on the porch of the church. I wanted to talk to her, but she slipped inside, and I did not feel it would be right to follow her in there.

I have a terrible fear, more an instinct, that Emmanuel is the killer. He lives with Jacques, but my village is not far away.

He knew how much I cared about Clemence. He hates what I love. I am haunted by the thought it was my interest in and involvement with Clemence which has led to her murder.

Emmanuel was questioned, as we all were who knew Clemence. There has been no follow-up by the investigating team. I have read about psychopaths and one of their features is a surface charm which deceives most people. And he would be cunning in covering his tracks.

All my life I have never been afraid of anything, but I am afraid of Emmanuel. I bolt the doors at night and check the window locks.

After two weeks of unquiet days and fitful sleep I finally voiced my suspicions to Jacques, first in a letter and later face to face. Jacques was the angriest he has ever been. He said I had always thought the worst of our son but had surpassed myself in accusing him of murder.

Jacques is still convinced I suffered severe postnatal depression after Emmanuel's birth. He went on to say that in most things I am rational and objective, but my illness clouded my judgement, and I am not to be trusted on the subject of our son. His Manu.

Jacques is wrong. I was never ill with postnatal depression. I am full of fear and dread these days, but I am rational.

Nevertheless, Jacques has a plan to use his academic contacts to arrange for Emmanuel to study in England, at the University of Portsmouth. He is twenty-two years old, and Jacques said we must continue to support him financially and give him a chance to build a good life for himself. I supported the plan and offered to pay half the costs. It will get Emmanuel out of the country, and it is my fervent wish he never comes back.

These are the most terrifying revelations yet and one sentence stands out for Holly:

I have a terrible fear, more an instinct, that Emmanuel is the killer.

The man Lillian feared of being a killer is *their son* Emmanuel Pichois. Holly reads the pages again, feverishly scanning the sentences. Surely Clemence is the little girl in an earlier journal entry? Holly gets up and retrieves the plastic folder from her desk. Yes, it was little Clemence who feared for her cat when the Cat Stabbing poster was up. And a few years later she is murdered. Strangled. A dreadful end.

Holly paces her bedroom from one end to the other and back again. Severe postnatal depression – this is Jacques's explanation of Lillian's suspicions their son could be Clemence's killer. But Lillian has roundly rejected this diagnosis. Who is right here – is it Jacques or is it Lillian? The date 1996 tugs at her mind. She flicks through the journal pages until she finds Lillian's draft letter tucked at the back. This draft letter was Holly's first discovery that something was badly wrong in Lillian's life.

Sure enough, it's dated September 1996. Holly shudders. This is what Lillian was writing to Jacques about: *I have hardly slept since so deep is my dread. I am consumed with the thought I have not done the right thing and should have reported my suspicions. He was in the area, and I know he is capable of killing. Remember Rabbit.*

Holly's left arm breaks out in a fiendish itch, and she feels it spread to her torso for the first time. It takes all her willpower to stop herself scratching savagely at her skin.

It is also a shock to learn Emmanuel was sent England, to study in Portsmouth. That jolts her. All this time Holly thought he was living in France. Is it possible he's still living in Portsmouth and is making the journey to Brighton to post these pages through her letter box? She picks up her phone and googles the distance. A mere 49.5 miles. An easy car drive or a train journey.

The pages have been left days, sometimes weeks apart. Is Emmanuel Pichois travelling to Brighton to terrorise her because she inherited Penumbra House? He has to be the prime suspect. Yet why does he want her to read these dreadful suspicions about him? Why does he want her to know Lillian believed him capable of murder? To terrify her?

Holly adds the latest pages to the other sheets wishing she had never set eyes on any of them. Her feelings about

Penumbra House are the most tangled mix of revulsion, fear, and attraction. She loves the large rooms, the high ceilings, the elegant windows. But her sense of being involved in a sinister drama, in the slipstream of Lillian's tormented relationship with Emmanuel, makes her feel she is falling into a deep dark spiral, losing her bearings. A dead rabbit and a dead young woman. *He hates what I love.* But was Lillian right?

Holly now fears Emmanuel Pichois as much as her aunt did. She has no idea what he looks like, and it is somehow worse to fear a man you have never set eyes on. It leaves everything to the imagination. But she must fight this campaign to drive her away from her house. If Emmanuel Pichois believes he has been disinherited, then let him stake his claim. Let him bring it out into the light of day and she'll fight him in court. His mother hated him and did not want him to have Penumbra House.

———

Holly's mood has not lightened all day. The murder of Clemence has been on her mind. As has Lillian's torment. How heartbreaking to be a mother who suspects her son of committing murder. Holly watches the ten o'clock news and the weather forecast predicts a storm. As she gets ready for bed her window flashes with lightning followed seconds later by the deep rumble of thunder. It has felt all day as if a storm was coming.

———

It is the banging of the door at 3am which wakes her. Not one bang, but a repeated squeak followed by a thump; a disturbing sound to hear in the dark. She doesn't want to get out of bed. It is her warm haven, the one place where she almost feels safe.

But the repeated squeak and thump cannot be ignored. She reaches out and switches on her reading light and sees raindrops are splattering the window. At least the roof tiles should stay secure this time.

Wearily she pulls on her kimono and feels for her slippers. She peers out at a dark sky, no moon, turbulence in the garden and the fig tree thrashing back and forth. She follows the thumping noise to the kitchen. A strong draught is blowing in and the kitchen door is wide open. The door, caught by the wind, slams against the frame and swings open again. Wet leaves have blown in and there are puddles on the steps leading down to the garden.

She heaves the door shut against the force of the wind and finds the key from the hook where she keeps it. Yet she is *sure* she locked it last night because it is part of her nightly ritual to check and lock the front door and kitchen door. Yes, she remembers turning the key in the door last night after putting a glass jar in the recycle box at the bottom of the kitchen steps.

She stands looking at the door, at the key in her hand, at the wet leaves strewn over the floor and shivers violently. How did the door come to be unlocked? Something is moving. She spots it and swings round. A frog crouches under the table. It is lying still, playing dead.

'I see you,' she says.

No choice but to catch the poor thing and put it out. Finding a plastic measuring jug under the sink and a piece of card she creeps towards the frog. As she bends down with the jug, the frog leaps away and wedges itself into the corner. She moves nearer, having to crawl under the table on her hands and knees and sees the frog's heart pulsing under its wet mottled skin. Poor terrified creature. She is spooked. Her heart beating fast too.

'Come on, I won't hurt you. I'm trying to save you.'

She catches the frog at her third attempt. Brings the jug

down and levers the piece of card under the opening so the frog is trapped. Crawling out and getting to her feet carefully, she fumbles to unlock the back door before letting the frog out onto the wet steps. He crouches there for a moment, before hopping down the steps and disappearing into the wet grass. The fig tree is groaning as it thrashes back and forth.

She locks the kitchen door again, checking it twice before she hangs up the key. Another unsettled night. *Don't ever come to Penumbra House if you want a good night's sleep*, she thinks.

The next morning Holly weighs herself on the scales in the bathroom and sees she has lost another pound. She isn't dieting yet her weight is dropping. She feels so listless and wanders into the kitchen. Maybe the weight loss is because she has little interest in eating. It's the regular bouts of nausea which are putting her off her food.

And she's gone back to snacks instead of cooking a proper meal for herself. Even the simple pleasure she'd discovered in cooking has gone, wiped out by her mysterious symptoms. When did she last cook a Sunday roast dinner for the men?

She unlocks the back door and hears Ray talking to Barry in the garden, a little surprising as they usually rub each other up the wrong way. The garden is fresh after its overnight soaking, giving off the rich smell of wet earth. She goes down to join them.

'It rained a ton last night,' she says.

'Garden needed it,' Barry says.

'A frog got into the kitchen, and I had to catch it and put it out at three in the morning!'

'Bummer. I've had no frog visits recently,' Ray says.

'Yes, there were all those dead frogs in the basement weren't there,' Holly recalls.

'I'm off. Too wet to garden today,' Barry says.

They watch him trudge up to the shed. Its door is swollen by the rain, and he has to wrench it open.

'You could do with a new shed,' Ray says.

'I know, but it will have to wait. I've been thinking, Ray, anyone can get into the garden down the side alley at the moment.'

'Yeah.'

'I think we should put up a gate.'

'We can do that.'

'I noticed we're the only house on the street without one. And a locking gate would make me feel, well, safer at night.'

He looks at her. 'Has something spooked you, Hol?'

She shrugs and gives a weak laugh. 'I was sure I'd locked the kitchen door last night, but it was open and banging. Everything's spooking me at the moment. Do you want a cup of tea?'

She's glad he agrees and follows her up the steps to the kitchen. She makes a pot of tea and sits opposite him.

'I'll look into garden gates for you. You buy them readymade, and I'll put up the posts.'

'Thanks. Sooner rather than later if you don't mind.'

He nods. 'Do you want a mortice lock or just a bolt?'

'A mortice lock please. The house stood mostly empty for all those years, yet Lillian never put up a gate. I think that's odd.'

'I think the odd thing is how seldom she used the house. Your aunt Lillian sounds a bit um…'

'A bit what?'

'Eccentric. By the way, the washer in your bathroom tap looked fine. I put a new one in anyway.'

'I don't understand why the water poured out. It was really gushing.'

He shrugs. 'Don't know.'

'*Another* mystery to add to the list,' she says darkly.

He is watching her warily, and she feels that, like James, he thinks she is indulging in neurotic fantasies. Maybe he thinks she's becoming eccentric. Like Aunt Lillian.

———————

Max packs up at six and Holly hears him talking to James, planning a run in Preston Park. They leave together and she watches from her sitting room as they walk up the road chatting. Buddies. It makes her want to talk to Laura. Holly's mobile isn't in her bag, and she looks in the kitchen but can't find it. She searches her bedroom and the sitting room and still can't find it.

With rising frustration, she thinks back to the places she's been during the day. Food shopping in the morning up the road, but she used her phone when she got home. She had sat in the garden for a while, and she retraces her steps and searches the ground under the loungers. No sign of her phone.

Back in the kitchen she gets out the footstool and searches the upper kitchen shelves, recalling her laptop lead had ended up with the tea bags. Nothing. A second more thorough search of the other rooms, looking under her bed, pulling up the cushions on the sofa, emptying the bathroom cabinet. All proves fruitless.

There's no landline in the house and she doesn't want to borrow James or Ray's mobile. She'd have to explain she's lost hers. After an hour of exhaustive searching, she gives up. She feels like weeping.

Chapter Thirty-Four

PENUMBRA HOUSE

How Holly wishes Spencer were back. The atmosphere in the house is tense. James living on the top floor has laid bare the old fissures in their relationship; his egotism and his need to always have the last word. She recalls his comment about Lillian's bedroom being wasted, and concedes he made a valid point.

Holly walks up to the room and stands on the threshold. Why did Lillian choose to sleep in a room which overlooked the street? It's quieter to sleep at the back of the house as Holly does. The new plaster is dry, but she hasn't had the room painted because she doesn't know what to do with it.

Several ideas occurred to her. One was to make it a study and move up her books, desk, and laptop. Yet she isn't an intellectual like Lillian and does not need a separate study. She briefly thought about letting it be a gallery space for Spencer's paintings. That would mean more people trooping into the house at all hours, and she dismissed the idea quickly.

Now she wonders if she could make use of it as a teaching room. It's over six months since she left the college, and she misses her students. Perhaps she'll advertise her services locally and take on individual students who need tutoring.

She wanders across the hall into Spencer's studio. When the sun shines these rooms are full of light and are a perfect space to paint in. Today the sky is overcast, and the light is soft. Spencer texted her when he arrived in Turin. With her phone still missing she hasn't heard from him since. She picks up one of his paint rags and smells the solvent. She longs for him to be back here, standing at his easel. His presence in the house makes it feel a better place to be.

Holly stretches out on the sofa in her sitting room. It's been another wasted day. She hears Max working in the hall, whistling tunelessly. Her mobile phone is still missing after three days and is causing her a stupid amount of anguish. When she lost it, she had emailed Laura from her laptop: *More trouble at the mill. Now my phone is missing!* Laura had emailed straight back saying she called the number, and it went to answerphone. Either the phone is off, or the battery has died. She suggests Holly buy a cheap burner phone until it turns up, adding 'you can't be without a phone'.

Holly hasn't got round to doing this yet because a new and alarming symptom has appeared. Over the last week sunlight has started to hurt her eyes. She always loved sunny days but suddenly the sun is making her eyes water and she has to blink a lot or close her eyes. Bright light in the house makes her headaches worse too. With its big windows Penumbra House is full of light.

She googled *can light hurt your eyes?* And discovers there is a condition called *photophobia*. The article said *photophobia* was not actually an eye disease. It recommended wearing sunglasses outdoors but to avoid wearing them indoors as this could make the *photophobia* worse by adapting the eyes to conditions which were too dark. It is also a common symptom in migraines.

Holly knows it's never wise to consult Doctor Google, but could she have developed a tendency to migraine at the age of forty-nine. It would fit with the nausea, the eye ache and the desperate headaches she has been suffering almost daily.

She pulls a mask over her eyes, blocking out the light and hoping she can sleep the afternoon away. Increasingly she feels cut off from the world, unable to experience things directly. This makes her utterly bleak. Untethered. She is also losing perspective on her relationships, has hardly spoken to James for days and finds Max's relentless cheeriness irritating.

What's worse is the way she keeps questioning her decision to take on Penumbra House with all its problems. Why didn't she just sell it? She has never felt more aware of the weight of the house pressing down on her, trapping her. There are all these rooms to be maintained; the long tangled garden; the petty conflicts with the men and, most troubling of all, the pages from Lillian's journal of misery which obsess her thoughts. She hears the front door open, and Spencer call out.

'Holly?'

She pulls off the mask and stumbles as she hurries to stand. She walks into the hall and is so moved to see Spencer standing there with his daughter.

'Oh, welcome back, welcome back!' Holly exclaims.

'I wanted you to meet Raffy straight away.'

'Hello, Raffaella. Good to meet you.'

'Ciao, Holly.'

His daughter is dressed in jeans and a denim jacket and

smiles shyly at her. They follow Holly to the kitchen and her despair is lifting at the sight of Spencer's face.

'What a *lovely* surprise.'

'Didn't you get my texts?' he asks.

'No, I haven't had my phone for days. It disappeared.'

'I wondered why you didn't text me back.'

'How was Turin?'

'It was great, so stimulating.'

'Papa was staying in a house with artists, and it was *disordinata*,' Raffaella says wrinkling her nose delightfully.

'Meaning messy,' Spencer adds.

'Was it? But your dad isn't messy. He always leaves his studio super tidy with all his brushes lined up,' she says to Raffaella.

'Raffy's right. The kitchen in Turin was a challenge, but the guys were great and took me to some galleries I'd never have found.'

He opens his rucksack and hands Holly a small package wrapped in brown paper. 'I saw this and thought you'd like it.'

She unwraps the paper to reveal a small vase made of opalescent glass. It has a long neck and opens into a fat bowl at its base.

'It's lovely.'

'I know you like to put flowers on the table.'

Holly sets the vase in the centre of the table, and it catches the light from the window and glimmers in shades of pale pink and blue. 'So pretty, like an opal. Thank you. I love it.'

She has an urge to cry with happiness. As she glances over at Spencer she sees he is looking at her with concern. She moves towards the fridge. 'We'll show Raffaella round the house. But first, what do you both fancy to drink? I've got apple juice, tea and coffee.'

'I can't drink milk from cows,' Raffaella says.

'Nor can I. I have soya milk,' Holly says.

'Do you have any hot chocolate?' Spencer asks.

'I do.'

Raffaella smiles. 'I'd love some hot chocolate.'

It's an odd request for a June day. Holly makes coffee for her and Spencer and heats soya milk for the chocolate. She beats the mixture until it froths nicely and hands Raffaella the mug. They take their drinks into the garden and sit on the loungers by the wall.

Raffaella sips at her chocolate. 'I like this. *Grazie.*'

'You should have seen the garden in January, darling. It was a proper wilderness with nettles up to your waist,' Spencer tells his daughter.

'I'd like to explore,' she says.

'Please do,' Holly says.

Raffaella gets up and stops at the fig tree, looks back at them. 'Here is the tree you keep painting, Papa.'

'It is indeed.'

They watch her walk to the top of the garden and peer into the shed.

'She's lovely, and she speaks English so well,' Holly says.

'She's a good kid. How has it been here?'

'Not brilliant. Rather miserable, actually.'

'Sorry to hear that. You've lost weight. And I don't like those dark shadows under your eyes. What's been going on?'

This is why he's still looking at her with concern. She isn't sure how much to tell him about the strange and inexplicable events that have made her days and nights wretched. She fears she's losing her grip on reality and can't bear Spencer to think she's turning into a neurotic woman.

'I've had some killer headaches recently. And waves of nausea. I wondered if it's migraine. And I missed you of course,' she says.

'I *was* worried you might pine for me.'

She gives him a soft punch on his arm. 'It's very good to have you back.'

'Have you been to the doctor about the headaches?'

'Not yet. But I should. And I will, soon.'

He's still gazing at her and does not seem reassured.

She stands too quickly and feels dizzy. 'Come on, let's show Raffaella round the house.'

They enter the sitting room, and Raffaella is drawn to the little liqueur glasses on the mantelpiece and holds one up to the light to see the engravings. Holly watches her face. She is a beautiful girl, the image of her mother, Sofia, and it's clear Spencer is immensely proud of her.

As they head upstairs, they pass Max. Spencer introduces his daughter.

'*Buon giorno*,' Max says with a little bow and Raffaella blushes.

They spend time in Spencer's studio, flicking through his charcoal sketches of the fig tree.

'Papa has made the tree like a horror movie,' Raffaella says.

'Exactly right,' Holly agrees.

Spencer smiles. 'Good, because I think horror sells.'

'Did you see the painting Papa did of me?'

Holly nods. 'I thought it was lovely.'

'Mama likes it,' Raffaella says.

The next day Holly comes down the kitchen steps to pay Barry. The garden has lost its look of a wilderness but has kept its austere feel. The fig tree dominates, will always dominate, but there must be ways to soften its impact. They need to introduce more colour; everything in the garden is green or brown at the moment.

'Shall we plant some bulbs next year, Barry? Daffodils and crocuses would look nice by the wall, and I love foxgloves and hollyhocks.'

He nods. 'Next year. That friend of yours, her dog makes a mess of the ground every time he comes here.'

'Does he?' She knows Cooper does, has seen his enthusiastic digging.

'He keeps trying to dig a hole by the fig tree.'

'Ah, no real harm then?' she says airily.

Barry grunts. She ignores it.

'Let's plant some bulbs round the fig tree too. Though we'll have to wait till we've explored the roots.'

'You still planning to do that?'

'I think I have to,' she says.

'Told you it's wiser to leave it be.'

It is early evening when Spencer lets himself in and heads to the kitchen where Holly is sitting with Max.

'Hi, both.'

'Hi. Where's Raffaella?' Holly asks.

'I left her at a screening of a teen film at the Duke of York's. I couldn't face it and I'll pick her up when it's over. Tell you why I popped round. Shortly after we left yesterday, Raffy started to get unwell. She told me she was dizzy and needed to lie down. She slept on the sofa for nearly two hours. It's so unlike her. Usually, she's an unstoppable force of nature. Her reaction was similar to how you've been feeling Holly. Do you think the soya milk is making you ill?'

'The soya milk? But I've drunk it for years.'

'Could the carton have been off?' Spencer says.

She gets up, takes the carton out of the fridge, and checks the date. 'The date's fine.' She smells it, pours some into a glass and takes a sip. 'Maybe it is off. It tastes slightly bitter. Oh God, I hope it didn't make Raffaella ill. I'm so sorry.' She tips it down the sink and rinses the carton.

'She's fine now. They bounce back. I was more concerned it might be affecting *you*.'

'I don't see how it's the soya milk. I can't have developed an allergy after all these years. Maybe I'll try a different brand.'

Max gets up. 'I'll be off, Holly. See you tomorrow.'

'Thanks, Max.'

They hear the front door close behind him.

'He's become quite the fixture round the place, hasn't he?' Spencer says.

'Why do you put it like that?'

'I don't know. It's just he's always so interested in everything about the house.'

'Do you think he's touting for more work?'

'It may be that. But…'

'But…?'

'I find him slippery. Don't you think his interest is a bit over the top?'

'Yes, probably a bit. But he doesn't know anyone else in Brighton, so he's latched on to James. They go running together and eat out at least once a week.'

It's rare for Spencer to voice a personal criticism about someone. He is a glass half-full man and usually sees the good in people.

'Getting back to you, I was thinking you should see a doctor as soon as possible if you think it's migraine. They'll have something which can help,' he says.

She doesn't want to talk about her headaches, or any of her other symptoms. She's just happy to have him back.

Chapter Thirty-Five

PENUMBRA HOUSE

I t's time to change the linen on her bed. Holly pulls off the pillowcases, the duvet cover and as she untucks the fitted bottom sheet, she finds her mobile phone wedged between the bed frame and the mattress. She snatches it up and looks at it in wonder. The screen is black.

Hurrying into the kitchen, she finds her charger and plugs it in. As the phone comes to life her screen is flooded with notifications of texts and emails. First, she reads the texts sent by Spencer. Next, she texts Laura:

> Hallelujah! My phone just turned up.
> Relief! XX

She carries the bed linen to the kitchen and loads the washing machine. But how did her phone get stuck down there? It was wedged right down the side of her bed. Sometimes at night she listens to a sleep meditation on her phone, and she rests her phone on the pillow. Could it have slipped off the pillow? Possibly. Had she meditated on the day it went missing?

Adding the soap powder and conditioner she turns the dial to a thirty-degree wash. She recalls wanting to call Laura in the evening. It's difficult to remember when the phone went missing, she's so distracted these days. It doesn't matter, she has it now.

Later, she asks Spencer if he'll help her put up the framed black-and-white photograph of Lillian and Jacques Pichois in her sitting room. He comes down at lunchtime and they agree the photograph should be centred above the mantelpiece. She holds it up while he steps back and assesses it until they find exactly the right height. Holly is meticulous with her measurements and precise with her strokes of the hammer. Spencer lifts the frame onto the brass picture hook.

'Thank you. I'm happy with it there,' she says.

'Lillian was a handsome woman, and you have her hair.'

'Laura said the same thing.'

'Your face is softer and sweeter though.'

Holly smiles. She has already hung the portrait he painted of her on the wall opposite and she looks at it and back at the photograph of Lillian and Jacques in pride of place.

'There's nothing of Dad in here. I must put something up,' she says.

'Do you have a favourite photograph?'

'I have several. I'll get one framed. I can't think why I didn't do it before.'

She feels an ache at this neglect of her beloved father.

'What's your best memory of him?' Spencer asks.

'Oh, there are so many to choose from.'

He sits on the sofa, and she joins him.

'I've remembered a good one. Dad loved the Popeye cartoons, you know Popeye the Sailor Man. Dad had an old tape and played them to me, a lot. I didn't really get them. I couldn't understand why Popeye and Bluto were fighting over Olive Oyl. All I could see was that she had very big feet!'

Spencer laughs. 'Did you tell him?'

'No. I liked sitting next to him, hearing him laugh.'

'Nice. What are your plans for the rest of the day?'

'My daily therapeutic walk by the sea,' she says trying to sound upbeat.

He takes her hand and squeezes it, and she likes that. 'Something else,' he says. 'I'm driving to Norfolk in July. My good friend Ben has a solo show in Holt. I want to support him. Would you like to come with me?'

'We could go to Blakeney! It's near Holt, and I used to go there with Dad.'

She has a vivid recollection of a walk she and her father did from Blakeney harbour over the marshes to Cley next the Sea with the windmill in the distance becoming larger as they strode towards it. Dad was a fast walker.

'I'd love to come with you. Dad and I had the best crab sandwiches ever in Cley.'

'I'll borrow a mate's car and drive us there.'

Putting on her sunglasses Holy takes the now-familiar bus route to the seafront, getting off at the Old Steine. She never lingers at the busy garish end of the beach. The ruined West Pier is her favourite destination, and she walks briskly till she reaches a kiosk and buys a coffee before settling on the pebbles opposite the pier. As the waves tumble in and sweep out she sips her coffee and reflects how Penumbra House feels so much nicer when Spencer is there. He is the person she turns to more and more for support.

A tall man approaches and sits nearby, but not too close to her. He's holding a polystyrene tray with fish and chips, and she smells the tang of vinegar as he eats with his fingers. She watches him discreetly. He eats all the fish and most of the chips. He gets to his feet and feeds the remaining chips to the seagulls by flinging them in the air. The gulls swoop down and gobble them. As she watches their clamour, she catches his eye.

'I usually get grief for doing this,' he says.

'Not from me. I admire seagulls,' she replies.

'Me too, they have as much right to our planet as we do.'

———

On the way home she stops at a supermarket before taking the bus the last stretch up the hill. As she comes into the hall, Max is folding a ladder away.

'I've finished the ground floor hall,' he says.

'Excellent. It's looking much cleaner and brighter.'

'I'm glad to catch you, Holly. I have a favour to ask.'

She's carrying a bag full of groceries and it's annoying to be asked for something the moment she walks through the door. 'I need to unload this lot.'

He follows her into the kitchen and watches her put the groceries away.

'Sorry, I really didn't want to spring this on you, but needs must. There's a good chance I've got a job in London.'

'Really?'

'Yes, your nice friend Laura put me up for a job decorating for someone called Saskia. She wants several rooms painted.'

'Saskia. Yes, I know her. That *is* good news.'

'It really is, and I need the work and am well pleased. But there's a problem.' He blinks at her.

'A problem?'

'Saskia wants the work done straight away you see. If I'm not available immediately I'll lose the job. That's the deal. Can I postpone painting the first and top floor halls for a couple of weeks?'

She stops arranging nectarines in her fruit bowl and looks at Max. He reads the dismay on her face.

'I know it's a big ask, Holly. Thing is, I was ground-zero when I arrived in Brighton. You and James have been brilliant to me. But it's vital I widen my contacts and I really don't want to miss this opportunity.'

Holly hesitates. He's guilt-tripping her into agreeing to the delay; a delay she doesn't want.

'I'd like to help, Max, but you know how keen I am to get the painting over and done with. It's been going on for months.'

'It's a big house and big houses take time. I get that you want it done, I really do. But it is only the hallways. The most important rooms, the ones you use every day, are sorted. And it was *Laura* who got me this job.'

'Let me have a word with Laura and see if Saskia will wait a couple of weeks.'

'OK,' Max says shortly, his friendly expression vanishing, his face closing down.

He leaves the kitchen, and she hears him packing his things away noisily in the hall cupboard. It's only four. Usually, he works later. Is he making a point? Showing his displeasure with her. She's hit with a wave of weariness and slumps into a chair thinking I'll discuss it with Ray and call Laura afterwards.

Once Holly hears the front door close behind Max she goes down to Ray's basement. It is locked and there's no sign of his van on the road either. She returns to her floor and stands at the sitting room window looking out at the front path. They are nearly six months into the renovation, and she wants it to be over.

Is she acting spoilt and entitled to feel this irritation with Max? Probably. But he did push to do her hall, stairs and landings. Or is it Laura's involvement in the matter which makes her feel uncomfortable?

———

Laura calls Holly around seven as she is in the middle of making a vinaigrette with her new resolve to eat more healthily.

'Hi, hon, I just wanted to check I haven't put you in a tricky position re. Max.'

'My hands are oily. Let me wash them and I'll call you straight back.'

As Holly runs her hands under the tap and soaps them, she thinks this could be an awkward conversation. She wanted a moment to prepare herself before she calls Laura back. She sits and selects the last number called.

'How are things with you?' Holly asks.

'Julie is as sly as ever. Whatever. I'm pleased with myself to have got Max a job. Saskia will pay him well and London rates are significantly higher than Brighton. I wanted to check you're OK with it?'

'It's good of you to have approached Saskia and I get that he needs the work, but I'm not thrilled at the idea of a delay. Would Saskia wait a couple of weeks?'

'Not really. She's going on holiday for two weeks and wants the rooms painted in her absence.'

'Oh, I see. Max didn't say that.'

Holly thinks how very nice it will be for Saskia to have everything done in her house in a mere two weeks.

'I wanted to help him. I think he needs a break after what his shitty ex did to him,' Laura says.

Holly experiences a spasm of irritation at how Max always attracts sympathy.

'Maybe we all indulge Max a bit, you know what I mean?'

'Maybe that's because we are in a far more privileged position than he is. He needs the work and it's only two weeks, Holly,' Laura replies with an edge to her voice.

'It's not ideal, but I guess I can live with it. I'll tell him to take Saskia's job. Now I need to get back to mixing my vinaigrette,' Holly says, wanting the call to end.

She's angry as she mixes the oil, vinegar and mustard in a glass jar and gives it a vigorous shake. There's something 'Poor Me' about Max which James bought into first. And Laura has just guilt-tripped her in the same way Max had done earlier. But it is Laura's use of the word *privileged* which has sparked her anger.

Yes, Holly has inherited a large house and yes, she is extremely fortunate, she knows she is. But let's not forget Laura has been helped on her way too. Her father, the judge, made sure his daughter had a lovely residence in a sought-after London square. Holly never made her friend feel guilty about that, did she. Are they drifting apart? Has her move to Brighton affected their friendship?

Holly's in the sitting room feeling miserable when she sees Ray's van pull up outside an hour later. She watches him unload his fishing equipment and carry it up the path. She'll give him time to sort himself out before going down to discuss the latest development.

. . .

'What the hell is Max playing at? You hired him first, and he needs to see your job through before taking on another one,' Ray says.

He's shown her into his kitchen, and is frying mince with onions. He is so sure of himself, and she wishes she had waited to talk to him before saying yes to Laura. Ray would have strengthened her resolve.

'You're right, of course. I was feeble about it.'

'Let me speak to him.'

'But I told Laura it was OK. She'll be on the phone to him pronto.'

Ray raises his eyebrows at that. 'Shouldn't *you* be the one to tell him?'

'Yes, but Laura's so pleased to have got him a job. I'm guessing she'll tell him.'

'He really pushed to do the hall, stairs and landings, touting for the job at our dinner, aided and abetted by James.'

'I noticed that! It had to be James who was behind Max's appearance on the doorstep shortly before we ate.'

'Course it was. And now Max is buggering off and leaving the job half-done.'

'I know. It's really annoying.'

'He'll like the London rates he'll get.' Ray lifts a bottle of beer and takes a deep sip. 'You're allowed to change your mind, Hol. Stand up for yourself.'

'I don't think I can.'

'Why not? You let people take advantage of you.'

She hears the frustration in his voice as he stirs the meat and onions.

'I mean look at Barry. He comes and goes when he feels like it. Never tells you what day or what time. Turns up when it suits *him*.'

'That's not a federal offence,' she says.

'He's taking the piss.'

'I like him. You know where you are with Barry.'

She's getting upset. They had similar arguments when they were together, Ray pointing out that Holly is naïve and does not know when people are on the make.

'I know you think I don't have any street smarts,' she says. She resents this perception of her. 'But I am *not* a helpless female.'

'Not saying you are. I just don't like to see you being messed around.'

She lifts her hands in a gesture of futility before resting them on the table. 'I haven't got the fight in me to make a fuss about *any* of this.'

Ray looks at her then, really looks at her. 'You still not one hundred per cent?'

'I've been better. Tired and headachey all the time. You sure there are no more poisonous materials lurking upstairs?' She tries to make light of it, hating to sound like a hypochondriac.

'You look washed out. Have you eaten?'

'I had a salad.'

'A salad! You need a bowl of my chilli con carne.'

He adds chilli powder to the pan and stirs it vigorously. His chilli is usually good. She has lost her appetite these days but does not want to be on her own this evening as she might brood on the edgy exchange between her and Laura.

'A small bowl would be nice, thanks.'

She goes to use his bathroom and, on the way back, peeps into his bedroom. She notices his new king-sized bed. When she was with Ray, he complained how she slept at a diagonal and took up too much room. She sits at his table and watches him add a tin of red kidney beans to the pan. He's irritated at her tendency to be a pushover yet he offers her food. That's Ray, a kind man. She is falling out with everybody. Penumbra House is causing fault lines in all her relationships.

The next evening James is visiting his mother, staying over at his sister's house in London. When she calls Laura, it goes to answerphone. Restless and feeling the need to get out of the house, Holly walks down to the Duke of York's cinema to watch a movie. The film runs two and a half hours, has had great reviews, and stars one of her favourite actors.

It's her second visit to the art house cinema and she pays extra to sit in the soft armchairs upstairs where she chooses a seat in the far corner. The cinema is half full downstairs and only five people are seated upstairs with her. The film starts and it's warm and dark and she feels very comfortable.

She wakes when the tall young guy who works at the box office shakes her gently.

'We're about to close up for the night,' he says looking awkward and quickly withdrawing his hand from her shoulder.

She sees the cinema has emptied and is embarrassed. 'Sorry. Sorry. I must have dropped off.'

She fumbles for her jacket and bag at her feet, clumsy after her sleep, and follows the tall young man downstairs. He locks the cinema after her.

As she walks home, she is in a bleary state. How much of the film did she miss? It's well after 11pm and the streets are dark and empty.

A bus trundles by and only two passengers stare out of the windows. She doesn't feel as much at risk after dark on Brighton streets as she used to on London ones but as she turns into her road she sees a parked car with its hazard lights on, flashing orange insistently. She approaches the car hesitantly and peers in.

The car is empty. She scans the houses nearby and all are in darkness. Odd. Up ahead she spots a lone figure shuffling along the pavement. Is it a man? An old man? It's hard to tell.

She opens her front gate and as she walks up the path thinks she hears something behind her. She swings round quickly, but must have misheard because she is alone on the path. Living in Penumbra House is making her scared of her own shadow.

The moon comes out from behind a cloud and the small white tiles of her path glimmer momentarily. There's a wavering light coming through her fanlight and she unlocks the front door. The house is in darkness, except for her bedroom where she sees the strip of light shining under the door. She thought she turned off all the lights when she went out hours ago. Could she have left her bedroom light on? She is so distracted these days.

She turns the knob on her bedroom door and as she opens it gasps at the swarm of brown moths fluttering excitedly around the light bulb. Her bedroom window is wide open, and the curtains are dark with the bodies of moths, hanging and stirring, those furry dark bodies, those ashy wings. There must be twenty, thirty, fifty hanging there or hovering around the room.

She gags and flees from the room, slamming the door behind her. James knows of her phobia about moths, but he's in London and can't help her. She won't wake Ray, not at this time. It's nearly midnight and she recalls his grumpiness when she roused him to deal with the rotting rat corpse. No, she must be a grown-up and deal with this horror on her own.

But she *cannot* spend a night in her bedroom with all that moth life swarming close by. One of them may land on her face, or in her mouth. Ugh! Finding the spare duvet, she makes up the sofa bed in the sitting room and locks the door.

Why was her bedroom window wide open like that? Had

she pushed it up so far before she went out? She is sure she did not. And is it wise to go to sleep leaving that window wide open all night? There's no gate to stop someone coming down the side alley, entering the garden and climbing into the house. She recalls the old man shuffling down the street. But she cannot go back into her bedroom. The moths are waiting for her.

No, it will have to wait till morning, till daylight. She'll be better able to deal with the infestation then. What caused it? What attracted the moths into her bedroom in such numbers? She has never heard of anything like this happening before.

She was so sleepy in the cinema but now sleep eludes her. How she longs to be back in the small cosy bedroom of her London flat. The bedroom opened from her kitchen/diner and cooking smells would linger. But she felt safe there; she could sleep deeply there. She doesn't feel safe in Penumbra House, has never really felt safe from the moment she started living in these huge creaky rooms, under these high ceilings.

Chapter Thirty-Six

PENUMBRA HOUSE

Max is working in London at Saskia's place and there has been a whole week without early starts, creaking of ladders or the smell of paint. It's a relief. Holly's in the bathroom when the doorbell rings and she makes no move to answer it as she isn't expecting anyone. Someone opens the door and footsteps go upstairs. No doubt another patient visiting James.

Spencer helped her clear the room of the beastly moths. Truth be told he had done the hard part, dealing with the fluttering creatures, using a broom to beat the curtains and drive the moths out into the garden. There were casualties and she insisted she sweep up the dead ones lying scattered around her bedroom.

The incident has left her with a slight revulsion for her bedroom which she can't seem to shake off. She makes a point of keeping the windows shut to avoid the possibility of a further infestation.

Holly would like to get away from Penumbra House and have a complete change of scene. A holiday with Laura in August seems appealing. She and Laura are good at doing holidays together. Maybe she should research some places to suggest.

Holly opens her laptop on the kitchen table. Laura suggested a beach holiday but their favourite places, the Greek islands and Mallorca, will be rammed in August. They need somewhere less crowded, and she spends the next hour googling locations and keeps coming back to the stunning images of the west of Ireland.

The doorbell rings again and she ignores it again. James has still not had a separate bell installed, in spite of their argument. And now he is qualified, more people will come to the house every day. She scrolls through the images on her laptop, but her concentration is gone, distracted by her irritation with him. It is of course her insistence on a second doorbell which makes James not want to do it.

Snapping her laptop shut she goes into the garden and looks up at James's floor. His treatment room is at the front of the house, and he'll be in there with his latest patient. Spencer is standing at his window and waves at her.

Next to the shed is the space where Barry dug up the barren blackberry bush and she's asked him to plant a white lilac bush there. Her father's garden had one, and the scent in the evenings was strong and lovely. This is what the garden needs – colour and fragrance to attract bees and butterflies. She heads to her sun lounger as Spencer comes down the kitchen steps.

'Are you taking a break? You usually work in the mornings.'

'Usually. The doorbell keeps going this morning, and it's distracting.'

'Have you been answering it?'

He nods. 'It's hard to ignore.'

'Spencer, please don't! James *promised* to install a separate bell that would ring on his floor only. We are *not* his doorkeepers.' She hears how irritated she sounds.

'He's offering sessions at half price for a few weeks to build up his practice, hence the surge in interest,' Spencer says.

'I bet he is, and they'll just keep on coming.'

'You want me to let it ring?'

'Definitely. Close your doors. That's why I'm out here.'

'Have you spoken to him about it?'

'Several times!'

'OK.'

'When we were together James used to say if I nagged him to do something it hardened his resolve not to do it. That's what he's doing over the doorbell. He can be such a jerk sometimes.'

They sit on the loungers, and she looks at Spencer.

'Why is it that when a woman asks a man to do something it's nagging? We don't call it nagging when a man asks a woman to do something.'

He smiles but doesn't comment. Spencer avoids conflict and his favourite saying is: *Remember what peace there is in silence.*

'I'm spending the rest of the day out here,' she says.

'I'll get my sketchbook and join you.'

She watches him walk up the steps to the kitchen. There is something touching about the back of his neck, and she regrets her sharpness.

What a bitch I'm turning into, she thinks. *Spencer's a good man, and was just trying to be a peacemaker.*

The next morning Holly hears the clatter of the letter box but lies on in bed not ready for her day to begin. It is too early for the postman and there is no point in leaping out of bed and trying to catch anyone. And maybe this time it will be an innocent delivery, a flier for cut-price pizzas or gutter clearing.

But her head is throbbing, and her mouth is dry, all-too-familiar symptoms these days; symptoms she associates with Penumbra House; the house that is making her ill. And her sleepiness has gone so she gets up and can't stop herself from looking at what's on the doormat. More pages lying there, waiting for her.

She snatches them up but needs tea before facing them and heads for the kitchen. Yet she is already scanning the words before the kettle has boiled.

BRITTANY 2014

Emmanuel stayed on in England after his studies were completed. I am deeply grateful he did not come back to live in France.

Jacques visits him in Portsmouth at least once a year, usually on Emmanuel's birthday. Jacques hinted to me there has been trouble with Emmanuel in England; but would not give me the details, whether the trouble was financial or something worse.

I do not want to know and ask no questions because when Jacques and I talk about Emmanuel it becomes strained between us. It is a chasm we cannot cross. I have however gleaned that Emmanuel is unable to hold on to any job for long and Jacques has to send him money on a regular basis.

Most of the time Jacques and I spend our days in harmony doing our work side by side. He often stays over at my house but has kept his house. I have no wish to stay there.

I am happy his last book received such good reviews. He deserved that. My translations are back on track though I feel they have never achieved the level of my best years.

BRITTANY 2015

The next time I set eyes on Emmanuel was at the funeral of my beloved, the saddest day.

A friend told me Emmanuel was staying in Jacques's house. Of course he was. He has been waiting for this moment, knowing he will inherit Jacques's house. What he does not know, and which will come as a nasty shock to him, is that over the last decade Jacques had to borrow money against the house. As an academic, however highly respected, Jacques's pension was not generous. Emmanuel's inheritance will be considerably less than he expects.

I organised the funeral, observing Jacques's wishes, made clear to me in his last days. As an atheist he wanted a Humanist celebrant and wished to be cremated. He said there should be no hymns and no flowers and asked for jazz to be played at his funeral. I booked a jazz quartet we had enjoyed in happier days.

The musicians set up at the top of the chapel, near his coffin. I was told later the music was of a high quality, though I hardly heard it. I was very tense, and my neck and shoulders ached. As I looked at Emmanuel sitting in the other front pew, acting the grieving son, I remembered him as a child who liked to witness suffering, indeed who liked to inflict pain.

I am certain he has grown into a man without a conscience. He came to the service on his own and I cannot believe him capable of forming a loving relationship with a woman or a man or an animal. Remember Rabbit.

I did not organise a wake on the day of the service. I managed to get through the day without talking to Emmanuel other than to say good morning and goodbye. After the cremation the undertaker told me Emmanuel had expressed no interest in taking Jacques's ashes and he handed me the cardboard box containing the remains of my beloved.

A month later I invited three close friends of Jacques's to my house. I cooked duck confit and tarte tatin, his favourite dishes, *and we shared memories of our precious Jacques. Later we went into the garden and scattered his ashes, and they blew across the field.*

Emmanuel put Jacques's house on the market straight away at an inflated price. It has not yet sold. I hope I will never have to set eyes on him again.

I have made my will in favour of my dear deceased younger brother's daughter, Holly. She will get Penumbra House. She has grown into a nice young woman; though not so young anymore. I forget she is in her forties. She is a teacher in London and was a devoted daughter to dear Leo who died so suddenly.

Holly sits at the kitchen table and her tea gets cold. She cries at the kind words her aunt said about her. There has been an eighteen-year break since the last of the journal pages. She wonders what the significance of this gap might be. Emmanuel was in England so Lillian found some peace with Jacques before he died. She hopes she did.

The funeral sounds utterly grim in spite of the jazz quartet. Lillian and her son in separate pews locked in their wordless feud. She recalls the first time she saw the words *Remember Rabbit* and thought it must be code for something. How innocent she was of the evil Lillian was referring to. The burning of the rabbit was the key moment in her aunt's rejection of her son. She writes here that Emmanuel has grown into *a man without a conscience.* And more to the point, Emmanuel stayed on in England.

This escalates Holly's fear. It *must* be Emmanuel who is posting these pages to her. Reminding her he has been disinherited and she is squatting in his rightful home. According to Lillian he couldn't wait to put Jacques's house on the market. She hears someone coming down the stairs from the top of the house. It will be James and she quickly throws a tea cloth over the pages. He doesn't come into her kitchen. She hears the front door click behind him. Recently, they have been actively avoiding each other.

Has the time come to report the appearance of these pages to the police? They're a form of intimidation and indeed have been from day one. She needs to think what she would say to the police. Would they say there is no direct threat to her in these pages and dismiss her as a hysterical woman?

No direct threat perhaps, but she's sure she's in danger and worse is yet to come.

Chapter Thirty-Seven

PENUMBRA HOUSE

Holly is in her sitting room and the warm evening light brings out the lovely colour of the walls. This beautiful room is hers and she should be thankful, but oh how she wishes her father was sitting next to her. He was a quiet thoughtful man and she turned to him for advice at every crisis in her life. He would know what she should do about the pages. She's not contacted the police. She fears they'll say, 'Why are you trying to involve us in what is a Hilborne family drama?'

Laura hasn't called her this week and Holly thinks it's a good time to suggest some places for their holiday in August. County Kerry and the Dingle Peninsula are top of her list, and maybe they should book two weeks away, a proper break from Penumbra House. She dials Laura's mobile, and it goes straight to answerphone.

It's after ten when Laura calls her back and she sounds like she's somewhere outside.

'Are you out?' Holly asks.

'I'm taking Cooper for his lamp post walk.'

Laura sounds different, not stressed exactly, but not quite herself either.

'Is everything OK?'

Laura gives a strained little laugh. 'I've a confession to make, and I want you to hear me out before you say a word.'

'O...K.'

'Max has been working flat out on Saskia's rooms because he's only got the two weeks to do it. Friday evening, he came round to say hi. We talked till late, and I said he was welcome to stay over in my spare room.'

Holly sits up straighter, sensing what might be coming.

'He stays over Friday night and works at Saskia's all day Saturday. Afterwards he comes round with the *biggest* bunch of flowers to thank me, and I invited him to supper.'

There's a pause, an awkward pause.

'One thing led to another and... I slept with him!'

'Oh!' Holly says.

'Just "oh"?'

'I can't think of anything else to say.'

That's a lie. What she wants to say is 'please be careful; you may get hurt again'.

'I know you think I'm taking a risk, but I've been living the life of a nun and sex is such a release. I find him very attractive.'

'Clearly.'

'Here we go.'

'What?'

'The usual sermon about me leaping into things too quickly with men.'

'I didn't say that.'

'You were about to. I heard it in your voice. I don't want to hear it tonight. It's a long time since I've felt like this, and I want to enjoy it. Saskia thinks he's a total charmer.'

'He's certainly charming.'

'There it is again. That *tone*.'

Holly sighs, her heart sinking at the implications of Laura being with Max. 'You're being over-defensive. I haven't said anything against Max.'

But Laura isn't listening. 'He's clever, you know, a graduate. I can't understand why he's not doing something more challenging.'

It's clear she wants to talk about Max and to get Holly's approval.

'I'm glad you're feeling happy. Really. And if you're still up for some time away in August, you're on. You're quite right; I need a break from the house. I've been doing some research for us.'

'Have you? That's good.' Laura's thoughts are elsewhere.

'The west of Ireland looks amazing. We'd need a car if we went there. I guess we could hire one.'

'Hon, I'm sorry but I can't chat now. I need to get back. He's at my flat, which is why I didn't pick up when you called. Send me some links via email,' Laura says.

And with that she is gone.

The next day a steady stream of patients turn up at the house and ring the doorbell, no doubt attracted by James's cut-price offer. Holly is raging inside as she stops herself from answering the door.

Several hours later, she hears James come downstairs and leave the house. She's been waiting and watches from the side window in her sitting room as he walks towards Hazel's house. Hazel is kneeling on a bean bag clipping the large rosemary bush which grows in her front garden. She stands and they talk for a while and James opens his rucksack and hands something to her, probably his business cards.

They talk some more, and Holly sees Hazel glance over at Penumbra House. What's he telling her? James walks away from their houses and Holly goes straight into her bedroom and takes a sheet of paper from the desk. She writes the note to James which she has been composing in her head all morning.

> *Dear James,*
>
> *In December, when we discussed you moving into Penumbra House, we agreed you would have a separate bell installed for use by your patients. A bell that could only be heard on your floor and therefore would not disturb the rest of the house.*
>
> *In late May, I reminded you and asked you to install the bell as a matter of urgency.*
>
> *It is now nearly the end of June. Your practice is up and running with a lot of people coming to the house every day. The ringing of the house bell disturbs both me and Spencer. If you do not have a doorbell installed by the end of this week, I will get Ray to organise one on Monday and will give you the bill.*
>
> *Holly*

She feels fully justified as she folds the note and slips it into an envelope. If it makes him so angry he decides to leave the house, well, that would fine by her! She can manage perfectly well without his rent. And his egotism.

She goes to the top floor and props it against the closed door of his treatment room. Yet she does not want to be in the house when James finds it, so she heads out for her walk by the sea.

As she gets to her front gate, she sees Hazel is back on the bean bag in her front garden. Holly thinks about turning and walking the other way, but Hazel has spotted her.

'Holly, Holly, my dear,' she calls out.

She walks towards her.

'Now, I'd love you to come in for coffee and a flapjack,' Hazel says.

'That's good of you, Hazel, but I'm heading for the seafront. I try to get a walk in most days.'

'*Do come in.* You've never seen my place and I should have invited you over months ago,' Hazel says warmly.

Holly reluctantly follows her into the house. Hazel's kitchen is bright with turquoise tiles and a shelf of colourful jugs.

'What a pretty kitchen.'

Hazel has a Nespresso machine and busies herself with the capsules. She takes down two Emma Bridgewater mugs and a matching plate and arranges a circle of flapjacks.

'I'll have it black please. I can't drink dairy,' Holly says.

'I have oat milk,' Hazel says triumphantly.

'Oh great. Thanks.'

Hazel froths the milk and puts a bowl of brown sugar lumps on the table.

'This is delicious, thanks, Hazel.'

'I was just talking to James. He's given me a stack of his business cards. I told him I'll share them at my next *Purl and Plonk* group. Lots of us have trouble with our backs so he may pick up some new clients.'

'I'm sure he'd really appreciate that.'

Hazel's expression becomes serious. 'He tells me there have been a few unexplained mishaps in the house.'

I knew it, Holly thinks. He's been gossiping, no doubt detailing Holly's fright at the tap which turned itself on in the middle of the night.

'A few mishaps, but the house was empty for so long and things are bound to go wrong during a renovation.' She tries to convey an airy lack of concern. She doesn't want to have this conversation with Hazel.

She bites into a flapjack, and it is soft, sweet and oaty in her mouth. Flapjacks are the universal panacea. 'Nice flapjack.'

'I use honey instead of syrup. Now please don't take this the wrong way, Holly, but I have been slightly *worried* about your gardener,' Hazel says conspiratorially.

Holly stiffens and looks up. 'Barry? You've heard something about him?'

'No, not as such. Nothing specific. It's more the way he *lurked* outside your house for years.'

'Really?'

'Oh, my goodness yes. Ian, my husband, used to see him on the pavement, just staring at the house, years before you arrived.'

'We talked about this before. I think it might be his grief. His wife, Rita, worked there for my aunt, and Rita died. I think he's a lonely man.'

'Surely it is plain *odd* to keep coming back to look at a house like that.'

'He feels something for the house. I know he didn't like the way Lillian let it go, especially the garden.'

'I hardly think he has the right to be critical about someone else's property,' Hazel says crisply. Holly has touched the property owner nerve in Hazel.

'Maybe not, but that's how he feels. And he's proving to be an excellent gardener.'

Hazel gives her a kindly and condescending look. 'You're most generous and tolerant. James considers him an odd character too, and I always say you have to be so careful who you let into your house.'

Ironic, Holly thinks, when the invitation she regrets most is the one to James.

As she walks to the bus stop Holly is irritated with both Hazel and James. Underneath it all Hazel is a bit of a snob and is status conscious. She thinks Barry as a worker should not be taking liberties and deciding when he wants to work. Or have the cheek to express an opinion about how Lillian neglected the house and garden. Does she expect her to sack Barry because he's not socially acceptable to her?

Holly has felt for years that gossip is toxic and the spreading of rumours can ruin careers. She has seen first-hand in the college where she worked how gossip does its insidious work in an institution. How a nasty story starts as a trickle, grows as it's repeated, gets exaggerated, gains momentum, and causes misery. Hazel is clearly suspicious of Barry. This is the second time she's raised the subject. Surely Barry is just a grumpy but essentially decent and hard-working man.

It's true many strange things are happening in the house, things she cannot explain. Lights on which she turned off, doors unlocked and left open that she is sure she locked, the dead rat in the cupboard and the hideous swarm of moths, all those brown fluttering bodies in her bedroom.

She'd been out for several hours on the evening the moths appeared. And she was also away the weekend of the rat's appearance in the house. She recalls she was staying with Laura. Is it possible someone's getting into the house? Somehow getting in while she's away?

But Barry? No. She can't believe Barry is a malignant man. There's no denying he resented Lillian's occupancy of Penumbra House. He made his opinion abundantly clear the first time they met. Yet she has given him work, and over the last few months reclaiming the garden has become their joint project.

She thinks he's getting fond of her, and sometimes smiles at what he considers her fanciful ideas. They've talked about how to introduce colour and fragrance into the garden next year. In truth, she's the one who did all the talking.

The bus arrives and she gets on and sinks into a seat by a window.

As she sits looking out, she reflects how difficult it is to know *who* to trust these days. She's wondered, briefly, if James is working against her, resenting her good fortune, resenting her *palace*, resenting having to pay her rent. But she dismisses this as paranoid thinking on her part. They may not be getting on and he is as egotistical as ever, but James is no psychopath.

She gets off the bus near the seafront feeling dejected. Her suspicions are growing like a virus and are poisoning her days.

Chapter Thirty-Eight

JULY

PENUMBRA HOUSE

Holly heads for the greengrocer near Penumbra House which she thinks has the best fruit and veg in Brighton. There's always a display of produce laid out on tables on the pavement in colourful mounds. She surveys the display and buys two mangoes, a pineapple and three fat lemons.

When she gets home Spencer's sweeping the stairs up to his floor.

'Thanks for doing that,' she says.

She won't tell Spencer about her letter to James. She doesn't regret writing it, is glad she's taken action, but this fight is between her and James.

She holds up her bag of fruit. 'I plan to make a lemon drizzle cake.'

She hasn't felt like cooking recently or eating much because of her nausea. Nor has she done a Sunday roast dinner for the men since May. But this morning she feels the smell of a cake baking in the oven will lift her mood. Entering the kitchen, she spots the note James has left for her on the table. He hasn't put it in an envelope, has left it open for anyone to see.

Dear Holly,

I will buy and install a bell by next Monday.

I have to say I thought our relationship was beyond giving ultimatums!

James

Patronising arse, she thinks, screwing the letter into a ball and throwing it in the bin. She shuts the kitchen door and takes out the mixing bowl, slamming it down on the worktop. She beats together her butter substitute, caster sugar and three eggs, sifts in the flour, and grates the zest of one lemon into the bowl. Lillian's cake tins are an eccentric collection of sizes and shapes. Holly's kept the best and she lines one of these with greaseproof paper, spoons in the mixture and levels it with a spatula. Her mood gradually quietens and then lifts. It is therapeutic to cook.

She knows Lillian's oven by now and when she takes it out the sponge looks a perfect pale gold. She squeezes the juice of two lemons into a smaller bowl and adds caster sugar, inhaling the delicious sweet and sharp smell as she stirs. The part she enjoys most is pricking the cake all over with a skewer and pouring the drizzle so it sinks into the holes and forms a lovely crisp topping. She sits by the kitchen window with a cup of tea, admiring her cake. Her mobile rings. Laura.

'Hi, hon.'

'Hi. I just made a lemon drizzle cake and I'm pleased with it.'

'Well done you. How are things Chez Holly?'

'Fraught with James.'

'As per usual.'

She recalls Laura's earlier rebuke that Holly only ever goes on about her own problems.

'But OK. How are things with *you*? Is the atmosphere at work any better?'

'Not at all. Face-Ache is throwing her weight around! I've had enough and started approaching other companies who have openings.'

'Good move. They don't deserve you. Oh, I hope you get something really good and can resign with a flourish.'

'I wish! My CV is out there. We'll see what happens. And I'm so sorry but I've realised I *can't* get away in August after all. It will be work or wedding stuff all the way until the big day.'

'Oh, I see.'

'Iona has asked me to design and write the menu and the place names. And she wants my advice on dressing the tables, you know, with my events expertise. Bless. Did I tell you I'm paying for the flowers? Let's aim for a break in the late autumn instead. After the wedding. Maybe do the Canary Islands again.'

'You didn't like Tenerife.'

Holly recalls Laura nicknamed it Tener-Rip-Off-A-Touristica.

'I liked the weather, and Saskia says Gran Canaria has some lovely beaches.'

'Does it,' Holly says, with little enthusiasm.

Laura is ringing from the office and Holly hears the thrum of a printer in the background. 'I better go. Face-Ache approaches. Talk soon, sweetie.'

She hasn't once mentioned Holly's suggestion of the west of Ireland. Has she even read Holly's detailed email? Holly gets up and a worm of suspicion grows. Laura usually takes a week off in August. Does she plan a week in the sun with Max rather than with her? Holly knows Max stayed with Laura most nights while he was working at Saskia's. What will they do now Max is coming back to Brighton? Will Laura go to his flat and stay there? Or will he spend his weekends in London, more likely given the space and comfort of Laura's flat.

She looks at her cake thinking she'll offer Spencer a slice later. As she feared, Laura's relationship with Max *is* creating a distance between them.

The next day Holly hears the text ping and it's a message from Nikki confirming their meet-up at the Wakehurst country house estate at eleven. Nikki was a colleague and kindred spirit at the sixth form college where she worked, and Holly has kept in touch with her by email since moving to Brighton.

This will be the first time they've seen each other since December and a day exploring the house and gardens followed by lunch in the National Trust tearoom is just what Holly needs. James is in London with his mother and Spencer is helping a friend move house over in Saltdean. Holly double locks the house when she leaves.

As Holly gets home that evening, she smells the gas so drops her bag and runs into the kitchen. The large back ring on her hob is on full, hissing out gas. She turns it off and flings open all the kitchen windows and the door to the garden, which she wedges open with a chair. She goes back into the hall, opens the front door wide and leans against the door frame.

Crushed and humiliated, her throat is on fire and her eyes are watering. She stumbles into her sitting room, sinks onto the sofa, and cries bitter tears. She knows she did not leave the gas on. OK, she concedes she's been losing it recently, has been preoccupied and forgetful, but she did *not* leave the gas on. She hadn't even used the hob this morning before she set off for Wakehurst.

But will anyone believe her? She cannot stop crying. There is a reservoir of unresolved grief, and it is flooding her, unstoppable. Her second miscarriage. The sudden death of her father. The mess she's making of living in Penumbra House. And underneath it all the knowledge she's being targeted by someone who wants to harm her. She staked so much on getting the house right and on creating a happy household with the men. But she's no good; she's a failure on every level.

Chapter Thirty-Nine

PENUMBRA HOUSE

R ecently Spencer has started to spend a few nights at
the house, sleeping on the camp bed in the front
upstairs room. He tells Holly he wants to work late and start
early to make the most of the long days and the summer
light. Yet she wonders if the real reason is so he can keep an
eye on her.

She'd caught his concerned look when he came back from
Turin. There have been other worried looks at her since. She
tells him to use her bathroom whenever he needs it and this
morning, she heard the shower running hours ago, at first light.

Later she hears him coming down the stairs.

'How did you sleep?' he asks.

'So so. You were up at the crack of sparrows.'

'I was. Shall I make us coffee?'

'Please.'

He fills the kettle. She has a recipe book open on the table and has been looking at recipes hoping to take her mind off darker things.

'I've always been nervous of cooking a whole fish. Having to deal with the head and the tail, but I'm going to try it,' she says.

'Do you have time to look at something? I've taken photos of my paintings to send to some London galleries. I'd love your feedback on which ones to send.'

'Of course.'

He pours boiling water onto the coffee and brings the cafetière to the table.

'You want soya milk or are you avoiding it?'

'I'm back on it.'

She boots up her laptop, and he forwards the photos on his phone to her account. The doorbell rings, and he looks over at her.

'Please leave it,' she says, getting up to close the kitchen door as the bell rings again, longer this time. They hear James walk down, open the front door, greet someone and their footsteps head up the stairs.

Holly and Spencer exchange conspiratorial looks. She sits close to Spencer, their heads together as they spend the next hour choosing the best shots. He has painted the fig tree in winter, in early spring and in June. His work is striking and his talent evident, but she can't shake the feeling that there is something unlovely about the fig tree. It is the rapacious way it has taken over the garden. Very little thrives beneath its thick and spreading foliage. They agree on the photos he should send to the galleries.

'This is your best work, Spencer.'

'That means a lot, thank you.'

'I want to buy one of the canvases for my sitting room. I'd like one of the less-tormented ones.'

He laughs.

Later, Spencer goes upstairs, and as she heads for her bedroom, she hears him talking to James who is on the first floor.

'Spencer, would you do me a favour? Will you answer the doorbell if you hear it? I don't always hear it at the top,' James says.

'Don't you know when your patients are coming? Surely they make appointments.'

'I hoped you'd help me out.'

'O... K...'

Holly experiences a pulse of irritation. Why can't Spencer just say no to James.

James continues. 'By the way, while you were away the tap started running in Holly's bathroom in the middle of the night. Freaked her out big time. Yet she swears she turned it off.'

'What are you implying?'

'This house seems to be accident prone; don't you think? Things keep going wrong and Holly is spooked by it. That night she woke me up she made me search *every bloody room* in the house. Absurd!'

'Something's going on and I don't like it. Where was Max?'

'Christ's sake, Spencer, it's not Max. He was in London.'

'I was only asking.'

'I think that Barry is an odd character. Have you noticed how he pops up unannounced?' James says.

'Odd maybe, but harmless.'

'He's a cantankerous old sod who spends a lot of his time on his own. His wife died years ago, and I think he broods.'

'You're making him sound positively unhinged.'

'He behaves as though he is at times. He chops at those plants as though he's enjoying killing them. And Holly's all over the place emotionally. She's not coping. I heard her talking about the house being malignant and making her ill. That's nonsense! The Holly I married had more common sense.'

'Lay off Holly,' Spencer says.

'Just saying.'

She hears Spencer go into his studio and bang the door shut. James carries on up to his floor and she leans against the wall in the hall before walking quietly into her kitchen.

Thanks for the character assassination, James – the Holly he married indeed. And they are still married, though once they reach the five-year mark of separation, and he can't contest it, she is going to divorce him. Though given the petulant way he's been behaving recently she wouldn't put it past him to argue against their divorce.

Spencer stuck up for her and she appreciates it, but honestly what's wrong with her? She keeps listening in to what people say about her and she fears there's a grain of truth in what James just said. She isn't coping very well, hasn't been for a while and fears she may be slipping into paranoia.

Holly's up early on Friday because she and Spencer will set off for their weekend in Norfolk this afternoon. She has been looking forward to it and packs with a sense of something promising yet also tentative between them. Folding her prettiest pyjamas and underwear into her case makes her feel foolish and girlish. She packs her perfume and a favourite pair of earrings. On top of her lacy knickers, she dresses for Norfolk in jeans, a shirt and sensible walking shoes.

As she comes out of her bedroom, she sees the white pages glimmering on her doormat. A groan escapes from her lips. She bends down addressing the anonymous poster of the pages in her head – you can't let me be happy for even one day, can you? Her eyes race across the words.

BRITTANY APRIL 2016

Looking back last year was the most terrible one, truly my annus horribilis.

The heartache started early in the year when my dear brother Leo died suddenly in February. It shocked me Leo died before me because he was eight years younger and appeared to be in good health. He was a keen walker and was temperate in other ways.

I loved my brother and tried to help him when his feckless wife ran off leaving him with a small child to comfort and care for. He was a good father to little Holly, and he deserved a longer life. What a cruel lottery death turns out to be.

I always planned for dear Leo to have Penumbra House when I die and had bequeathed it to him. I was sure Leo would have appreciated the house and brought out its qualities. It could be a very fine house, but I have neglected it for too long and am now too sad and too weary to do anything about it.

After Leo's death I changed my will and bequeathed the house to my niece, Holly.

In the autumn came the deepest cut of all when my beloved Jacques died.

I have not had a moment of peace or even mild contentment since he passed away. He was my soulmate and my life partner. We could not agree about Emmanuel, yet we had such deep love and respect for each other for over forty years. It is utterly bleak to carry on without Jacques.

I have been reading Tennyson's In Memoriam, recommended to me as the greatest poem ever written on bereavement. Tennyson loved Arthur Hallam and was shattered at his death at the age of twenty-two. He writes that time softens the pain, and he had his religious faith to turn to. I have no faith and cannot believe that time passing will lessen my grief.

After I held the wake for Jacques and we had scattered his ashes, I lowered the portcullis and have hardly ventured out. I did not care if I survived the winter.

Now it is spring, and I must try to carry on. I have decided I will not go to England again. I cannot face another visit to Penumbra House, which was to be the home where Jacques and I would live out our days.

I have been troubled by a sense of unfinished business and the only way to allay this was to travel to Rennes to meet with my solicitor again. He is an honourable man and I trust him. I made the journey and gave him a letter for my niece Holly to read after my death.

We discussed Emmanuel Pichois and his possible claim. My solicitor is crystal clear on my unshakeable wish that he gets nothing from me and because Penumbra House is in England, he cannot claim it under French Law.

Holly feels on the edge of a panic attack as dots dance before her eyes. Her aunt was a broken woman in the last years of her life. Heartbroken and alone. If Emmanuel Pichois is posting these pages through her door, why has he allowed her to see that last paragraph? There it is in black and white. It was Lillian's last, rational, and unshakeable wish to disinherit her son. She was of sound mind when she made her will. It doesn't make sense for him to let her see this.

Holly's left arm and torso start up their familiar itch and her temples throb. What scares her the most is that it feels like they are approaching the end game. These are likely to be the last pages of Lillian's journal. Emmanuel Pichois is the only person with the motive to drive Holly out of her mind and out of Penumbra House. He is succeeding in destabilising her.

She is barely coping these days and is convinced all the things going wrong in the house are connected to these revelations about Lillian's life. Maybe all her symptoms are the result of stress too. Stress makes you ill and she's been stressed for months.

With no more pages to torment her, Holly fears his next step will be to appear in person and attack her physically. How will she protect herself? She doesn't know what he looks like or when it might happen. She adds the latest pages to the others in the plastic folder and is suddenly clear what she must do.

While they are in Norfolk, she'll show *all* the journal pages to Spencer. And Lillian's draft letter too. Holly will ask him to read them and seek his advice on what she must do to save herself. There are such dark and fearsome secrets here, and she cannot carry them alone anymore.

Chapter Forty

PENUMBRA HOUSE

At 5pm on the Friday Spencer texts he is on his way over and Holly places the plastic folder with all the pages at the top of her small case.

She is in the hall talking with Ray when they hear footsteps and laughter on the upper stairs. She is surprised to see Max walking down with James. This is the first time she has seen Max since Laura's disclosure and she waits, feeling awkward. James is in front, and he adjusts the rucksack slung over his shoulder and nods at her case.

'You off somewhere?' he asks coldly.

'A weekend in Norfolk,' she says.

'I'm away this weekend too,' Ray says. 'Spending the weekend with my lad in Milton Keynes.'

Max is right behind James, looking delighted with himself. The cat that got the cream, she thinks.

'Max, hello. How's it going?'

'Great, thanks, Holly, *really good*. I hope to be back at work on your hallways next week.'

'That's good to know. Thanks.'

He's positively beaming. 'And Laura says hi.'

Holly blushes. It's the first time either of them has made any reference to her best friend sleeping with him. She hates the way he said that; his little smirk as if he has one up on her. She's sure Max has told James about his new relationship. James probably confided to Max too about what a bitch she's being about the doorbell.

Is Max heading up to London to stay with Laura? Probably. It appears Laura has thrown caution to the wind. As she closes the door behind the two men she sighs, wishing she could be genuinely pleased her friend is happy to be in a new relationship.

'What was that all about, with Max?' Ray asks.

'You probably don't know yet. Laura's involved with him.'

'Blimey! That was fast work.'

Holly agrees. 'I hope she isn't opening herself up way too soon.'

'On the make, he is. Has been from the start.'

'Well, Laura likes him,' she says gloomily.

Spencer has borrowed a friend's car for the weekend. As he drives them out of Brighton, Laura and Max are still on her mind. She hadn't told Spencer about the affair because she needed time to process her feelings about it, her negative feelings.

'Did you know Laura and Max have become an item?' she says.

'No way!'

'It's the truth.'

'When did this happen?'

'He was working late at Saskia's and got himself an invitation to stay in Laura's spare room. One thing led to another and now they're dating.'

'How do you feel about that?'

'Uneasy actually. It's all happened so quickly. Laura is impulsive and, oh I don't know, she's been looking for a relationship. She wants to have someone to accompany her to Charlie's wedding. But she's happy about it and she's my best friend, so I'm trying not to say anything negative.'

'I hope she'll be all right.'

'Why do you say that?'

'She has this confident devil-may-care manner, but I suspect there's something more vulnerable underneath.'

Spencer increases his speed as they head along the A23, and Holly thinks about his words. She's pleased Spencer has seen beneath the shell Laura puts on to face the world.

'She *is* vulnerable,' Holly says. 'She has moments of acute self-doubt and self-criticism. Both about her work and about herself. It's not helped by her father and brother implying she's failed somehow. The whole unmarried mother nonsense. I love her dearly and it makes me sad she's pulling away from me.'

He glances at her. 'I'm sorry about that. You're a good friend to her.'

'She's been a good friend to me. I suggested she come down again soon, but it seems her weekends are now with Max.'

Holly doesn't tell him she's also smarting because Laura rejected her idea of a holiday in Ireland. And if Max is to be Laura's plus-one at Charlie's wedding, that'll change their stay in the Lake District too. She and Laura had planned to build a break around it. She looks at Spencer's profile. Should she raise the subject of Lillian's journal? He's intent on driving, and

Holly will wait till they get to the place where they're staying in Holt.

They pass the sign proudly welcoming them into *Norfolk, Nelson's County*.

Soon after Spencer finds the old coaching pub on the outskirts of Holt where they've booked adjoining rooms. They arrive minutes before nine and are lucky to get food as the kitchen stops serving at nine. They order sausages and mash and Holly turns off her mobile.

'I'm going off-grid for the weekend,' she says.

'Good plan. I will too.'

When their food arrives Holly toys with it but eats little.

'You OK, Holly?' Spencer asks.

'Not really.'

She puts her knife and fork together on the unfinished meal and takes a breath. 'Something awful's been going on for weeks, at the house. I wish I'd told you before. I should've told you before, but I'm telling you tonight.'

'What is it?'

'Lillian kept a journal, a personal one. For years. Someone, I don't know who, has been posting pages from it through the door. I've brought all the pages with me. They are, well, they tell a really disturbing tale, and it scares the hell out of me. Will you read them? I need someone else to read them. Someone I trust.'

'Of course I will. *This* is what's been worrying you?'

'Yes. So much. I'll go and get them.'

'I'm done here. I'll come up with you.'

They walk up to their adjoining rooms, and she retrieves the plastic folder and hands it to him.

'It's quite a few pages to read. There's also a draft letter from Lillian which I found ages ago.'

'I'll read it all in bed.'

He gives her a tender look and kisses her before opening his door. 'Try to get a good sleep. I want those dark circles under your eyes to go.'

The hotel phone by her bed rings shrilly the next morning. It's Spencer.

'Hope I didn't wake you?'

'No, I've been lying here awake for a while.'

'I've read it all. I see what you mean. Do you want to come to my room? I'll order us coffee and toast, or do you fancy a cooked breakfast?'

'Coffee and toast will be fine. I'm going to have a quick shower. Give me ten minutes.'

As she showers, she feels better already. Spencer has read Lillian's journal and she's no longer alone in carrying the burden of her aunt's secret torment.

When she gets to his room, she sees Spencer has laid out the pages on his bed in chronological order.

'It *is* disturbing, especially the later stuff,' he says.

'I have a cousin I knew nothing about, and he hurts animals, and he may be a killer.'

'Poor Lillian. An unwanted pregnancy and a child she cannot love. And keeping all this a secret from her family. What a burden it must have been.'

'I can't understand why she didn't tell Dad. He loved her and he wouldn't have judged her.'

'Older generation. Different values maybe.'

'I guess so.'

'And these kept appearing on the doormat.'

'Yes. For weeks now.'

'This is what worries me most. The way someone is targeting you and wants to scare you,' Spencer says.

'I *am* well and truly spooked.'

'Could it be Emmanuel Pichois?'

'That's what I think. He has the motive. If Penumbra House was in France, Emmanuel would have inherited it, even though Lillian hated him. That's French inheritance law for you. But Lillian employed a British succession lawyer to make sure I got the house legally. If Emmanuel ever turns up, he can't get his hands on the house. But it's the idea of his turning up which terrifies me. I'm sure he wants revenge.'

'When did the pages start arriving?'

She thinks back. 'February. I'd only been in the house about a month I think.'

'And then what, every few days?'

'Every couple of weeks. Once I heard the letter box clatter and I ran to the door, but there was no one on the street.'

'We have to do something about it.'

He looks serious.

'You think I'm in danger?'

He hesitates a moment before answering. 'Yes, I'm afraid I do.'

'It's not just these pages, Spencer. It's all the other things going wrong in the house. I didn't tell you, but I came back to a gas leak the other day. The back ring on the hob was left on high and the whole place stank of gas.'

'Bloody hell! There might have been an explosion.'

'I did *not* leave the gas on. Please believe me.'

'Course I believe you. You should have told me. It must have been horrible keeping all this stuff to yourself.'

'It's been a nightmare. And now I'm convinced it's all connected. Someone's trying to drive me out of the house.'

The coffee pot is empty, and Spencer rings for a second pot. 'James told me your bath tap started running in the middle of the night, while I was in Turin.'

'It did and it scared me. James thought I was overreacting massively.'

'Too many things have happened. Lillian had the house for decades. She may have given a key to various people over the years.'

'You think Emmanuel Pichois could have a key?'

'It's possible.'

Holly, agitated, gathers up their used plates and cups on the tray and puts them outside the door.

'She was an intensely private person. I feel she would have guarded her keys. Although…' Holly turns. 'Barry's wife, Rita, used to clean the house. Back in the day. She would need keys because she cleaned the house before Lillian arrived.'

'Good point. And they were never given back?'

'I don't know.'

Spencer and Holly join the crowd that evening at the exhibition of his friend Ben which is called *The Vaulted Sky*. It features large and small landscapes of Norfolk. The hall has stained-glass window panels, rich red and green oblongs, and is churchy in feel.

Ben is delighted to see Spencer. Ben looks a good decade older than them and has grey in his beard which he strokes as he walks them round his paintings. They are clutching plastic cups of white wine and Holly notices the red dots underneath some of the paintings, indicating sales.

A young woman, pregnant and in a flowered smock dress

comes up to Ben and he puts his arm around her and introduces his daughter, Saffron. She is at the radiant blooming stage of pregnancy, probably in her second trimester, and as Holly looks at Saffron, she feels no pang.

The hall empties by nine and Spencer, Ben, Holly, and a few others go to a pub and stay till closing time. Holly drinks little and is thinking about her father and their last visit to Norfolk and how much she wishes she could have talked to him about Lillian's secret life. But Spencer has been brilliant. The pub closes, and they say their goodbyes.

As they reach the pub where they're staying Spencer takes her hand. 'Come on, let's go into the garden at the back.'

She lets him lead her. 'It's very dark.'

He stands behind her and puts his arms around her waist. 'Now look up.'

She does and they stand for an age witnessing the inverted bowl of stars which spark and pulse above their heads. 'Extreme and scattering bright,' she says.

'Good words.'

'Not mine; John Donne.'

She turns round and initiates a kiss. It is a long exploratory kiss, and her body heats up.

———

Holly wakes the following morning and stretches luxuriously after the best night's sleep she's had in months. It's so lovely to have a warm sleepy body next to hers, to have *Spencer's* body next to hers, skin on skin. It had been ages since she'd had sex.

They order room service again and she pours him a coffee.

'This morning I've been thinking back to the reading of Lillian's will. Going over it all in my head. It was a strange experience, uncomfortable really, and what I want to know is did the solicitor know Lillian had a son.'

Holly had been summoned to Brittany in October last year for the reading of the Last Will and Testament of Lillian Hilborne. Shamefully, she had not even known her aunt had died. And there had been no funeral because Lillian had donated her body to medical science, which was very much in character.

'You haven't told me about the reading of the will,' Spencer says.

'I'll never forget it. His office was in Rennes, a building on a square and this elderly man introduces himself. He's English and says he's a specialist succession lawyer. Honestly, Spencer, he looked like someone out of a Dickens novel, all stooped and whiskered in a black suit. We go upstairs and he asks when I'd last seen Lillian. It was three years ago because she'd stopped coming to England.

'I explained my annual visit to Brighton, feeling guilty about how little I kept in touch with her. Had we ever met in France, he asked? I told him I'd never been to Lillian's house in Brittany, which is odd when you think about it. He cleared his throat and read the will out loud. It wasn't a lengthy document, but it had the whole *She was of Sound Mind* preface, you know.'

Spencer nods. Holly looks into her coffee cup, recalling the sensation she experienced sitting there with the elderly solicitor in his poorly lit office.

'He was uneasy about something in the will, or maybe it was *me* he was uneasy about. It wasn't anything he said. It was more the way he paused and looked at me after he read that Penumbra House was coming to me as the sole beneficiary.'

'It does sound positively Dickensian.'

'It *was* like that. His office was up narrow stairs, and his room was gloomy. He even had a fountain pen lying on a blotter; so old-world as if time had stopped, though I heard the clock in the square chiming the hour. He finished the reading and said my aunt was a remarkable woman and he was privileged to have served her. He said Lillian had left a letter for me, and he handed me an envelope, the deeds to the house and the keys. It was unreal and I felt stunned and undeserving.'

'Why undeserving?'

'I didn't make enough effort to see her. Sure, I came to Brighton once a year, and I sent Christmas cards with my news, but I didn't do enough. She acted as if she was indestructible, but she was in her eighties. And I sensed he was doubtful about me.'

'He was probably just being all lawyerly and inscrutable. It's their big moment, isn't it, the reading of the will.'

'I guess it is. But now I'm thinking he must have known Lillian had disinherited her son, hence his long troubled stare at me. He didn't know how much I knew. Or rather how little I knew.'

After breakfast they drive to Blakeney and park in the harbour. The water is low, the boats are moored in mud, and there is the unmistakable tang of stagnant water. Her senses are sharper. She notices the sickly smell of frying onions coming from a food truck in the car park.

She takes off her sunglasses and the light does not hurt her eyes as much. The colours of the boats look vibrant. For weeks she's had an awful muffled feeling of there being a film between her and the world. It is quite wonderful to experience things more clearly.

'I'm feeling good. My head is clearer. Maybe I just needed to get away from the house.'

'I'm glad.'

'Let's walk to Cley next the Sea.'

He reaches for her hand and a delicious warmth spreads up her arm. The path is bordered by high rushes which ripple as if moved by an invisible force. The sunlight is sharp, and the dark brick windmill with its white sails dominates their view. They agree they will have to order crab sandwiches at the café in Cley in honour of her father.

They're in no hurry to get back to Brighton. It is early evening when they stop the car further down the coast in Norfolk and get out to admire a small parish church with a perfectly round tower.

'So many lovely churches in Norfolk,' Holly says.

The door is unlocked, and they step in. The stained glass is long gone, and the light through the clear glass brings out the simple beauty of the nave.

'Come look at this.' Spencer is kneeling on the floor leading to the altar. There is an engraved stone slab with a carving of a skull with empty eye sockets etched above the words *Here lyeth ye body.* The name is difficult to decipher, but they make out the words *Relict of Edward.*

'Relict is such a dreadful word for a widow. As if her life was over once her husband had gone,' she says.

'1707,' he says.

It's dark on the motorway when Holly turns on her mobile and sees four missed calls from James.

'James has been trying to get in touch with me.'

She punches in his number, and he picks up on the second ring.

'Where are you?'

'About an hour from Brighton.'

'You *won't believe* what's been going on here.'

Her stomach clenches at the tone of his voice. Something bad is coming.

'Hang on, I'll put the phone on speaker,' she says.

She turns up the volume button and Spencer slows the car.

'What's been going on?'

'I get back from London to find the police here.'

'The police?'

'Just listen. Max and Barry got into some huge fight in the garden. They made such a racket the Neighbourhood Watch called the police. I've had it all from Hazel *in great detail*. It was her husband who made the call. Apparently Max was digging a bloody great hole by the fig tree and Barry went berserk. Two officers arrived quickly, and Barry and Max were still slugging it out. Don't know how it happened exactly, but Barry was arrested, and Max did a runner.'

'Barry? Arrested? What for?'

'Oh, this is the best bit.' James is almost gloating. 'One of the cops spotted some black plastic at the bottom of the hole. They called for reinforcements and dug deeper. They found a *body*, Holly. The police reckon Barry knew the body was there.'

Holly jerks with shock.

'That body has been buried under the fig tree for God knows how long. Your garden is the scene of a crime. It's been sealed off and an officer left on duty to keep people out.'

Spencer pulls onto the hard shoulder and turns off the engine. Holly sits back and closes her eyes. She feels him grasp her hand and squeeze it tight.

'Breathe,' he says.

Chapter Forty-One

PENUMBRA HOUSE

First thing Monday morning Spencer calls a household meeting and they assemble in the sitting room. There is still a police presence in the garden, and he thinks it best to avoid the kitchen. Ray has just got back from seeing his son in Milton Keynes.

'I don't get why they arrested Barry if Max was digging the hole,' Ray is saying as Holly comes in carrying a full cafetière and four mugs, and places these on the coffee table.

'Help yourselves.'

After they settle she holds up the sheaf of pages from Lillian's journal.

'You need to know some stuff I've learned because it has to be connected to the body in the garden. Lillian had a lover and they had a son – Emmanuel Pichois. She hated and feared him, and she disinherited him. I learned all this from these pages. They've been cut from a journal Lillian kept, and someone has been posting them through the front door for weeks.'

'Your aunt had *a son*?' James says.

Holly nods. 'Yes, and my dad and I had no idea.'

James leans forward. 'Why did she keep it a secret?'

Holly puts down her mug and looks over at James. 'Because her lover was married and because Lillian suspected her son was a killer.'

There's silence in the room as they take this in. Holly touches the sheets of paper in her lap.

'It's all in here. The whole sorry tale. Her son, Emmanuel Pichois, came to live in England in his early twenties. He studied at the university in Portsmouth. We think he is still living in England.'

To her surprise Spencer gets up from the sofa and approaches the mantelpiece where the black-and-white photo is hanging. He stares at the framed photo.

'Didn't Lillian say her son took after his father?' he says. 'Look at Jacques Pichois, Holly. Come and look at his face.'

Holly joins him by the fireplace and stares at the face of Lillian's lover. She experiences a jolt of recognition. Max has the same striking eyebrows as Jacques Pichois. It can't be missed. How could she not have noticed this before?

'You're right! Those eyebrows. They're the same. That's his father. Must be. It's been hanging there for weeks, and *he* would have seen it,' she says feeling weak and foolish that she could have missed so clear a clue.

Spencer turns to face the others. 'Max is Emmanuel Pichois.'

'Max?' James looks stunned.

James and Ray join them by the photo and the four of them stare at the black-and-white photo of the lovers. There is an unmistakable likeness to Max.

'How did Max first make contact?' Ray asks eventually.

'Don't you remember, he saw the skip outside and asked me if there were any decorating jobs going,' James says.

Holly thinks he looks uneasy because he was the one who introduced Max into the house.

'Max Clancy *is* Emmanuel Pichois,' Spencer says again.

'The ages fit,' Holly says.

The realisation sinks in that Max has been lying to them for months. Manipulating them all.

'That's why there was nothing on the internet about him. I thought it was strange,' Holly says.

'And his story about the wife doing him over was probably bullshit,' Spencer says.

'I doubt there was ever a wife,' Holly says.

'He targeted the house. He wanted to get in. And being a decorator gave him all the access he needed,' James says.

'Could Max have had a key?' It's Ray.

Holly looks at him for a moment, thinking back. 'Oh it was me! I loaned him my keys one day. Ages ago. He wanted to move the bedroom furniture and I was at the bus stop.'

'Dead easy to get copies cut.'

It hits her then. 'He's been getting into the house at night, while we slept,' she says.

'First thing we do is change the locks,' Ray says.

'Can I look at those pages?' James asks.

She hands the sheaf of papers to him. Her hands are shaking, and she's finding it hard to catch her breath. The image of Max creeping around Penumbra House at night, going into the bathroom, going into the kitchen, hiding, and waiting, fills her mind. Another chilling thought strikes her.

'Do you remember the dead seagull, Ray?'

'Yeah, I remember the dead seagull all right.'

'It was when we had the scaffold up.'

'Start of the year,' Ray says.

'He was watching the house *before* he approached James.

He climbed the scaffold and left the dead seagull to frighten me,' Holly says.

'If he had a key, he could have done all those other things to frighten you. The rat and the tap on in the night,' Spencer says.

'He probably flung the brick through the window,' James says.

'I thought they must be connected. But what was his plan?'

'To punish you,' James says. 'You had the house he thought he should have.'

'The body under the tree,' Ray says. 'He's a killer, right? Did he know you were planning to dig up the roots of the tree?'

'Yes! He asked me about the fig tree.'

Spencer looks at Ray. 'He came here to cover his tracks?'

'He knew about the body because he put it there,' Ray says.

'Of course. He had to get the body away before the roots of the tree were examined, and your trip to Norfolk gave him the opportunity,' James says. 'And I think he was building up to something even worse. I think Barry saved your life by exposing Max. The man is a killer, and you were next.'

Holly goes pale, and Spencer shoots James an angry look.

'He must hate me so much and want me dead.' Her voice shakes. 'It's been a slow torture for months. I felt I was losing my mind.'

James has been flicking through the journal pages. He tidies them into a neat pile and puts them on the coffee table. 'Incredible.'

'He was a deeply disturbed and cruel child,' she says.

'What do we do now? The police have his details but he's still out there, somewhere,' James says.

'But they *don't* have his details do they. They think he's Max Clancy,' Spencer says.

'And they arrested *Barry*. Poor old Bazza,' Ray adds.

Holly heads for the door. 'I need to call the police.'

'Wait, just a minute. I have a suggestion,' Spencer says. 'We change the locks today and until Max, sorry Emmanuel, is caught, the three of us take it in turns to keep guard. We don't leave Holly alone in the house, *ever*.'

She looks at Spencer. 'You think he's coming back?'

James nods. 'I think he will. You're in danger as long as he's on the run. The disinherited son. He thinks Penumbra House should be his.'

'I'll call the locksmith.'

They watch Ray tap on his phone. 'Can you do it by close of play today? Tomorrow morning, then. First thing? Cheers, mate.' He puts his phone in his pocket. 'Locksmith will be here tomorrow at nine.'

'Thanks, Ray,' she says.

'When are you going to tell Laura about her beloved Max,' James asks.

'Oh God! I must call her. He wouldn't go to hers, would he? He's a killer.'

'You call Laura and I'll call the police,' Spencer says firmly.

Holly hurries out of the room.

Spencer turns to James. 'Will you please go easy on the doom and gloom.'

'What do you mean?'

'This is bad enough without you laying it on with a trowel. Telling her she's the next to be killed!'

'She needs to know how bad things are. Trying to protect your girlfriend, are you?'

'Stop being a prick, James,' Spencer says.

Ray gets to his feet. 'Focus. Who's going to sort out this rota then?'

'I'll do that, and I'll stay here today and tonight,' Spencer says.

'OK. I'll do tomorrow,' Ray says, and he leaves the house.

It is a difficult call with Laura. Holly gets through to her office and Laura starts by saying she can't really talk. Holly tells her it's urgent and she must listen. When she gets to the fact of the body in the garden and Max's fake identity Laura stops her.

'I'm taking the rest of this call outside.'

Holly hears her walk across the office and down the stairs. Laura's voice is tight with anxiety.

'You're saying he's a killer.'

'We think so. He was digging up the body. If he turns up *do not* let him in.'

'Christ! I'll bolt my doors and windows. Oh God...'

'Any sign of him you call 999 at once. Then call me. OK?'

Laura exhales shakily.

'OK, yes. I slept with him, Holly. I had sex with him. Sex with a killer.'

'How could you have known? He took us all in.'

Ninety minutes later the doorbell rings and Spencer opens the door to two men. Holly is standing just behind him.

'Spencer Penfold? You called us.'

They introduce themselves, Detective Nick Monkton, and his Sergeant Wayne Smith.

'You have more information about Max Clancy?' Nick Monkton asks.

'Yes, we do, please come in.' Spencer shows them into the sitting room.

'I'm Holly Hilborne, the owner of the house. Can I get you anything?'

They turn down her offer of tea or coffee. 'We're working on identifying the body in the garden. We need any information you have,' Nick Monkton says.

'It's not Barry Pumphrey you need to question about the body,' Holly starts.

'The man who was digging the hole went by the name Max Clancy and we think he put the body there and was trying to get it out. Then Barry disturbed him,' Spencer explains.

'Go on.'

'And now we're sure that Max Clancy's real name is Emmanuel Pichois.'

'He's the son of my aunt Lillian Hilborne and her lover Jacques Pichois. They lived in Brittany,' Holly adds.

'Lived?' Nick Monkton asks.

'They're both dead.'

'You're saying this man is a French national?'

'Yes, but he's been living here a long time. He was at university in Portsmouth. Hang on, let me check the dates.'

Holly flicks through the pages of Lillian's journal, still lying on the coffee table, and finds the right entry.

'At Portsmouth University probably from 1997.'

Nick Monkton looks at the pages in her hand. 'What are those?'

'From my aunt's journal. They only came to light recently. That's how we found out about him.'

'Can I see them?'

She watches his face change expression as he scans the pages. 'There's more detail further on. My aunt was afraid of her son,' she says.

He speed-reads the later pages as Holly and Spencer exchange glances.

'We need to take these with us. We'll make copies and return them to you.'

'Of course. I think he wants to kill me too.'

'Why does he want to kill *you*?' Nick Monkton demands.

She nearly wails. 'Because I inherited his mother's house! This house. Don't you see, he thinks this house should be his.'

'He's a very dangerous man,' Spencer says. 'Yet he comes over as charming and helpful. He got access to the house because he was painting it. Was here for weeks and none of us sensed anything was wrong. But now we're keeping watch round the clock.'

Nick Monkton looks at Holly. 'Does he have a key?'

'Yes, I'm afraid he does,' Holly says.

'Change the locks at once.'

'The locksmith is coming tomorrow first thing,' Spencer says.

'Do you have any photos of this man, Miss Hilborne?'

'I took some photos of my sitting room, and he's in one of those.'

She spools through the shots on her phone and finds the one she'd shown to Laura. 'That's him at the edge of the frame.'

'Please send it to me.'

'And I've got the number of my aunt's solicitor in Rennes. He may know something. He's English,' Holly adds.

She finds the number and the sergeant writes it down.

'Thank you. We'll follow up on all this.'

They stand and Holly follows the two men into the hall.

'Do you think he's still in the country?'

'He could still be in the country. There'll be an officer in the garden for the foreseeable. We'll be in touch as soon as we have anything. Please be vigilant.'

Spencer bolts the door behind the men and Holly leans against the wall.

'They're worried he's on the loose. Don't leave me,' she says.

'Not for a minute.'

That evening Holly puts two large potatoes in the oven to bake for their supper. She and Spencer look at the yellow and black tape stretched around the fig tree and surrounding area of the garden. They've been told they are not allowed to go anywhere near it as it's a crime scene and evidence is still being collected.

'To think there was a body buried there all the time. I know you'll say I'm being fanciful, but I *always* felt there was something unhappy about the fig tree.'

'You did.'

'This will be the talk of the street.'

'At least Hazel gets a major story for her newsletter.'

Holly grimaces.

'Sorry, sorry, it's far too serious to joke about,' he says at once.

'I hope they've un-arrested Barry. Unfair that they automatically thought that he was the villain.'

They eat the jacket potatoes with smoked salmon and salad.

'Thank you for organising the meeting this morning. It's such a relief to know I won't be getting any more pages on my mat.' She tries to smile.

'But you're still looking worried,' he says.

She hesitates a moment before opening up and telling Spencer all the weird symptoms she's been suffering since she moved into the house.

'I'm worried there might be something wrong with me. With my head.'

He reaches for her hand.

'I'm glad to be honest with you at last,' she says. 'I've been keeping too many secrets haven't I.'

He nods, his face serious. 'Tomorrow you make an appointment to see your doctor. How does it work here?'

'You have to call at eight if you want an appointment that day.'

'Please, Holly. Call them first thing. Tell them you need the full works: blood tests and allergy tests, X-rays, the lot, because you haven't been well for weeks.'

'The headaches are awful. But the dizziness is the worst. It frightens me. I shouldn't have let it drift.'

'Why *did* you let it drift?' he asks gently.

She squeezes his hand, and her eyes fill with tears. 'It's my stupid fear. Dad died so suddenly.'

'Oh, darling Holly.'

'If it's something sinister, I need to know.'

'I'll come with you.'

'I need a hug,' she says.

They stand, and she rests her head against his chest.

Later, when they get into bed, he holds her close, cuddles her and strokes her hair until she falls asleep.

Chapter Forty-Two

PENUMBRA HOUSE

When Holly wakes on Tuesday Spencer is gone from her bed. She is groggily aware he's talking to someone in the kitchen. She needs to get up because she's planning to do something. What is it? Call the surgery; that's it. But it's already after eight. She swings her legs out of the bed as Spencer comes in with a cup of tea.

'I got through to your surgery, eventually. You're booked in for an appointment at 12.15.'

'You're the best.'

'We'll walk down together.'

She takes the cup from him.

'You get some work done. I'll be fine. Ray will be here soon with the locksmith,' she says as brightly as she can manage.

She knows Spencer does not like to be away from his painting for long. When he's engrossed in a painting it gains momentum each day and he can't wait to get back to his canvas. She thinks how lucky Spencer is to have something he can lose himself in.

———

Ray arrives at nine and the locksmith turns up five minutes later. He works on the front door first. Holly makes tea for them while he changes the lock on the kitchen door.

'I'll need four sets please,' she says.

'I've brought two sets. You'll have to come down to the shop for more.'

He tests both sets of keys front and back and packs his tools away. Holly pays him in cash.

After he's gone Ray hovers in the kitchen. It's his day to be on vigil duty and he looks at a loss as to what to do.

'Honestly, Ray, there's no need for you to stay while Spencer is upstairs. We've got the new locks now so Max... Emmanuel can't get in.'

'OK. But give me a shout if you have the slightest concern. And keep the front and back doors locked.'

———

Just before noon Holly and Spencer walk down to the surgery, across the road from Preston Park. He points to a bench near the ancient elm.

'I'll wait for you here,' he says.

———

Forty minutes later Holly joins him on the bench, giving him a thumbs up and an uneasy smile.

'I'm all booked in for a battery of tests and they took some blood today. The doctor tried to reassure me; said they'll find out what the trouble is. Thank you for making me do this. I should have gone ages ago.'

It's a perfect July day and they sit for a while. The four-hundred-year-old elm is clothed in green, a miracle that a tree so ancient still puts forth buds and leaves.

'I noticed your joy in the renovation stalled a while ago,' Spencer says. 'Actually, Laura noticed it before I did.'

'I've been afraid for weeks that something malignant is growing in my head. It's possible I might be quite ill, Spencer.'

In the surgery, as she listed her symptoms to the doctor, she thought how could she have been so stupid as to wait weeks before getting checked up. Will her delay prove fatal? Spencer puts his arm around her, pulls her to him and kisses her.

'If it turns out there's something wrong, they'll know how to treat it. I'll be with you every step of the way. Come on now, it's time for tea and a jam donut at the Chalet café.'

'Can I have lemon drizzle cake if they have it?'

'It was always donuts before.'

In the afternoon Ray comes up and sits in Holly's sitting room with a stack of bills and receipts, doing his accounts on an old calculator. He offers to spend the night on her sofa bed, but she tells him Spencer is staying the night, so around six o'clock Ray leaves.

Holly walks up to James's floor. It's Wednesday, his day to be on watch.

'I need to go out and get two more sets of keys cut,' she tells him.

'Do you want me to come with you?'

'It's not necessary, really. I'm sure you've got things to do.'

'I *have* got a stack of admin.'

'I'll be fine. See you later.'

'Keep your phone with you, Holly.'

She walks down to the key shop, glad to be alone if only for an hour. She appreciates what the men are doing to keep her safe but how long will they want to carry this on. Her fight with James over the doorbell has been eclipsed and seems trivial now.

The police haven't found Max. Is he hiding somewhere close by, or has he headed for France? She finds it difficult to think of him as Emmanuel Pichois and keeps telling herself I have a cousin and he is a killer. It nags at her that the solicitor in Rennes must have known Lillian had a son. She *knew* something was amiss as she sat in his office. That strange look when he said Penumbra House was coming to her as the sole beneficiary. She should have trusted her instincts and asked more questions. How long ago that all seems. It is less than a year ago, only last autumn, yet the axis of her life has shifted forever.

———

In the afternoon Nick Monkton turns up again, without his sergeant, and joins her and James in the kitchen. Holly wishes he would let her make him a coffee as she is so agitated she needs to be doing something, anything. It is all the waiting which is so hard to take. But he turns down her offer of refreshments.

'You've got some news for us?' James asks.

'I have. We've identified the remains in your garden. Georgina Arnold, a student at Portsmouth University. She was doing the same course as Emmanuel Pichois, and she disappeared in November 1999. She was twenty when she disappeared,' Nick Monkton says.

The body which lay hidden under the fig tree all these years has a name at last.

'Twenty,' Holly says quietly.

'Her family has been informed. They're grateful they are able to give her a proper burial at last. We have collected all the evidence we need, and your garden is no longer a scene of crime, Miss Hilborne.'

'That's good to know,' James says.

'Any news on Max, I mean Emmanuel Pichois?' she asks.

'I'm afraid not. He has left his Brighton flat. Looks like he left in a hurry. We've enlarged and circulated the image you sent me. And we're in contact with the police in France. Once Emmanuel Pichois is arrested, he'll be questioned both about the murder of Georgina Arnold and about a cold case in Brittany, the murder of a young woman twenty-three years ago. This is from information we received from the solicitor in Rennes, backed up by those pages from your aunt's journal, so thank you for that.'

'You spoke to her solicitor?'

'Yes, I did. Your aunt shared her suspicions with him, but it was never followed up officially.'

He looks faintly disgusted as he says this. He stands to go and she sees him to the door. 'Don't worry. We will get him. It's just a matter of time.'

As Holly closes the front door, she feels rage building in her. Lillian shared her fears about Emmanuel with her solicitor, but she hadn't warned her niece about her evil son. Is Emmanuel the challenge she referred to in her short cryptic letter? *I believe you have it in you to rise to the challenge of Penumbra House.* Was having to deal with Emmanuel part of the legacy? *Courage,* she had said. That was all.

You left me vulnerable, Holly thinks. *I didn't know I had to protect myself against a killer.*

James comes into the hall and sees her leaning against the wall. 'You've gone white again.'

'He said they'll get him, but I'll never feel safe again, not until he's locked up in a psychiatric prison.'

'Is Spencer coming back tonight?'

'He has to check in at Saltdean and said he'll be back if it isn't too late.'

'Do you want me to sleep on the sofa bed in your sitting room?'

She shakes her head. 'It's not necessary, James. Really. You're upstairs if I need you.'

Chapter Forty-Three

PENUMBRA HOUSE

Thursday morning comes. The curtains lighten and birds chatter outside her window. She lies on in bed utterly exhausted after a night of bad dreams. Spencer texted her fairly late saying he was sorry, but he needed to stay over in Saltdean after all.

She'd dreamed Penumbra House was on fire, was full of choking smoke, and Spencer was trapped in his studio. He was wrestling his canvases out of the studio window. The noise of the fire was rising, a terrifying cracking sound and he couldn't hear her voice screaming at him to leave the paintings and get out of the house.

He threw one more canvas out of the window and ran from his studio. The first-floor landing was full of smoke, a deathly thickness, and the wooden banisters had burst into flames. 'Too late! Too late!' she shrieked. This is what woke her; her scream had jolted her out of the nightmare.

She sits up in bed, her mouth is dry, and she wishes Spencer was with her. The sense of being under threat all the time has invaded her sleep.

Spencer's back in the house just after nine. It's his day to be on vigil duty and after she unbolts the door to him, she hugs him tight.

'That's a nice welcome,' he says.

She doesn't tell him about her nightmare.

He brings his sketchbook down to the garden and they block the alleyway with the bins and a chair from the kitchen as there is no side gate yet. Holly joins him in the garden, lying on the lounger in the little patch of sunlight. She takes off her sunglasses and lies with her eyes closed. The sun on her eyelids and face feels nice, but the nightmare has lingered, Emmanuel is still out there somewhere and the imminent results of her blood tests are all filling her with quiet dread. A headache has started to throb again, too. She felt almost normal during their weekend in Norfolk.

Back in the house and the symptoms are returning. It's fanciful to imagine Penumbra House is making her ill, but she can't quite dismiss the thought. Emmanuel Pichois has poisoned her experience of the house. He is a man who knows how to bury his anger deep, to disguise his real feelings and to wait for his moment to strike.

Now and then she opens her eyes to watch Spencer sketching. He is always motivated, always fully absorbed in what he is doing, and she wonders if he ever suffers dark nights of the soul.

'I'm making coffee; do you want one?' Spencer says.

'Let me do that.'

In the kitchen she fills the kettle and thinks back to January when she moved into Penumbra House. Those early months she was full of hope. Renovating the house was something she felt Lillian and her dear father would have applauded. Those feelings are long gone.

How naïve she was to walk away from everything she knew, her safe cosy life in London. She has done nothing about researching how to get students for home tutoring. Indeed, she cannot see beyond the next few days. Her life is at a standstill until they catch Emmanuel and until she knows what is wrong with her.

The house is quiet. James waited for Spencer to arrive this morning, then left for London to see his mother, so thankfully no patients will be ringing the doorbell today. Holly pours boiling water onto the coffee and inhales the aroma; one of the great smells and one guaranteed to lift the spirits. She tells herself to get a grip and less of the self-pity. At least the men are united at last in their commitment to protecting her.

After lunch Holly is in the sitting room and sees the same young guy in the brown council uniform she spoke to before. He is standing outside Penumbra House by the elm tree, with another man. She goes outside, and he recognises her.

'Hello again. We're going to try to save her,' he says.

'Oh, I hope you can.'

'We think we got here in time.'

Holly watches them for a while then returns to the sitting room as the men pack up their equipment and leave. She slips out of the house again and looks up and down the road. No one is around. She reaches out and strokes the bark of the sick tree, identifying with it.

'Be well,' she whispers.

She smiles at the thought that if Laura could see her now, she'd say Holly has turned into a tree-hugger.

Back inside, she joins Spencer in his studio, asking if it's all right for her to sit and watch him work. They spend a peaceful hour together, not talking as he paints. His mobile buzzes, and he reaches for it.

'Yes, that's my address, who is this?'

Holly looks up at the tone of his voice.

'What? When? Just now?'

He glances over at Holly and shakes his head, looking troubled.

'OK, and you called the police? OK, OK.' He ends the call. 'Shit!'

'What is it?'

'That was a neighbour in Saltdean, though I didn't recognise his name. Someone is trying to break into my place. This guy says I'm needed there.'

'A break-in? You better check it out.'

'But I don't want to leave you here alone. Is Ray around?'

'He's gone fishing. Look, it's four o'clock and I'll bolt the front door till you're back. I'll be OK.'

'Why don't you go sit with Hazel while I'm out.'

'I'd rather stay here. Really. She'll just want to talk about the buried body. In great detail, and I can't face that. You should go, Spencer. You're needed.'

They walk downstairs together.

'I'll be as quick as I can, and bolt the door behind me,' he says.

She watches him race off on his bike, then bolts the front door and checks she's locked the kitchen door. She reminds herself Max/Emmanuel doesn't have a key that works anymore but the empty house makes her feel vulnerable.

She wanders into her sitting room. As she gazes up at the photo of Lillian and Jacques hanging above the mantelpiece her feelings about her aunt are in turmoil. She feels rage towards Lillian, but also pity. Her lifelong clandestine affair and to have a child by your lover and hate that child. And the unhappy fate of Penumbra House, a place her aunt had such dreams about. If only Holly's father were still alive, and she could turn to him for his wise counsel.

She has three short videos of her father talking, small intimate moments caught on her phone camera at earlier Christmases. After he died, she found these almost unbearable to watch. Now she wants to hear his voice and see his beloved face again. She settles herself on the sofa and opens the files on her phone, watching them one after the other several times. They make her heart ache, but she is glad she has them.

Someone is hammering on the front door. She is frightened and coming into the hall stands by the bolted door, making no move to unlock it.

'Who is it?' she calls out.

'It's James.'

She unbolts the door.

'Why did you bolt the door?'

'Because I'm on my own.'

'But Spencer should be here.'

'He had to rush off to Saltdean.'

'Some guard he turned out to be!' James says.

'I thought you had to be with your mum?'

'Her appointment was cancelled, so I came back early. Just as well. You look very tense, all knotted up.'

'This whole situation is making me tense.'

He looks slightly sweaty.

'Do you want a cup of tea?'

He follows her into the kitchen.

'I've got a better idea. Come on upstairs and let me iron out some of those kinks in your spine. It'll help you relax.'

'Oh, I don't know.'

'Trust me, I've been told I'm a genius with my hands,' he says.

He is proud of his skill and she feels it will be churlish to refuse his offer.

'I need a quick cuppa first,' she says.

'None for me. I've spent the morning drinking bad tea at that bloody overheated and overpriced care home.'

Holly makes herself a mug. 'How was your mum today?'

'Her mind's going. She's retreated into her inner world, and you can't have a real conversation with her anymore. But I'm told she's in good physical shape and will probably go on for years.'

He hasn't sat down at the table. He's clearly had a bad day with his mum, is fed up and is keen to demonstrate his skill at osteopathy. Holly only drinks half the mug of tea, puts it in the sink and follows him upstairs.

He pulls off his jacket, switches on the lamp in his treatment room, and leaves the room to wash his hands. The room has subdued lighting. He comes back and pulls on thin plastic gloves which snap at his wrists. There is a fat roll of blue paper in the corner, and he stretches a new sheet of it over the treatment bed as she takes off her shoes.

'No need to undress fully but take your top off,' he says.

She does this and gets up onto his treatment bed.

'Now lie on your stomach.'

He rips a hole in the paper where your head goes and she rests her head in the hole and tries to breathe slowly. The table smells faintly of an aromatic oil, something osteopaths use on taut muscles, she guesses.

James starts to manipulate her back, working his fingers up from the base of her spine. His touch is not gentle, but she knows her muscles are tight and resistant from the last few days of high tension. Since the body was discovered and Max's identity revealed she has found it almost impossible to relax.

James's hands move up to her shoulder blades and she hears him breathing as he works on them.

'God, your shoulders are like rocks,' he says.

His fingers are on her neck, and he presses down firmly.

'Ouch, that hurts!'

This doesn't feel good at all. Is he trying to hurt her? Is he taking his frustration out on her? He continues to press her head down into the hole, and she experiences the deepest, the most instinctual, urge to get away from him. She tries to lift her head from the hole, but his powerful hands move around her neck. She tries to push herself up onto her arms using her elbows, but he brings his knee up onto her back and pins her to the table.

'You want to hurt me,' she gasps.

'But they'll think it was Max,' he says.

She screams once, a long, terrified and despairing wail.

He presses her skull down hard and squeezes her throat with a tightening grip.

'I found the journal. Your aunt was a bitch, like you. Runs in the family,' he hisses.

She screams again but weakly this time and gags as his fingers close ever more firmly around her throat. His knee is digging into her back, pinning her to the table. She flails uselessly with her arms but cannot reach him. She cannot breathe or make any sound or even move. He's strangling her, and she's starting to black out.

He's killing me, she thinks. *I'm going to die.*

Suddenly James's hands stop squeezing, she sucks in air desperately as she feels his body slump heavily onto her, then he rolls off and drops to the floor with a thump.

She pulls her head out from the hole, turns over wincing at the pain in her throat and sees Spencer standing over James with the stone Buddha in his hands.

Chapter Forty-Four

ROYAL SUSSEX COUNTY HOSPITAL, BRIGHTON

H olly's mind is starting to work again when the consultant sweeps up to her bed that morning. She sits up with difficulty. Her neck and shoulders are painful, and her throat is severely bruised. The consultant explains how her blood tests revealed Diazepam.

'Were you dosing yourself and misread the instructions?' he asks, rather sternly. 'There are very high levels in your blood.'

'I've *never* taken Diazepam!' she says, feeling insulted he thinks she's the sort of scatter-brained woman who would misread instructions.

'I assure you we detected *dangerously* high levels.'

'I don't understand how that can be. Will I be OK?'

'You'll make a complete recovery as long as you don't swallow any more tablets.'

After this salvo he strides away to the bed at the other end of the ward, and she dislikes him. An arrogant man who doesn't believe her and thinks she's been overdosing on tranquillisers. But there *is* Diazepam in her blood; excessive levels, he said. That would make her sick; that would make her tired and dizzy and nauseous. That would explain her mysterious symptoms.

Who has been doing this to her? And how?

It doesn't take her long to work out that only she drinks the soya milk in her fridge. Someone must have been spiking her milk. It explains why Raffaella was affected, after the hot chocolate. When did this start? She recalls the day she caught Max in her sitting room, she'd heard the creaking floorboard. He was painting James's rooms, but he was *in her room.* He said he needed a glass of water. But had he been tampering with her soya milk?

Or could it have been James? James knows she is lactose intolerant, and that the soya milk is for her alone. One of them must have been getting into her kitchen and upping the dose of the tranquilliser for months, watching her fall apart. Both Max and James wanted her to be in a wretched and weakened state. And it worked. This is her mystery illness, the cause of her dreadful headaches, her dizziness, and her despair.

———

It's mid-afternoon when she sees Barry approaching her bed. He stands at the end as she struggles up into a sitting position.

'My neck is hurt,' she says.

He nods solemnly. 'He did that? James?'

'Yes.'

Barry curls his lip. 'A coward.'

'I'm sorry they arrested you, Barry.'

He shrugs. 'I told them. Max helped himself to my tools. He didn't ask. I wasn't having that.'

She's glad to see him; glad she's right about him being a good man. 'Won't you sit down?'

There's a chair by her bed.

'I prefer to stand.'

She wonders how much Barry knows about what has been going on. 'We know who Max is now. He is Aunt Lillian's *son*. None of us knew she had a child.'

'Her son, eh. I thought he was shifty the first time I saw him.'

'Did you? We were all taken in. You told me a little boy came to Penumbra House once. Could it have been him?'

'I didn't see the kid. Rita said he was Lillian's godson.'

'Believe me, Lillian would not have agreed to be a godmother to anyone. She was an atheist.'

'Might have been him then. Only the once. Why did she keep him a secret?'

'It's hard to know. But she didn't want a child.'

'Very reserved wasn't she, Lillian Hilborne. A closed book.'

'Yes indeed.'

'What did the doctor say about you?'

'He says I'll make a complete recovery.'

'Glad you're OK. You best rest now. I'll be off.'

'Thank you for coming to see me. It's *really good* to see you.'

He gives an awkward little nod and hurries away.

EARLY EVENING

Holly is sitting up trying to read a newspaper, without much success. She keeps getting flashbacks of her last encounter with James. He was sweaty and intense, a man in the grip of an obsession.

He made that call to Spencer because there was no

burglary in Saltdean. It was a hoax call to get Spencer out of the house and he knew he didn't have long. He knew Spencer would race back to her as fast as he could.

James is under arrest for her attempted murder. Her estranged husband had wanted to kill her.

Spencer, Ray and Laura come into the ward together. It is their second visit, but they hardly talked before as Holly was dosed up on painkillers. This evening Laura looks tired and unkempt, not like Laura at all.

'It's so nice to see you all,' Holly says.

Laura leans in to kiss her and flinches as she sees the extent of bruising on Holly's neck. 'You're so pale, darling.'

'They said I'm fine to leave tomorrow and I'm going to be OK.'

'Great news,' Spencer says.

'Someone was spiking my milk with Diazepam, for months. I think it must have been James. He found Lillian's journal you see, and he wanted me to fall apart. The cold-bloodedness of it all has stunned me.'

'Two evil men, James and Max,' Laura hisses bitterly.

'I *knew* I hadn't left the gas on, or the tap. But the other things; I wasn't sure if it was me. I thought I was losing it.'

'It was the Diazepam and you'll be fine now,' Spencer says.

'Is there any news on Max? On Emmanuel I mean,' Holly asks.

'They haven't got him yet.' It's Ray.

Laura looks down at her hands. 'What I can't get over is there were *two* murderous men in your house. Quite extraordinary.'

Holly leans back against the pillows thinking that Max might have hurt Laura if he'd had the chance. Who knew the extent of his anger against women?

'Extraordinary yes. It was my getting Penumbra House. Max thought he should have it. His mother's house. And James always liked money and he was jealous. Very jealous as he started his campaign against me almost as soon as he'd moved in. I'm still here and sort of in one piece.' She tries unsuccessfully to smile. 'Remember Lillian's letter, Laura: *you have it in you to rise to the challenge of Penumbra House.* What bullshit! She didn't warn me. She knew her son was out there and dangerous, and she didn't warn me.'

They must be able to hear the bitterness in her voice. She is suddenly weary.

'I think I need to sleep now.'

'Of course. I'll see you tomorrow.' Laura kisses Holly on the cheek. 'Forgive me,' she whispers.

The three of them leave together. When Spencer reaches the exit, he stops.

'I'm not happy about leaving her. I don't like her being on her own. She's had some horrible shocks and there's so much to process.'

He heads back to Holly's ward, and she is lying curled on her side, her eyes closed. He settles himself on the chair by her bed and watches her face. After a while she opens her eyes and reaches out her hand to him.

'I'm glad you're still here,' she says.

She wriggles up into a sitting position and he caresses her wrist gently with his thumb. A health care assistant approaches and asks Holly if she would like a cup of tea.

'No thanks.'

The assistant looks over at Spencer.

'Can I stay?' he asks.

'Twenty minutes more, then we like to clear the ward and get supper sorted.' She walks away and he pours a glass of water for Holly.

'I hadn't made a will, Spencer. It was one of those jobs I kept putting off because it felt morbid to think about my own death. James and I are still married. And he was living under the same roof as me. It gave him a strong claim to Penumbra House if I was gone.'

How is it possible to tell Spencer the incredulity and devastation she feels that the man she married and lived with for twelve years, a man she once wanted to have children with, a man she's tried to help when he's on his uppers, has betrayed her so completely? She has to keep telling herself James wanted her dead.

'I've been lying here trying to work out who did what to harm me. I mean there were two types of abuse going on – the physical threats like the brick through the window and the dead seagull and the rat. I think Max did those things. He hates me. Lillian said he hated whatever she loved. And he has a record of hurting animals. But the other things, the Diazepam in my milk? The drip, drip, drip, of the journal pages. The gas leak? The psychological torture of thinking I was losing my mind. That was worse and I think James did all that. It's more his style. He knows my insecurities and how to manipulate me.'

'Vile, just vile. A campaign to destabilise you,' Spencer says.

'Yes, and it almost worked. I don't know if he was trying to string out the divorce to get a better claim to the house, or whether he thought he could influence me when I was feeling so low and vulnerable. If he convinced everyone I was losing it maybe he could even have gone for Power of Attorney.'

She looks at Spencer's face, a face she knows so well. He is a kind man; a man she knows she can trust.

'What I want to know is did James know Max was Emmanuel Pichois?' Spencer says.

'I don't think he knew at first, when Max turned up and offered to paint the rooms.'

'OK, but James must have found the journal soon after he moved in, poking about in your boxes probably.'

'You're right! There was a box sent from France. Full of Lillian's manuscripts. I thought it looked like it had been opened and resealed.'

Holly exhales.

'And did you see how at our household meeting he asked to look at the journal pages, as if he was seeing them for the first time. He's such a fake! I should have guessed it was him. The very precise way he cut the pages out of the journal. That was pure James.'

She leans back against the pillow. Everything James has done since he arrived in the house has taken on a new and sinister complexion.

'He may not have known who Max was at first,' Spencer says, 'but he sure as hell realised who he was when he was caught digging up the body. And of course it played right into his hands, didn't it?'

'What do you mean?'

'Once James knew Max was a killer, he had the perfect patsy. Max was on the run and known to be dangerous. If James killed you suspicion would automatically fall on Max. He didn't need to settle for half of the house in a divorce; he could get it all with you gone.'

Holly nods.

'But we stopped James,' Spencer says quickly.

'*You* stopped James. You're a hero. You saved me, just in the nick of time. I was passing out.'

'He's stronger and fitter than me so I needed the stone Buddha.'

She smiles wryly. 'You do know the Buddhist mantra is *no harm to self or others*.'

'It's not my habit to go around bashing people over the head, but I had to stop him and make sure he didn't get up in a hurry.'

'I sensed he was in a strange mood when he arrived at the house. But I still did as he asked and got up on his table. What a fool I was. I couldn't fight him. He had his knee on my back.'

'Stop knocking yourself.'

'I thought it would be churlish to refuse his massage. I'm a coward.'

'I don't think you're a coward. You took on Penumbra House.'

'The house of horrors.' She smooths the sheet on her lap. 'Barry came to see me this afternoon. I was touched he came to visit.'

Spencer smiles at her, and she likes the way the shape of his eyes changes when he smiles. They interlace their fingers, and he is looking at her with such tenderness her heart squeezes and her stomach flutters pleasantly. They sit in silence for a while and watch the light from the sun move slowly down the wall of the ward.

'I've been thinking about what to do about the house. Part of me wants to sell up and leave it behind forever. But there's another part of me which feels why should I go. It's starting to look as it should. I love my yellow sitting room. You love your studio and Ray is settled in the basement. He's been a good friend and I owe him something. Lillian gave me the house and she'd want me to have the courage to stay.'

'Give yourself time to think about it.'

'If I ran away, would it haunt me forever?'

'Traumatic memories have a habit of doing that wherever you are. There's beauty in Penumbra House as well as horror.'

'You just don't want to lose your studio.' She says this with a teasing smile.

'I don't want to lose my studio. What I really don't want to lose is you.'

They are bringing round the trolley with the supper for the patients and Spencer has to go.

Holly picks at the hospital food. She stretches out to rest and is bruised and sore, but deep down she feels a contentment growing. Whether she stays in Penumbra House or goes, she and Spencer are going to be together.

He was her soulmate all along, but they met when they were too young, and had drifted apart. How delicious to find each other again when they are both on the brink of turning fifty. Late love is even richer than early love.

Chapter Forty-Five

AUGUST

PENUMBRA HOUSE

Holly decides she'll stay at Penumbra House. It's *her* house, and she's survived everything her legacy triggered. She'll not let the malignancy of Emmanuel or the greed and malice of James drive her way.

This morning she receives news that the UK police working with the French police have established a lead on Emmanuel Pichois in Marseille. She tells this to Spencer as they go upstairs to clear out James's treatment room. It's a task she's put off for a few weeks. This will be the first time she steps into the room where James nearly succeeded in strangling her.

It'll have a new user soon enough. Trisha approached her about a friend who wants to run small classes in creating stained glass, and Holly agreed she can rent the top floor. You exorcised a room of its toxic memories not by shutting it up and locking the door but by letting in new life.

As they are packing James's stuff into cardboard boxes, she finds the leather-bound journal written by her aunt tucked behind his reference books.

'Well, look at this. It's Lillian's journal,' she exclaims.

The journal is ruined. Many of the pages are cut out but Lillian had pasted reviews of her translations in French and in English and these remain intact. One reviewer describes Lillian as the finest translator of her generation. There is a final short entry in Lillian's handwriting. Holly reads it aloud to Spencer.

> *BRITTANY APRIL 2018*
> *This will be my last entry.*
> *Who did I write this for anyway?*
> *I have regrets. I sinned.*
> *Some things sustained me – the life of the mind, my translations, my one true love.*

'Her last entry. She died that autumn. So sad,' Holly says, closing the ruined journal.

'Yes. She deserved a better, a happier life. Let's go into the garden. It's sunny and we've done enough for today.'

They walk down the kitchen steps into the sunlit garden, and she carries the journal with her.

'Let's sit here.' Spencer spreads an old towel under the fig tree.

'Really?'

'It's OK. I love this tree and I think you'll come round to it.'

They sit down with their backs against the trunk.

'We are doing the right thing staying here aren't we? The body in the garden, the evil of that won't ruin it for us,' she asks.

'The *house* was never evil, just neglected.'

'*They* are evil.'

'Yes.'

Holly knows Emmanuel is still out there somewhere. Will the lead the French police reported result in his arrest? She cannot say. The difference is now she knows he represents a threat, and she has the strength to live the life she wants. She opens the ruined journal and reads the last heartbreaking entry again.

'Lillian felt she had sinned. I guess she had. She should have reported Emmanuel, shared her suspicions with the police. Who knows? It might have saved his second victim. This journal destroyed my peace of mind. I took on her turmoil, I think. And I've been feeling so angry with her. But what a sad life. She loved a man passionately, but she hated the son she had with him.'

Holly puts the journal aside. Can she forgive her aunt for not warning her about Emmanuel? Maybe. Given time.

They're in no rush to leave the garden. Next spring there will be flowers by the wall and white lilac will bloom near the shed. The leaves of the fig tree rustle soothingly and peacefully above their heads.

THE END

Holly's Pea And Pesto Soup

Ingredients:

4 medium sized white onions
910 gram bag of frozen petits pois
I tablespoon of sunflower oil
4 teaspoons of Bouillon powder
1 heaped teaspoon of wholegrain mustard
Dessert spoon of balsamic vinegar
3 or 4 teaspoons of pesto

Method:

Use a decent-sized stockpot. Slice the onions finely and sauté them in the oil until they are soft and transparent. Do not let them go brown.

Add one litre of stock using four teaspoons of Bouillon to make the stock.

Add the whole packet of petits pois. Stir and let the mixture simmer.

Add the heaped teaspoon of wholegrain mustard and the dessert spoon of balsamic vinegar.

Simmer until the peas are cooked.

Turn off the heat and add the 3 or 4 heaped teaspoons of pesto according to how strongly you want the pesto taste to be.

Let the mixture cool before using a hand blender to puree it to a consistency you enjoy.

Warm the soup and serve.

If you are not dairy intolerant, it is nice to add a swirl of single cream.

Acknowledgements

I had the idea for *The Exes* two and a half years ago. It took me a while to achieve what I wanted, and my literary agent Gaia Banks worked closely with me on the various drafts. I am lucky indeed to have such a champion as Gaia.

Thanks also to Alba Arnau of Sheil Land Associates for some wise words along the way.

I am delighted to join the Bloodhound Books family and have had fantastic support at every stage from Betsy Reavely, Morgen Bailey, Tara Lyons, Kate Holmes and Fred Freeman.

I have many people to thank for the information I needed to tell this tale.

First, my thanks to Jonathan Hearsey for details on the training and practice of osteopathy, and for the many times he has helped my back!

I am indebted to Clive Edwards for describing the building processes as you renovate a dilapidated house and to George Walter for outlining the stages of restoration.

For the wallpaper scene I consulted Lucinda Hawksley's book - *Bitten by Witch Fever: Wallpaper and Arsenic in the Nineteenth-Century House*, Thames & Hudson.

Thanks also go to: Amelia Clarke Terry for helpful discussions on the evolving plot; Gloria Mura for advice on Italian; the Brighton Council arborist who told me about the problems facing Elm trees in Brighton; Nick Clarke Terry for bringing his artist's eye to the task when we brainstormed book cover images and Peter Florence for details on Spencer Gore

(1878–1914) as a painter of fig trees and because Peter's own giant fig tree in his garden inspired me.

My warm thanks to Chris Briscoe and Chris Maddison for inspiration.

Remembering Thomas Stephen Vladimir Bostock.

A large bouquet to Phil Viner for his feedback on the opening chapters of the book which was so helpful.

Thank you Caroline Matthews for reading a near final draft and your wise comments.

Many thanks to admired fellow writers Claire Douglas, Essie Fox, Emily Freud, Louisa Treger and P.D. Viner for agreeing to read advanced copies.

I must mention my dear writing group members who have been a source of encouragement and support for the last five years: Phil Viner, Laura Wilkinson, Kate Harrison, Sarah Rayner and Susan Wilkins.

To the book bloggers and readers who review my books – you need to know how much we writers appreciate your reviews. Thank you.

Finally, as ever, thank you Barry Purchese for your loving support and masterly feedback.

A note from the publisher

Thank you for reading this book. If you enjoyed it please do consider leaving a review on Amazon to help others find it too.

We hate typos. All of our books have been rigorously edited and proofread, but sometimes mistakes do slip through. If you have spotted a typo, please do let us know and we can get it amended within hours.

info@bloodhoundbooks.com

Ingram Content Group UK Ltd.
Milton Keynes UK
UKHW012046300323
419432UK00006B/360